HOLIDAY WISHES
&
MISTLETOE KISSES

Praise for M. Ullrich

What the Heart Remembers Most

"Ms. Ullrich has written a beautiful romance with this book that delves into how a loving couple can end up almost destroying their love through neglect and lack of communication. This is an angst ridden story that will pull at your heartstrings so hard you may hear them protest the harsh treatment, but don't let that stop you from reading this book. It is beautifully written with characters you can easily connect with because they are so human."—*Rainbow Reflections*

"[T]his is an emotional roller coaster, full of angst and drama… but the characters were so lovable and vulnerable that it made it easy to get into. Ms. Ullrich takes her time to develop the story, with small details that seemed apparently unimportant but later gained crucial relevance."—*LezReviewBooks*

"*What the Heart Remembers Most* is a romance that tears through the readers' hearts. It is a reevaluation of what is important in life. As we experience the traumatic recovery of Gretchen along with all the characters, we feel the desperation and tension and love. We live it all through with Jax and Gretchen, and upon finishing, dare to believe in forevers again."—*Hsinju's Lit Log*

Top of Her Game

"[T]his is a beautiful sports-related romance that I thoroughly enjoyed."—*Rainbow Reflections*

Pretending in Paradise

"*Pretending in Paradise* has real depth while still maintaining the lightness and sexiness of a true romance novel and it is this unique mix that really makes M. Ullrich's books the ones to look out for when you're on the search for the next steamy romance read."—*Curve*

Against All Odds

"*Against All Odds* by Kris Bryant, Maggie Cummings, and M. Ullrich is an emotional and captivating story about being able to face a tragedy head-on and move on with your life, learning to appreciate the simple things we take for granted and finding love where you least expect it."—*The Lesbian Review*

"I started reading the book trying to dissect the writing and ended up forgetting all about the fact that three people were involved in writing it because the story just grabbed me by the ears and dragged me along for the ride…[A] really great romantic suspense that manages both parts of the equation perfectly. This is a book you won't be able to put down." —*C-Spot Reviews*

Love at Last Call

Love at Last Call is "a very well written slow-burn romance. Another great book by M. Ullrich."—*LezReviewBooks*

"[I]f you enjoy opposites attract romances—especially ones set in bars—you'll love this book! I'll definitely be looking up the rest of the author's work!"—*Llama Reads Books*

Love at Last Call is "exciting, addictive (I was up all night reading it) and still gave me all the major swoon moments I've come to love from this author. Can I give it more than five stars?"—*Les Rêveur*

"This book was like a well-crafted cocktail—not too sweet, not too bitter, and left me with a warm feeling in my body."—*Love in Panels*

"*Love at Last Call* is M. Ullrich's fifth full-length novel and it's truly excellent. The writing is smooth and engaging, with perfect pacing and a plot that's sure to please fans of contemporary romance. If you're looking for a book to sink into, have some fun, and get away from it all, you'll want to pick this one up."—*Lambda Literary*

Against All Odds

"*Against All Odds* by Kris Bryant, Maggie Cummings, and M. Ullrich is an emotional and captivating story about being able to face a tragedy head-on and move on with your life, learning to appreciate the simple things we take for granted and finding love where you least expect it."—*The Lesbian Review*

Time Will Tell

"I adored the romance in this. I got emotional at times and felt like they fit together very well. They really brought out the best in each other and they had a lot of chemistry. I really did care whether or not they were together in the end…It was a very enjoyable read and definitely one I'd recommend."—*Cats and Paperbacks*

"M. Ullrich just keeps knocking them out of the park and I think she's currently the one to watch in lesbian romantic fiction."—*Les Rêveur*

"*Time Will Tell* is not your run of the mill romance. I found it dark, intense, unexpected. It is also beautifully romantic and sexy and tells of a love that is for all time. I really enjoyed it."—*Kitty Kat's Book Review Blog*

Fake It till You Make It

"M. Ullrich's books have a uniqueness that we don't always see in this particular genre. Her stories go a bit outside the box and they do it in the best possible way. *Fake It till You Make It* is no exception."—*The Romantic Reader Blog*

"M. Ullrich's *Fake It till You Make It* just clarifies why she is one of my favorite authors. The storyline was tight, the characters brought emotion and made me feel like I was living the story with them, and best of all, I had fun reading every word."—*Les Rêveur*

Life in Death

"M. Ullrich sent me on a emotional roller coaster…But most of all I felt absolute joy knowing that in times of darkness you can still love the one you're meant to be with. It was a story of hope, tragedy, and above all, love."—*Les Rêveur*

Life in Death "is a well written book, the characters have depth and are complex, they become friends and you cannot help but hope that Marty and Suzanne can find a way back to each other. There aren't many books that I know from one read that I will want to read time and time again, but this is one of them."—*Sapphic Reviews*

Fortunate Sum

"M. Ullrich has written one book. That one book is *Fortunate Sum*. For this to be Ullrich's first book, well, that is just stunning. Stunning in the fact that this book is so very good, it was a fantastic read."—*The Romantic Reader Blog*

By the Author

Fortunate Sum

Life in Death

Fake It till You Make It

Time Will Tell

Love at Last Call

Pretending in Paradise

Top of Her Game

What the Heart Remembers Most

Holiday Wishes & Mistletoe Kisses

Against All Odds
(with Kris Bryant and Maggie Cummings)

The Boss of Her: Office Romance Novellas
(with Julie Cannon and Aurora Rey)

Visit us at www.boldstrokesbooks.com

HOLIDAY WISHES
&
MISTLETOE KISSES

by

M. Ullrich

2021

ISBN 13: 978-1-63555-760-2

This Trade Paperback Original Is Published By
Bold Strokes Books, Inc.
P.O. Box 249
Valley Falls, NY 12185

First Edition: November 2021

CREDITS
EDITORS: JERRY L. WHEELER AND RUTH STERNGLANTZ
PRODUCTION DESIGN: STACIA SEAMAN
COVER DESIGN BY TAMMY SEIDICK

Acknowledgments

I am grateful for so much and for so many. Thank you to Radclyffe and Sandy for their continued leadership and encouragement, and to the rest of the team at BSB who work hard at producing the best novels possible. I have a very big, very special thank you to every reader of mine who waited patiently for this release. It was a long road to completion, but we made it. Thanks to my support system, the ones who kept me on my feet and my head on my shoulders throughout the craziest year of my life.

I'm thankful for Thanksgiving because of you, Leg.

For those who aren't afraid to wish for more.

THANKSGIVING: BILLIE AND LEAH

CHAPTER ONE

I think we're good to go," Billie said, making sure the potted mums and several wine bottles wouldn't topple over in the trunk of her car. "We just have to stop by Lena's bakery for the pies." She slammed the trunk shut and turned back to Leah, who stood on the stoop of her modest home, beautiful in the autumn sunshine. "How are you feeling?"

Leah tucked a strand of her chin-length red hair behind her ear and smiled softly. Her eyes were closed, and she faced the sun. "I feel fine, but the more you ask me, the more I feel like I should be worried." She cracked one of her blue eyes open and looked at Billie.

"Meeting the parents for the first time is a big deal." Billie walked over and wrapped her arms around Leah's waist. The breeze around them was brisk and smelled of dry leaves and the start of the holiday season. "It's completely understandable if you're nervous."

"Except I'm not nervous," Leah said as she adjusted Billie's necktie. She ran her fingertips from the Windsor knot to where the tie disappeared into Billie's V-neck sweater. "Where did you manage to find a tie with turkeys on it?"

"You can find anything online." Billie kissed Leah's forehead and relished its warmth. She thought for a moment about her own nerves and found it hard to believe Leah had no concerns. "Not even a little nervous?"

Leah held Billie's face in her hands. "Do you want me to be nervous?"

"No, I just—"

"Good," Leah said, kissing the tip of Billie's nose.

Billie turned and watched as Leah skipped toward the Prius. She couldn't help but imagine what her dad would think or how her mother would act around Leah. Billie had never brought someone special home for a holiday, and as far as she was concerned, Thanksgiving was the major leagues.

Leah stuck her face out of the open passenger window. "Are you coming or not? I'm starving, and I will leave without you."

Billie laughed and went back to the car. She waited until she was settled and had her seat belt buckled before leaning across to kiss Leah sweetly. "I love you, and I'm very excited about today." She started the car and pulled out onto the empty street. "Thanksgiving has always been big in my family, but the guest list has slimmed down over the years thanks to petty family feuds." She glanced over to catch Leah craning her neck to watch the trees pass the windows. "Do you want to go over everyone's names again? We have a thirty-minute ride to study." She knew Leah had everyone memorized, but Billie was a firm believer in being triple-study-safe instead of sorry.

Leah rolled her eyes, but her small smile let Billie know she wasn't truly annoyed. "I got the names. I promise."

"Humor me." She lowered the radio and hooked her fingers around the steering wheel. Out of the corner of her eye, she noticed Leah starting to play with the belt of her wool trench coat and wondered if she was starting to maybe get a little nervous.

"Well, I already know Jesse. I'm very happy she'll be there because I know we'll have plenty to talk about if you get pulled away from me."

"Just no trash-talking me." Billie raised a finger.

"No promises, babe." Leah pinched her thigh. "Your mom and dad and your aunt Tiffany, who's your mom's sister and a pity invite."

Billie winced. "For lack of better wording."

"And Pops."

"Who will disagree with everything you say."

"I will let him."

"Even your personal life experiences."

"Old men love me."

Billie placed her hand on Leah's thigh and squeezed. Leah's thick tights made her muscular thigh feel firmer. "Pops is a tough one to soften." Leah traced the sensitive skin between Billie's fingers, her touch soft and teasing. Billie felt it in her chest.

"Some people said the same thing about you in the beginning."

Billie couldn't control her squawk of surprise. "What? What do you mean? Who? Who said that?" She kept turning her head from the road to Leah and back again at such a fast speed her neck started to hurt.

"The first year I saw you at Career Day."

"I talked to you."

"That wasn't the first year—that was the second year."

Billie racked her brain for the memory, but nothing came. "You were there, and I didn't know it?"

Leah nodded coyly. "I was new to the squad, and they thought it would be good to send a fresh, young face to meet with the high schoolers. At that time everyone with the EMS was over forty. Old? No. Old to teenagers? Yes." They shared a laugh. "I mostly stood there and let the veterans field any questions, but having me there did help. They had double the turnout."

Billie could very easily picture Leah, young and eager, surrounded by chatty teenagers. "Were most of kids who approached boys?" Billie said with a smirk. She could practically feel Leah's eye roll from across the car.

"Actually, smarty-pants, a lot of young women didn't even know they had a place in emergency services." Leah poked Billie's arm. "But yeah, that year it was mostly boys." Billie snorted. "*Anyway*, the point to this story is about how I saw this striking woman standing in the corner of the gym with her arms crossed and all authoritative. I kept watching you walk around and talk to students or workers. Each and every time you came close to our table, I'd be too intimidated to talk to you."

Billie couldn't believe what she was hearing. "I am not intimidating."

"I'm serious. I waited until we were just about ready to go and thanked the principal for having us. I tried to be cool and asked a bit more about the school's staff and thought I was very casual when I pointed to you."

"And what did Principal Whitman say about me?" Billie fidgeted a bit in the driver's seat. She and Mr. Whitman didn't always see eye to eye.

"He told me the students seemed to like you, but that you were a bit of a loner among the teachers. Imagine that."

"You know it takes me a while to warm up to people," Billie said earnestly, her defenses going up immediately. "Now everyone loves me."

"All I'm saying is maybe Pops has been waiting eighty-plus years to warm up to the right person."

Billie had to laugh at Leah's reasoning. She shot her a sideways glance. "Were you really too intimidated to talk to me?"

"I was," Leah said, shrugging as if being intimidated was normal for her, which was not the case. "I was completely out of my element, and you were totally in yours. It also didn't help that I thought you were really hot. I was basically drooling." Leah started chuckling, the memory obviously tickling her now. "I was very obvious, too. My chief teased me about it for the rest of the week."

"You didn't say anything when we met at Nancy's party later that year."

"Because I was also introduced to your girlfriend."

Billie slowed to a stop at a red light. She looked over at Leah and couldn't help but get lost in a gigantic what-if. What if Leah had talked to during her first Career Day? Would they have hit it off then? "And then the next time we talked—"

"*I* had a girlfriend," Leah said, finishing Billie's sentence and proving, yet again, they were on the same wavelength.

"Three years and several broken hearts later, we're finally getting our chance." Billie knew her smile was goofy and beaming, but she could never control the happiness Leah made her feel. "Eight months together, and you're finally meeting my parents," Billie said, leaning across the center console and watching Leah start to pucker her lips. "You should be nervous."

Leah dodged Billie's kiss. "You're a jerk. Turn the car around. I changed my mind about Thanksgiving. I'd rather spend it alone."

Billie laughed much harder than she should've. "I'm sorry." She tried to kiss Leah again but was swiftly denied. "Come here." She made kissy noises as she strained her neck for a kiss. "Let me make it up to you."

A blaring car horn from behind forced Billie back into her seat, and she paid attention to the road. She never got a kiss, but judging by the small smile on Leah's full lips, she knew she'd get one soon enough.

Chapter Two

Leah was nearly caught up on all the latest celebrity gossip and couldn't understand why Billie was begging her to run into the bakery. She didn't even look away from her phone when she spoke. "You could've had the pies and been back in the car already." She needed to know whether Kim K. was going to stay with that leech of a boyfriend or not.

"Because Lena will chat my ear off, and I'll never make it out," Billie said, her voice reaching a whiny pitch. "Please, babe. Please do this for me?"

Leah could hear the pout and puppy dog eyes in Billie's tone. Against her better judgment, she looked at Billie and knew she'd get a pie from every bakery in the area for this woman. But that didn't mean she'd make it easy for her. "Hurry up," Leah said, ducking her head to hide her smile. "I don't want to be late. That's a terrible first impression." She could feel Billie staring at her and barely held back her laughter. "Lena will be so happy to see you. How long has it been?"

"A year."

Leah faked shock. "That's such a long time. I can't imagine going an entire year without seeing your adorable face." Leah bit the inside of her cheek. Billie blinked, her expression blank. "And from what you've told me, she's like a second mother to you. Imagine not seeing someone who's like a daughter to you in a year? Wow." Leah made a sound of disbelief in the back of her throat.

Billie pursed her lips, distracting Leah momentarily. Billie's lips had a personality of their own. The bow of Billie's upper lip was deeply defined, and the shape of her mouth was perfectly pouty and decadent. Those lips were moving again.

"I guess I'll be right back." Billie reached for the car door handle, but Leah stopped her.

"You know I'm a sucker for when you beg. I'll run in for you." She pulled Billie in and planted a scorching kiss on her mouth. She savored the way their lips fit so perfectly together. She pulled back slowly. "You owe me, though."

Billie touched the tip of her nose to Leah's softly. "Anything."

Leah ran her hand from the back of Billie's neck down her throat and chest and came to rest on her thigh. "I'll be thinking about that all day." She climbed out of the car before temptation for another kiss grew too intense, and she fixed her coat. She didn't want to look rumpled if she was about to meet Lena for the first time. A thought hit her, and she turned back to the car. She tapped on the window and waited for Billie to roll it down. She leaned into the car slightly. "You're not going to formally introduce me?"

Billie shrugged, looking only mildly ashamed. "You're on your own."

"And you're lucky you're cute."

Leah turned back to the bakery and fixed her hair. The bell above the door shouldn't have surprised her, but Leah jumped a little at its loud chime. A line of eager waiting patrons filled the small space. Many pressed their faces to the glass showcases, and small children stood on tiptoe to stare at baked goods in awe. Leah fell immediately in love with the charm of the bakery.

Christmas lights already lined the shelves, and a cornucopia filled with individually wrapped muffins caught her eye. She grabbed a corn muffin for Billie and a pistachio one for herself. A small display of house-made brittles caught Leah's attention next. She took a few packages and moved to the next station, where plastic containers were stacked in the shape of a Christmas tree. They appeared to be filled with chips of some kind. Leah leaned in closer to see what they were, and a young woman popped up from behind the counter.

"Those are cannoli shells cooked flat. We sell the filling on the side as a chip and dip dessert." She finally looked up from the box she was filling with pastries and gave Leah a brilliant smile. "Leah!"

Leah stared at this stranger who apparently knew her. Nothing about the woman was familiar, not her perfect teeth, wavy blond hair, or her vibrant eyes. "I'm sorry, do I know you?"

"No, oh God, I should be the one apologizing." She fumbled with the eclair in her hand before fitting it into the bursting box. "Give me a minute, and I'll explain."

She walked away and left Leah to consider whether she should just leave or if cannoli chips and dip would make for a nice dessert bonus to bring to Thanksgiving. "There's no such thing as too many desserts," Leah said quietly.

"I'm so sorry about that," the worker said as she reappeared in front of Leah. "I'm Eloise." She reached her hand across the counter.

Leah shook her hand and smiled as if the name meant something, but she was still drawing a blank. "Nice to meet you, Eloise."

"I know you because I'm friends with Billie. You two are very cute together." Eloise wiped her hands on her spattered and smudged apron.

Leah was intrigued by Eloise's almost nervous behavior. She was also intrigued by this friendship she knew nothing about. "Billie never mentioned you." She didn't mean for the words to come out as harshly as they did. Leah winced. "I just mean I haven't heard much about her old friends."

Eloise's smile looked stiff as she nodded. "We're mostly friends online now. We used to be really close through grade school and high school. But I went away to college, and we sort of went our separate ways then. I'm grateful for social media because it keeps me in the loop, but it also makes me look like a total creep." Eloise laughed quietly, a sweet and self-deprecating sound. "Are you headed to the Mullins' for Thanksgiving?"

The freshly baked loaves of bread and rolls displayed on the wall behind Eloise momentarily distracted Leah. "I am. We just stopped for the pies. Are those rye rolls?"

"They are. Fresh baked this morning. I'll grab the pies for you."

"I'll take a dozen rolls, too." *We can always freeze them.*

"You got it."

Leah watched Eloise disappear into the back before continuing to shop. How much was too much when it came to bringing food to Thanksgiving dinner? She noticed chocolate-covered graham crackers surrounding a charming Hanukkah display. Leah had a weakness for anything involving graham crackers.

"Here we go," Eloise said as she reemerged. "Two pumpkin and a pecan for Pops."

Leah heard Billie's earlier words echo in her head. "Pops even gets his own pie?"

Eloise snorted. "Or else." She fit the three pie boxes in one bag and started to fill another with all the goodies Leah had accumulated. Leah topped the bag with a container of cannoli filling and chips. "I think that'll satisfy everyone."

Leah lifted and tested the weight of the bags. If these treats didn't win the Mullins over, nothing would. She smiled to herself, feeling quite smug. "How much do I owe you?"

"Nothing," Eloise said with a wave of her hand. "The Mullins never get charged, but please tell Billie I said hi, and I'm not mad she didn't come in herself. I know how my mom can be with her." Eloise opened and closed her hand like a running mouth.

"Your mother?" Leah knew her brain wasn't connecting something. The light bulb finally went off, and she wanted to smack herself. "Lena's your mother."

Eloise nodded.

"You're Ellie!"

Eloise's cheeks grew a touch rosier. "Wow, I haven't heard that nickname in years." Eloise touched her hand to her face.

"I'm sorry. If I had known you were Ellie, I wouldn't have been so stiff before. Billie talks about you and Lena all the time. Is she here? I'd like to meet her."

Eloise shook her head. "Mom had to have knee surgery. That's why I'm here. She'll be sad to know she missed you, though." She smiled, but the corners of her mouth barely turned up. "Billie and I were inseparable as kids."

Leah leaned forward on the counter and lowered her voice. "What happened?"

Eloise shrugged and turned her attention to the corner of her apron. "Life."

Leah was more curious than ever about Billie's past and the people who'd shaped her into the adult she was now, but she knew no more answers would be found here. "Thank you for the pies and the treats, Eloise. At least I know if meeting the parents doesn't go well, I won't starve." She held up the two bags.

"Oh my God," Eloise said with wide, bright eyes. Her mouth fell open into a gigantic smile. "You're meeting Billie's family for the first time." Eloise started clapping and nearly startled Leah. "This is so exciting."

Leah looked around, embarrassed. "It's really not a big deal. I've already met her aunt, and I'm pretty sure she's more important to Billie than her parents are." Every ounce of cheerfulness and color drained from Eloise's face. She started to worry she had said something wrong. "That was just a joke," she said quickly, desperately trying to backpedal. "Billie loves her parents very much."

A smile returned to Eloise's face, but it lacked sparkle and authenticity. "You're right. The bond Billie shares with Jesse is really something. They care very much about each other." Eloise wouldn't meet Leah's eyes again. "I have to get back to work. It was nice meeting you, Leah. I hope you enjoy the pies."

Leah couldn't get another word out before Eloise turned away. She couldn't sort out what had just happened, and she was more confused by the time she got back to the car. Billie lowered the radio as she got in.

"I thought you were lost forever. Did Lena get you? I'm really sorry if she did."

Leah shook her head, feeling the intensity of her own frown. "Lena wasn't there. She had to have surgery."

"Oh no, I hope she's okay. I'm sure my mom knows the scoop." Billie started to back out of the spot.

"Eloise helped me."

Billie looked at Leah quickly with wide, surprised eyes. "Ellie's back? No way," she said, smiling. "Last I knew, she took a job in Baltimore. Her Instagram and Facebook went stagnant a few months ago." Billie looked back at the bakery as if contemplating going in. "I'll have to reach out."

Leah noticed the difference between Billie's reaction and what she had seen on Eloise's face. She wondered about their past relationship and the rest of the story. "Yeah. You should do that." She turned back to look out the window and the bare trees that passed by.

CHAPTER THREE

Billie knew her grip was a bit tight, but she didn't want to let go of Leah's hand for any reason as they walked up to the front door.

"So, this is where you grew up?" Leah's tone wasn't judgmental.

Billie tried to see their modest home through Leah's eyes. Leah didn't come from money, but she grew up in a nice home in a flourishing neighborhood, and while Billie never felt inferior, she'd never shake being self-conscious. "It's not much," she said, starting the well-rehearsed brush-off she'd used all through her young adult life, "but between here and Jesse's house, I had a great childhood."

"I love it, and I love you." Leah kissed Billie's cheek.

Billie couldn't get enough of these moments, where Leah seemed to know just what she needed to stand taller, feel better, and be happier. These were the moments that told Billie she was right for wanting to spend the rest of her life with Leah. She choked back a strong swell of emotion and brought Leah's hand to her lips. "Are you ready?" She kissed Leah's knuckles softly.

"I am."

"Are you nervous yet?"

"Still not nervous."

Billie didn't get it, but the front door opened suddenly and any time left to dwell on Leah's surprising behavior evaporated. She smiled at her father, who stood tall and took up most of the doorway. "Hey, Dad."

"Hey, kiddo. Do you like standing out in the cold?" He looked from Billie to Leah, his smile growing exponentially. "Come on in." He ushered them both into the house, where smells of Thanksgiving dinner engulfed them. "Let me take your coats. Billie's here," her dad said loudly enough to be heard across the home.

Billie's heart sped up the moment she heard approaching footsteps. Her father was easy. He loved everyone, and everyone loved him. But her mother? Different story. Claire Mullin carried herself quietly but judged loudly, and a lot of her judgment was directed at how Billie lived her life. Regardless of their rocky relationship, Billie smiled the moment her mother entered the living room. Holidays made her mushy, and it had been months since they had seen each other.

"Did you get the pies?" her mom said with little regard for their guest.

Billie just stared at her mom, her smile falling away. She chose to ignore the sting and press on with the introduction she had been imagining for weeks. "Mom, Dad, this is my girlfriend, Leah."

Leah extended her free hand to Billie's dad and raised the bag in her other hand. "It's so nice to meet you, and I have the pies right here."

Billie watched the easy way Leah smiled and giggled as she was pulled into a big bear hug. Her mom was a bit colder with her welcome, unsurprisingly, accepting the handshake and the pies with barely a word spoken.

"I'm glad you were able to make it to dinner," her mom said. She turned her attention to Billie and scowled. "A tie? Do you really think that's necessary?"

"It's not every day you get to wear a tie with turkeys on it."

Her mom's eyes widened in what looked like horror. "Do you wear ties often?"

"Let's sit down and catch up," her dad said. He always knew when to step in to avoid an argument.

"You all relax," her mom said. "Pops and Tiffany should be here soon, and I'm sure your sister will stroll in whenever she feels like it. I'll be in the kitchen."

Dad rolled his eyes, and Billie bit the inside of her cheek to keep from laughing.

"Would you like some help, Mrs. Mullin? I'm a very good cook," Leah said eagerly.

Her mother narrowed her eyes and looked Leah up and down. If Billie had to guess, she was trying to figure out if Leah was lying or not. Billie tugged at her collar, her tie feeling a bit tight suddenly.

"No, thank you. You sit with Dad and Billie. Make yourself at home."

Billie took Leah's hand and led her to the couch. They sat together but kept a small space between them.

"I'll get us some drinks," her dad said. "I have a pot of coffee on, or I could get you water or juice?"

"Nothing for me," Leah said.

"I'll take a water. Thanks, Dad." Billie waited for him to leave the room before turning to Leah and taking her hands. "Nervous yet?"

Leah shook her head. "They're sweet."

Billie frowned so deeply it hurt. "My mother barely said two words to you."

"But your dad is very kind, and if he's been married to your mom for this long, she's got to be sweet."

"Interesting logic but prepare yourself to be very wrong."

"Here's your water," he said cheerfully as he entered the room. The doorbell rang. "I wonder who that could be."

Billie took her water as he passed. "I hope it's Jesse."

Leah placed her hand on Billie's thigh and leaned in to whisper, "I get the distinct impression your mother doesn't like Jesse very much."

"Oh, she loves Jesse, but she loves her like a real sister." At Leah's curious look, Billie elaborated. "She loves her, but sometimes she can't stand her." She could tell Pops was there by the shuffling sound behind her. She looked over her shoulder in time to catch Pops swatting Dad's hand away as he reached for his coat. "That's Pops and Aunt Tiffany," Billie said, disappointment heavy in her tone.

"Should we get up and say hello?"

"Nah, let them come to us." Billie just wanted a moment to read Tiffany's mood. Tiffany looked a lot like Billie's mother, except she was two inches taller and slimmer, a fact her mother never let her live down. Both women had aged gracefully and chosen to keep their shoulder-length hair a light shade of brown. Tiffany looked tired and already irritated by the world.

"Billie, dear, do you know if your mother has made mimosas yet?" Tiffany leaned down and kissed Billie's cheek. She moved on to kiss Leah's cheek without even an introduction.

Billie watched the exchange in confusion. "No, she, uh, hasn't made mimosas in years. Aunt Tiffany, this is my girlfriend, Leah."

Tiffany patted Leah's shoulder and sighed. "The one tradition I was counting on. I'm sure she has booze somewhere." Tiffany made her way to the kitchen, shrugging off her puffy jacket and leaving it on her dad's recliner along the way.

"I didn't really know what to expect from her today," Billie said to Leah quietly out of the side of her mouth, "but I don't think this was it." She wondered if Leah's eyes were wide with terror or amusement, but Pops hit her leg with his cane before she could ask.

"Move over and let the old man sit on the end." He plopped down beside Billie with a grunt. "What's with the tie? I didn't know this was a formal occasion."

Billie touched her hand to her neck and smiled. "I thought it'd be nice to dress up for Leah's first Thanksgiving with us. And it has turkeys on it."

"It's just a meal," Pops said in a grumble. "We should wear whatever we want."

She turned back to Leah and lowered her voice. "I'm beginning to regret the tie."

Leah pressed her shoulder into Billie's. "I love the tie, and I appreciate how you wanted to dress up to make today special."

Billie looked at Leah's face, focusing first on her full lips and sparkling eyes, and then at the way the slope of her neck was defined by the choker she wore to complement her black and burgundy dress. "I really want to kiss you right now, but I don't want to give Pops a heart attack."

"I guess you'll just have to wait, then."

"Or…" Billie stood and tilted her head to get Leah to follow. "I'm going to show Leah around. She wants to see my childhood home. Be right back."

"Don't take too long," Dad said. "They're going to show the parade again soon."

"We won't miss it." Billie placed her hand on the small of Leah's back and led her out of the room. Her smile was less than innocent. They walked down a narrow hallway that took them to the opposite end of the house from the kitchen. "My parents' room is just off the kitchen. My room is just over here." She swung the door open and closed it behind Leah. "They changed everything a minute after I moved out, but once upon a time this was a really cool room."

Leah looked around at the plain oak furniture and lacy window treatment. The bedspread was a deep green, and pictures of the ocean took up two walls. "It's hard to imagine what you were like in high school."

Billie stepped into Leah's space and reveled in the effect she had on her. Leah was very responsive. Even sharing body heat made her eyes get heavy. "I was a bit of a geek but still popular. I think it's because I was kind of taboo."

"What do you mean?" Leah tilted her head, and her eyebrows pulled together slightly. She always had such a serious look on her face when she listened to Billie tell a story, and Billie always felt really seen and heard.

"I was out in high school and didn't look much different from this," Billie said, motioning to her body, "except I had zero fashion sense."

Leah laughed. "I'm glad that improved."

She kissed the deep dimple in Leah's right cheek. "The way I looked confused people, and kids didn't really know what to make of me. Was I a girl who wanted to be a guy? Was I really gay? Was I the only gay person they ever knew or would ever know? It also didn't help that I was painfully shy, so as much as I stuck out, I also disappeared into the crowd."

Leah ran her hands up Billie's arms and put on a playful pout. "Were you lonely?"

"No."

"Did you have a high school sweetheart?"

Billie laughed and snorted faintly. "Definitely not."

"No? No one special?" Leah touched the prickly buzzed hair on the back of her head. "Not even a friend with benefits?"

Billie noticed the way Leah's eyes stayed on her chin as she spoke. The line of questioning was interesting, but Billie wanted to keep her focus in one place only. "Nope," she said with an exaggerated pop. She put her hands on Leah's hips and pulled her closer. "I never even kissed a girl in this room."

"My, my. Are you asking me to be your first?"

Billie wanted to ask if Leah would be her last, too, but instead of risking the moment, she leaned in and kissed her gently. She'd never grow tired of the softness that came effortlessly for them.

Leah snaked her hands into Billie's jacket, and the urgency bubbling beneath the surface was palpable. Leah ran the tip of her tongue along Billie's upper lip before pulling back. "Is it weird that the smell of Thanksgiving dinner is making this even hotter for me?"

Billie chuckled while she reached down to squeeze Leah's full behind. "If that's the case, I'll be making turkey a lot more often." She burrowed her face into the crook of Leah's neck and nipped at the sensitive skin there. Her mom called out for her, her voice carrying through the house the way only a mother's could. "I guess that's our cue." Billie took Leah's hand and led her back into the hive of Mullins.

CHAPTER FOUR

Leah kept trying to peek into the kitchen to see what Billie was up to. Billie's mother—Claire—had demanded Billie help her and insisted in a not-so-subtle way that Leah not join them. She wiped her sweaty palms on her thighs and forced a smile. She listened to Greg, Billie's dad, argue with Pops about the tradition of the parade. Pops stood his ground that everything in American tradition has changed for the worse, including the Macy's Thanksgiving Day Parade. Leah simply nodded when anyone spoke.

"So, Leah, what's your story? Billie hasn't really told me much." Tiffany sat back and crossed her legs. She was slumped into the couch, her burgundy high heel dangling from her foot as she bounced her leg.

Leah felt a momentary sting from the words. Billie had no real reason to talk about her with Tiffany—they weren't close like she was with Jesse—but something about Tiffany's phrasing caused an affliction. She was jaded about love, Leah reminded herself. "I'm an EMT in Seaside Heights."

"Yikes. That's a rough area to work in. I bet you see a lot of crazy things."

Leah thought of at least a dozen horrendous and amusing calls from that past summer alone, but she kept each one to herself. None of it was appropriate Thanksgiving chatter. "It can be pretty wild, but it's balanced by everyday accidents."

"Doesn't really seem like a job for a woman," Pops said.

Leah wished he would keep his opinion to himself this one time. She took in a deep breath. "There's a lot of women in my field, actually."

"Just because there is, doesn't mean there should be."

He's old, he's old, he's old. "Well, I happen to be one of the best in my region. My male captain told me so."

"Probably because you're pretty."

Greg cleared his throat loudly. "Pretty young. You must feel very accomplished."

Leah appreciated the save. "I do, and I love my job. I can't imagine doing anything else with my life." She fussed with the hem of her dress and wished Billie would come back into the room now.

"Billie comes from a family of teachers, which I'm sure you already know." Greg placed his mug on the coffee table and reclined in his chair. "But when she was six, she wanted to be a weatherman."

Leah perked up and her heart swelled. "Did she really?"

He started chuckling, his rounded belly bouncing. "Oh yeah. She was obsessed with watching the weather. She would get so mad at me when I'd change the channel."

"I guess you didn't know this about your sweetheart?" Tiffany's tone was unnecessarily snarky. "Everyone is full of secrets, hon. Get used to it."

"I hardly think this is a secret," Leah said, trying her best to tamp down her defensiveness. "But it's definitely something I'll be teasing her about."

Tiffany's coffee almost spilled over as she waved her hand. Leah wondered what else might have been in that cup. "Everyone lies, and everyone hides things. The sooner you accept that, the sooner you'll avoid a broken heart."

"Tiffany," Greg said firmly, "I don't think Leah needs to worry about Billie breaking her heart."

Tiffany snorted, and Leah felt torn between the two and the desire to stand up for her relationship—the relationship she'd felt one hundred percent secure in until that morning. She shook off Tiffany's implications and the questions she had since meeting Eloise. "Thank you for the advice, Tiffany."

"You mean a lot to my daughter," Greg said. "She's never brought anyone home for a holiday, not even a Fourth of July barbecue."

Even though Leah already knew it, hearing him confirm Billie's lack of serious relationships made her grow uneasy. She was beginning to understand why Billie expected her to be nervous. "She means a lot to me, too, sir."

"Oh God, do not call me sir." He pointed his finger at Pops. "Sir him. He's the old one."

Pops looked at Greg with a mean frown. "I may be old, but I can still kick your ass."

Leah forced a laugh and knew it sounded stiff. She glanced at the doorway to the kitchen one more time and prayed Billie would appear to save her. She even considered getting up and finding Billie, but she had no idea if what was happening in the kitchen was a better situation than the one she found herself in now. Leah stayed put and listened to Tiffany talk about her ex-husband's trampy new girlfriend.

❖

Billie leaned back against the counter as she watched her mom baste the turkey. The outside was turning the perfect tempting golden brown. "No one's turkey compares to yours."

"It's all in the Gravy Master." Her mom closed the oven and took off her oven mitt. "Leah seems nice."

"She is."

"Why isn't she with her family today?"

"Because I invited her here."

"Does she have family?" Her mom checked the cranberries bubbling away on the stove top.

"She does, but they're not very close."

"Is it because she's gay?"

Billie crossed her arms over her chest and stared at her mother. "If you're so interested in her life story, she's just in the other room. You can ask her yourself."

Her mom looked at her like she had just suggested she fly to the moon in the family Cadillac. "Are you going to have an attitude all day?"

She bristled. "I don't have an attitude. I'm just curious why you suddenly have a hundred questions about my girlfriend. I basically left her in a den of wolves to help you in here."

"I'm sorry helping me is such a burden."

Billie clenched her jaw to rein in her rising aggravation. "It's not a burden, but you're also not letting me help you. I haven't done a thing since coming in here."

"Get the rolls from the refrigerator."

"Fine." Billie did as she was told and placed two tubes of refrigerated rolls on the counter.

"The turkey will come out in ten minutes, and then those will go in. I need parchment paper."

Billie lined two baking sheets with parchment paper. "Leah is a great baker. She's constantly making different treats and sending them with me to work. The whole faculty loves me."

"They love you for you. Don't think some girl made that happen."

"Leah isn't *some girl.* I'm serious about her."

"Okay." The way she said it made Billie's blood boil.

"What is your problem with Leah?"

"I don't have a problem with Leah. I just don't think you're doing this right."

Billie pressed her fingertips to her temples. This Thanksgiving was going to drive her crazy. "How? How do you know I'm not doing this right?"

"You haven't had a real relationship, and now suddenly this girl shows up and she's perfect? It's unrealistic."

"We were friends for years and have been dating for eight months. This didn't happen overnight."

"Then why am I just meeting her now?"

"Maybe this is why," Billie said between clenched teeth, struggling to keep her voice down.

Her mom stopped dead in her tracks, breadbasket in one hand and decorative napkin in the other. "Forgive me for being critical of the first girl you ever brought home. Did it occur to you that I've been mentally preparing myself for this moment since you were fourteen? Since you told me you were, well, you know."

Billie widened her eyes and leaned in. "Gay?"

"I want you to be happy. I want you to find someone who makes you happy. But right now, I feel like you're making the same mistake as your aunt. You're going to end up as miserable as she is."

Billie knew her mom was making zero sense. "Aunt Tiffany was with Uncle Bob for eleven years, and it was a train wreck from day one."

"I'm not talking about Tiffany." Her mother grabbed the tablecloth neatly folded over the back of a kitchen chair and threw it on her shoulder. The burgundy and greens in the floral pattern brought out her dark eyes. "You always insist on following in Jesse's footsteps, and I really wish you wouldn't."

She watched her mother march out of the room toward the dining room, almost colliding with Leah. Despite Billie's confusion, she grinned at Leah. Her gorgeous face could always brighten a moment, no matter how dark.

"Is everything okay in here?" Leah said, peeking into the oven window.

"I'm more worried about how things were going out there." Billie reached out for Leah's hand and pulled her to lean against the counter with her. She played with Leah's delicate fingers and marveled at how strong her feminine hands really were. "They were nice to you, I hope."

"I hate to admit it, but you were right."

"About what exactly?"

"I'm nervous."

Billie smiled triumphantly for a second before falling into a panic. "No, no, no. You're supposed to be relaxing as the day goes on, not *getting* nervous. What happened?"

"Pops is something else."

She knew avoidance a mile away. "What did they say to you?"

"Nothing," Leah said, but the deep crease between her eyes told Billie otherwise.

Billie let out a long, slow breath. "If we leave now, I can stop at a store and pick up a turkey and some sides. We can have our own Thanksgiving at my place. We're taking the pies, too."

"We are not running away." Leah framed Billie's face in her hands. Billie was soothed and lost in Leah's soft eyes. "We are here to spend Thanksgiving with your family, and we are going to do just that."

The security she felt with Leah allowed Billie to bare it all. "What if they scare you away?"

"They won't."

"What if they make you realize I'm not worth it?"

"You are totally worth it." Leah kissed her softly.

"What if you don't see the same future for us as I do, because you don't want to be a part of this dysfunctional family?" Billie waited, but Leah's touch never wavered.

Her mom stomped her way back into the room before Leah could speak. They separated like criminals caught in the act. "Do you need help setting the table, Mrs. Mullin?" Leah fidgeted with her hands.

Billie could've laughed at the absurdity of being thirty-one and shy in front of her mother, but some tendencies ran deep. "I'll get the rolls in the oven."

Her mother looked between them, her cheeks a shade redder than before. "I would appreciate the help from both of you. Leah, I have some napkins for you to roll. You can do it at the dining room table. That'll keep you far away from the grouch." Leah followed her out of the kitchen, but not before shooting a wink over her shoulder.

Billie didn't know what to make of the afternoon thus far. What did her mother mean with her odd hints at Jesse's romantic life? She knew Jesse's latest relationship had gone up in smoke, but what did that have to do with her and Leah? Billie groaned as she popped open the cardboard tube, no longer frightened by its unpredictability.

She had all but told Leah, point-blank, that she planned on marrying her, and all she got was a delayed wink in return. If her family wasn't going to ruin her perfect relationship, she'd more than likely do the dirty work herself. She distracted herself with the monotonous and calming task of rolling dough into perfect crescent rolls. The shape, size, and curve of each buttery delight were the only three things Billie was capable of controlling.

Chapter Five

L eah stood back and watched Billie greet her aunt Jesse. She adored their bond and had never seen family be so effortlessly close. Part of her was jealous. Leah's own aunt disappeared from her family more than fifteen years ago, thinking she was better than everyone else. Jesse wasn't like that. Jesse was there and treated Billie like a best friend, all while carrying her close to her heart and under her wing. Leah considered herself lucky to have Jesse in her life now, too.

Jesse went to Greg next. No one would know they were siblings, the resemblance between them unnoticeable until they were side by side. Jesse was ten years younger than his fifty-one, but she looked much closer to thirty. Leah couldn't help but smile as they hugged.

"It's about time Jesse showed up," Billie said as she returned to Leah.

"I know. I could see you panic-sweating from the dining room." She elbowed Billie gently and continued to act the voyeur. Jesse's hello to Claire was stiff and left Leah cringing with secondhand awkwardness. "Seriously, what is the beef between your mom and Jesse?"

"I don't know. They've been like that for as long as I can remember. It's never caused any major family drama, but the tension has always been there."

"Aw, Pops is so sweet with Jesse." Leah covered her heart with her hands as they embraced. Tiffany stepped up next and nearly pushed Pops out of the way. Tiffany's hug was longer than necessary, and her smile fit the textbook definition of flirty. "And what is happening there?" She looked at Billie, who stood immobile, positively horrified.

"Oh my God."

Tiffany held Jesse's bicep as she lamented how long it had been since they'd seen each other. She insisted on taking Jesse's jacket and even helped slip it off Jesse's shoulders. Tiffany took the bottle of wine Jesse brought and giggled like it was a personal gift just for her.

"Oh my *God*," Billie said again, looking away. "Jesse's not into it, is she? Right? She can't be. What is happening?" Billie sounded panicked.

"She's breaking free and coming over here." Leah tried her best to read Jesse's face as she approached but couldn't. "Hi, Jesse."

Jesse offered a hug to Leah immediately, not bothering with a verbal hello. "I can't believe you're here."

Leah wanted to scream at another mention of Billie never bringing anyone home. "I know, I know, I'm the first girlfriend to be brought home for the holidays."

Jesse hummed and nodded. "I actually mean I cannot believe you willingly came here to be with this family for Thanksgiving," she said, turning to Billie. "Did you not prepare her? Oh my God, did you send her into this without warning?"

Jesse was relieving some of Leah's earlier stress. "I came here with both eyes open, yes."

"You're either really brave or really in love."

"Both." Billie snaked her arm around Leah's waist. "Definitely both."

Leah touched her rapidly warming cheek. Time to deflect. "It's a shame you're single. I would've loved to have had an equal number of gays and straights. They always outnumber us."

Jesse chuckled. "Maybe next year."

Billie's eyes lit up. "Does that mean you have someone in mind?"

Jesse started shaking her head furiously. "No, not at all."

"Come on, that's impossible. How long has it been?"

Jesse looked at her boots and then the window. She puffed out her cheeks with a long breath. "I, uh, Stacy was my last long-term relationship."

"You haven't dated anyone since the beginning of the year? That's crazy." Billie's face was comically shocked. "I've never known you to go that long. Not since you and Carole split."

Leah winced. Everyone knew Carole was a sore subject, but Billie still felt the need to mention her. She said the first thing that came to mind to defuse the bomb. "Ugh. Carole. The worst."

Jesse looked at Leah, and the likeness to Billie sparkled in her eyes. They had the same charm and the same easy smile. "You didn't even know Carole."

"I've heard enough stories, and from what I've gathered, the only person worse than Carole is Stacy."

Jesse looked between Leah and Billie. "I really do like this one," she said to Billie. "Let's hope she lasts the day." Jesse clapped her hand on Billie's shoulder and sauntered off to the living room.

Leah loved how Billie looked just a little bit scared. "I will make it through today, just like you'll make it through tomorrow when I drag you shopping."

Billie's fright turned quickly into exasperation. "You're nuts for going out on Black Friday."

"It's a tradition."

"A crazy one."

"One I want you to be a part of now." She checked over Billie's shoulder to make sure the family was occupied with each other. She kissed her quickly. "I promise to make it up to you." She poured every ounce of seduction she could muster into her tone. "I'll give you or let you take anything you want."

"Uh—" Billie looked down at Leah's chest and licked her lips. She was definitely getting flustered. "You don't have to do that."

She raised her eyebrows. "Are you saying no?"

"No," Billie said, a little too loudly. She cleared her throat and lowered her voice. "I just mean, like, you don't have to do that."

Leah shook her head and searched Billie's eyes for the clarity she wasn't giving verbally. "You said that."

Billie clamped her eyes shut, impatience written clearly on her face. "If we leave here together, and you still want to be with me…"

"Billie—"

"I'll be the one trying to make it up to you. And I owe you for running into the bakery."

Leah fixed the knot of Billie's tie and left her hand on Billie's chest. "And what if I said being taken by you *completely* is all I could ask for in return?" She pulled Billie in for what looked like an innocent hug any couple would share in front of family without a second thought. Leah tilted her head to press her lips to Billie's ear. "I want you to fuck me so hard I forget today even happened." She heard Billie swallow and pulled back.

Billie wouldn't even look at her. "Do you need a drink? I need a drink." Billie marched off to the kitchen, Leah hot on her heels. Billie swung the refrigerator door open, right into her knee. "Son of a bitch," she said, the words coming out like a squeak.

Leah covered her mouth to hide her laughter while Billie rubbed her knee furiously. "Are you okay?"

Claire breezed into the kitchen. "Billie. Stop messing around, and check on your rolls." She breezed out of the kitchen.

Billie stood upright and waved at her mother's retreating form. "I'm fine."

"Are you really hurt?" Leah said, wincing the whole time.

"I'm fine. I'll bruise, but I'm fine." Billie walked over to the oven and opened it. "Shit."

"Are they burned?"

"Almost." Billie pulled the two trays of rolls out of the oven. Each little crescent was definitely on the darker side of brown.

"Wait," Leah said, rushing to the stuffed bakery bag and pulling out a bag of rolls. "I got these for us, but we can use them now."

"Brilliant." Billie took the bag of rolls and kissed Leah's cheek. "A brilliant and beautiful lifesaver."

"A tad bit of an exaggeration, but I'll take it." A loud shriek broke them apart.

"The rolls." Claire started picking them up one by one and checking their bottoms. Leah worried she'd get burned, but the heat didn't faze her. "I gave you one job, and now we won't have any bread with dinner."

"It's fine, Mom. We have these rolls from the bakery. They'll be even better."

Claire stared at the rolls in Billie's hand. "We always have crescent rolls."

"And we can try something new this year."

Leah felt her anxiety mount as she watched Claire evaluate the rolls with a critical eye. She should've never distracted Billie from her baking duties. Guilt flooded her. Thanksgiving dinner could've been ruined because of her.

"We don't have much of a choice, do we?" Claire said, opening the bag and squeezing a small round roll. "Warm them in the oven, and please set a timer. Leah, keep an eye on her."

Billie looked at Leah once Claire left the kitchen. Her mouth was agape. "I should tell her this is your fault."

"I'm really, really sorry." Leah rushed to Billie and almost grabbed her but thought better of it at the last second and pulled back. "I'll tell her it was me. I don't want your mom to be mad at you all day." Billie replaced the burnt rolls with new ones and stuck them in the oven. She was completely silent as she set the timer for five minutes. "I don't want you to be mad at me all day."

Billie stepped back from where she was dutifully watching the rolls warm. "You think I'm mad at you?"

Leah felt silly instantly but couldn't help it. "Well, yeah. I got you in trouble with your mother and almost ruined Thanksgiving."

Billie laughed and shook her head. "I'm always in trouble with my mom," she said, prepping the breadbasket, "and something always goes wrong with dinner. We were lucky it was something small this time. Last year the yams bubbled over onto the bottom of the oven and caused a small fire, and we couldn't get the smoke alarms to shut off for an hour."

"Okay. That's a little worse."

"Then there was the year Pops thought he was having a heart attack, but it was just gas." Billie smiled at Leah's laugh. "The food was cold, and the paramedics burped my grandfather in front of an audience."

Leah straightened her back, feeling a bit better about the situation. "I have to be careful and make sure not to distract you again."

Billie handed a now full breadbasket to Leah. "Lucky for me, dinner's just about ready. You can go back to distracting me all you want."

Leah was tempted by Billie's smirk and the way her jaw muscle pulsed. She was tempted by how warm Billie's neck would be against her lips.

"Leah?"

She spun around to face an expectant Claire. "Yeah?" She sounded out of breath.

"Put the rolls on the table."

"Yup. You got it. Going now." Leah marched out, a tight grip on the basket, and didn't look anyone in the eye as she settled at the dining room table. She really needed to get herself together if she was going to survive this Thanksgiving.

CHAPTER SIX

Billie filled her wineglass after making sure everyone else was set with beverages. She sat back and placed her napkin on her lap. Jesse, Tiffany, and Pops sat opposite her and Leah. Her parents took their spots at each end of the table. Her stomach growled the moment her dad cleared his throat.

"Who wants to say grace?" His smile was polite, and he folded his hands on the tabletop. Not one person volunteered, and Pops reached for a spoonful of cranberry sauce. "I guess I'll do it." He made the sign of the cross. "Thank you, Lord, for giving our family another year together and for this wonderful meal. We are grateful for the love in our lives."

Billie peeked at Leah out of the corner of her eye. Leah's head was down, and she wore a small smile. She grabbed Leah's hand and gave it a squeeze.

"Amen." The sentiment echoed around the table.

"Let's eat," her dad said, standing and grabbing a large serving fork.

Everyone helped themselves to heaping amounts of steaming food. Billie waited patiently for Tiffany to finish with the gravy, and in the meantime, Leah buttered a roll for her. Jesse laughed when both she and Billie reached for the canned cranberry sauce, foregoing the homemade stuff every year. It was almost like a mutual boycott.

Moments of silence passed as everyone devoured the feast. Billie's favorite meal was always Thanksgiving dinner. Ever since she was little, she lost herself to clouds of mashed potatoes, rivers of gravy, and the perfect balance of savory turkey to sweet cranberry and yams. To her, the meal was perfection.

"Where are you from, Leah?" her dad asked. Billie was so happy with how interested he was in getting to know Leah.

Leah set her fork down and wiped her mouth before answering. "Actually, I was born in Florida, but my family moved to Michigan not too long after that."

"What brought you to New Jersey?"

"My mom had some family up here. After she and my dad divorced, she wanted my brother and me to have a fresh start. I've called Jersey home since I was eleven. I can't imagine living anyplace else." Leah gave Billie a coy smile.

"Billie always talked about leaving New Jersey the first chance she got," Tiffany said, raising her wineglass. "Isn't that right, Billie?"

Billie looked at Tiffany in horrified confusion. "Yeah, years ago, like when I was getting ready for college and wanted to move out." She started to panic that Leah would misunderstand. "I love my life here now."

"It's okay, babe." Leah rubbed her shoulder, instantly soothing her. "I think most people who live in New Jersey dream of running away at one time or another. Remember how much I complained last winter?"

Billie definitely remembered the complaining, but she also remembered the warm bed they spent a few snow days in. "I don't think I've ever met someone who hates snow as much as you do."

"None of you know what snow is," Pops said loudly. "You think you have it bad when you're driving along salted roads in your big trucks."

Billie said, "I drive a Prius—"

"When I was young, we walked almost everywhere, and if we did drive, our cars could only handle a couple of inches before you'd slide all over the place. Stores would close, and people would stay home." He slammed his fist for emphasis. "Nowadays you're all so worried about getting what you need right away. You're spoiled." An awkward silence followed his tirade.

"You really should get something better than a Prius," Jesse said, effectively breaking the tension.

Billie held up her hand, offended. "I love my Prius. Your Blazer is a joke. Did you even fit it out front, or did you have to park it on the football field around the corner?"

"My Blazer is sexy, and I can actually buy more than a bunch of bananas and one roll of paper towels when I go food shopping."

Leah chimed in with, "Oh, come on, Jesse, you're exaggerating."

Billie smiled. "Thank you."

"I can fit in the car, too. Even with the bunch of bananas and the roll of paper towels."

Billie's face fell, and everyone around the table started laughing. She was ecstatic that Leah was fitting in and getting along. She deepened her frown. "Whose side are you on?" She added a dramatic pout.

"Aww. I'm always on your side." Leah smooshed Billie's cheeks. "But I have a purse bigger than your car."

"Whatever." Billie picked up her fork and continued eating. "At least I won't go broke when gas costs more than four dollars a gallon," she said in a mumble. She felt Leah's hand on her thigh and then a gentle tap. She looked at Leah and knew by the way she raised her eyebrows she was checking in on her. Billie winked, a silent way of saying everything was great. Because it was.

"The rolls are different," Pops said. "Why are they different?"

Her mom shot her a look. "We had a mishap in the kitchen, but these came from Lena's bakery."

"How is Lena? Pass the green beans." Her father reached out and took the serving dish from Jesse.

Billie tilted her head. "She had some kind of surgery, is that right?"

"Knee surgery," her mother said as she delicately cut a slice of turkey into bite-sized pieces. "Her right knee was completely shot after standing for so many years in that place. It's truly a wonder she's made it this long without a replacement."

"What a terrible time for it," her dad said. "Who's working the bakery during the holidays?"

Billie perked up. "Ellie's back in town."

The loud clatter of silverware hitting fine china quieted the room as Jesse started coughing. She waved off anyone who showed concern. Half a glass of wine later, the coughing subsided.

Jesse pointed to her throat. "Cranberry sauce got me."

"I like the canned jelly stuff," Pops said as he poked at the small pile of cranberries on his plate.

Tiffany nodded. "I prefer canned over homemade, but it has to be whole. Not that log of jelly." She shivered.

"Oh." Her mom sat back and squared her shoulders. "So no one likes my homemade cranberry sauce."

Billie knew it was up to her to stop the argument before it escalated. "I like both, and the mashed potatoes are incredible."

Her mom relaxed slightly and smiled. "You've loved my mashed potatoes since you were in diapers. I still remember your first Thanksgiving. Your face was covered in them, and you were smiling the whole time."

Billie couldn't remember her first Thanksgiving, of course, but hearing her mother speak about it fondly made her heart smile. "I guess some things never change."

"When did Eloise get back?" Jesse said.

Billie looked at Jesse and tilted her head. "Uh, I don't know. Leah talked to her."

Leah nodded and finished chewing. "She didn't say. The bakery was so busy, we didn't really talk much." Leah cast a quick glance at Billie and then looked down.

"Last week," her mom said. "I invited them to dinner, but some of the women from church had it taken care of already. Rose made a whole turkey for them and everything."

Tiffany pushed her empty plate aside and refilled her wineglass. "Those holy rollers are really something."

"Don't be rude, Tiffany." Her mom shut down and focused on the last bits of her food.

Billie observed her family in the tense silence as they finished their meal. If anyone asked her right then and there what she was most thankful for, it would be that her time at home would be drawing to a close soon enough. She was ready to be alone at home with Leah, safe and sound.

Chapter Seven

Leah was more than happy to help clear off the table. She needed somewhere to channel her anxious energy after feeling the odd shift when Eloise was mentioned. Leah knew Jesse was in on the secret—that much was obvious. She hated feeling like she was in the dark about someone in Billie's past. And for Jesse to act so strangely, Eloise must've been very important.

"Are you going to put the dish in the sink, dear?" Claire said, saving Leah from her overactive imagination.

She placed the plate in the basin and continued to help with cleanup. Before her chest had the chance to fully loosen, she was back at the table with three pies before her. Dessert passed with very little conversation and a lot of Tiffany looking at her phone and commenting on what her ex was doing for Thanksgiving. She stared ahead at the pecan pie. Only one slice was gone.

"How's the pecan pie, Pops?" Leah said, still determined to win over the cantankerous old man.

"The best I've ever had."

Jesse laughed. "You say that every year."

"I mean it this time. Probably has something to do with that pretty young thing making it."

Leah rolled her eyes. The last thing she wanted was for the conversation to come back around to Eloise. "I make a pretty good pecan pie, actually. If I had known it was your favorite, I would've made one."

"Save yourself the trouble, Leah." Greg added another dollop of whipped cream to his slice of pumpkin pie. "Nothing beats the Grant women's pies. Lena has a magic touch and definitely passed it down."

"They really are the best," Billie said with her mouth full.

Leah was starting to hate the Grant women. "Guess I won't be baking you any pies."

Billie's eyes widened. "Let's not say anything crazy."

"Well, if I already know you won't like it—"

"I didn't say I wouldn't like it."

"That's exactly what you said." She knew her tone was sharp, and she took a deep breath. Now was not a good time to forget her surroundings. "I always want my cooking to be the best."

"And your *cooking* is the best, but I grew up with the best bakery in New Jersey ten minutes away. Their pies are the best pies, but that doesn't mean they're the only pies I like."

"This is the weirdest lovers' quarrel I've ever witnessed." Tiffany sipped more wine.

Leah's cheeks were on fire. "I'm sorry."

"Hey," Billie said, taking Leah's hand and lowering her voice, "I would love it if you baked a pie for me."

Tiffany snorted. "Glad that's settled."

"What's everyone's plans for Christmas?" Greg's voice was awkwardly loud.

"I'll be right here again," Tiffany said drolly.

Claire didn't look up from her pie. "Maybe with less wine."

Billie wiped her mouth. "We're heading to Leah's family's house in upstate New York."

"For the day or eve?" Claire said.

Leah answered, "Both. It's about a six-hour drive, so we'll head up on Christmas Eve, spend the night, and then head back after dinner on Christmas Day."

Greg chimed in. "What about you, sis? Will we be seeing you?"

"No. Liv and Theo invited me for Christmas dinner, and I promised a friend from work that I'd stop by their party on Christmas Eve."

"Who's having a party?" Billie asked, her brow pinched.

Jesse pulled a face like something stank. "It's a department thing."

Billie sat back with a huff. "Science nerds."

Leah could tell it genuinely bothered Billie to not be invited to a party. And Leah would say anything to make Billie feel better. "What kind of fun would the science department have anyway?"

"Please," Jesse said, all cockiness, "our parties are better than any snoozefest the English department would throw. What do you all do? Recite Shakespeare?"

Greg raised his hand. "Hey, hey now. The English department is not for the faint of heart."

"Sorry, bro. You all bore me." Jesse faked a yawn.

A thought struck Leah. "How's that one teacher in your department? The one you were telling me about that had a car accident and needed a bunch of surgeries."

"Terry? She's doing much better. I told her about the orthopedic doc you recommended, and he's helped her immensely." Jesse relaxed into her chair, the drowsiness that accompanied a full stomach evident in her heavy eyelids.

"What teacher is this?" Claire held her coffee mug in two hands.

"Terry Dorsey. She got into an awful accident at the start of the school year. Both her legs were broken. She was a mess."

"Jesse told me about her, and I know a lot of doctors because of my job. Dr. Lustgarten sees a lot of the traumas we bring in. I'm glad he was able to help."

Claire was shaking her head. "How long ago did she tell you about the accident?"

Leah was confused by the question but didn't think much of it. "Not too long after."

"Which helped with her recovery immensely." Jesse raised her glass to Leah.

"How long ago did you two meet?" Claire said.

Leah opened her mouth to answer, but Billie stopped her by sitting forward abruptly. "A while ago, but we have a lot of the same friends."

Claire stared at Billie, unblinking and intense. "Of course." She stood and collected the dessert plates without saying another word.

Leah felt paralyzed. She feared any sudden movements would detonate the bomb that was clearly about to go off. She looked at Billie, making her eyes as wide as she could, and tilted her head toward the kitchen when Claire walked away.

Billie lifted her shoulders. "What?"

"Go apologize."

"For what?"

"I don't know. Whatever upset her. Make it better," Leah said desperately. "We're not leaving until you make this better." She looked at the rest of the table, and everyone but Pops had the decency to act like they weren't just leaning in to listen. She had felt more embarrassment during this gathering than any other day in her life. Even when she'd peed her pants in the third grade.

"Fine." Billie tossed her napkin on the table and stood. She looked back at Leah once before disappearing into the kitchen.

"I'm going for a smoke." Tiffany picked up her plate of pie, grabbed her coat from the chair, and walked outside.

Greg watched Tiffany leave. "I think it's time for Charlie Brown. Care to join me, Pops?"

"Anything would be better than this." Pops used the table and the chair next to him to get up.

Leah wanted to help him, but she knew Pops wasn't the type to willingly accept assistance. The awkwardness was heavy. "So, Jesse, any big plans for winter break?" She hated the question the moment it left her mouth. She was talking to Jesse like she was a stranger, which she obviously wasn't.

Jesse's smile was small and knowing. "Lesson plans and test prep. I'm a wild child. How did you manage to get today and Christmas off?"

Leah groaned, thinking of all the favors she owed. "It wasn't easy, but it's worth it."

"How are you holding up?" Jesse's tone was uncharacteristically serious.

"I'm fine but thank you for asking. I was mentally prepared for today, thanks to Billie asking me if I was nervous a million times. I'm also one of the few that doesn't think meeting the family is that big a deal." She shrugged.

"Okay. How was meeting Eloise?" Jesse wouldn't look directly at her.

"Fine. Should it have not been fine?"

"Of course it should've been fine. I bet you were surprised to see her there."

Her mind was reeling. "I didn't even know who she was at first."

Jesse pulled back. "You don't know who Eloise is?"

"I knew about Ellie. When she introduced herself as Eloise, I didn't know."

"She hated that nickname, but Billie refused to drop it. It's like hanging on to a piece of her childhood."

This was her chance to learn more. "How close were they?"

"Billie and Eloise? God, thick as thieves doesn't even come close. They were inseparable. I still remember the tears when Eloise said she was going away to college."

Leah started to feel sick. "Wow, that's a serious bond."

"They really loved each other."

Billie stomped back into the room. "She's mad because Jesse met you first. Do you believe that?" Billie looked between them. "What's going on in here?"

Leah didn't even realize she had tears in her eyes until she saw the concerned look on Billie's face. She took a deep breath. "We were talking about you and Eloise."

"Okay, then why are you crying?" Billie said, approaching slowly. She looked at Jesse. "What did you say?"

"Nothing."

"Why didn't you tell me how much you loved each other?" Leah knew the tears were coming again, and she used every ounce of energy she had to will them away.

"I did. She was my best friend."

Leah lowered her head, hating the betrayal she felt in the form of a hot tear traveling her nose. "But you were in love and didn't tell me."

"You were in love with Eloise?" Jesse said loudly.

"Wait, what?"

"I don't care that you were," Leah said. "I just don't know why you hid it. We share everything, but she was your first love and you didn't tell me."

Jesse stood. "Why didn't you tell *me* about it?"

Billie waved her raised hands. "I was never in love with Ellie. I loved her like family. I still do."

Leah didn't know what to believe. "Then why has everything been so weird since she got back?"

"I haven't been weird about it," Billie said, pointing to herself.

Leah turned and pointed at Jesse. "You've been weird. Like you're keeping some big secret."

Jesse made a small choking sound. "No, I haven't."

Leah grabbed Billie's hands and looked up at her. "Please, just tell me the truth. Was there ever anything between you and Eloise?"

Billie knelt in front of her and looked in her eyes. "No."

Leah closed her eyes and let the answer sink into her heart. She weighed its truth, and her earlier worry began to ease. "I believe you."

"Good," Jesse said with a relieved sigh. Leah and Billie looked at her strangely. "For you guys."

"But because I don't want any secrets between us, I have to tell you—we did hook up in high school. It was a one-time thing."

Jesse dropped her head into her hands. "Oh God."

"That's it? Just once?" She held Billie's hands tighter.

"Once. We were so close. I was gay, and she was unsure…" Billie shrugged. "We didn't know anyone else who was queer in any way, so it felt natural to be together, so we wouldn't be alone. I regret it, that's for sure."

Leah reached out and caressed Billie's cheek. "Why?"

"I think our friendship changed after that."

"I'm sorry, sweetheart."

Jesse dropped her hands on the tabletop loudly. "Can you define *hook up*?"

"I would prefer not to in my family's home on Thanksgiving when anyone could hear it."

Jesse nodded rapidly, clearly not respecting Billie's wishes. "Give me a hint?"

"No. And I hardly think Leah wants details," Billie said in a fierce tone Leah had never heard before.

Leah held up a hand. "I do not."

"Please," Jesse said through tight lips.

"Why? Why is it so important to you?"

"I think it's important."

"Well, I don't, and quite frankly you're starting to piss me off."

Leah looked back and forth between them.

"Just tell me."

"No."

"Please."

"Jesus Christ, Jesse," Billie said loudly. "Why does it matter so much to you?"

"Eloise and I had a thing."

"A thing?"

Leah's mouth fell open. "A *thing*."

"You slept with Ellie?" Billie said with wide eyes.

Claire stood frozen in the doorway. "Oh, my."

CHAPTER EIGHT

Billie took Jesse to her old bedroom, closed the door, and stood with her arms crossed, staring at her like she about to scold her. "I don't understand."

"I don't really know how to explain it." Jesse sat on the edge of the twin bed. Her shoulders were slumped. "It wasn't planned or anything. I had barely seen her."

"Then how did it happen?"

"We ran into each other one night at Sylvia's. I was there just trying to be social again, and she was waiting for a blind date. She got stood up, and since we knew each other, we talked and hit it off."

"And then you slept together?"

"God, no," Jesse said, clearly disgusted. "We kept talking. One message turned into two, and before I knew what was happening, we were talking all day. I couldn't stop." Jesse chewed the inside of her cheek. "And I didn't want to."

Billie had a million questions but wasn't sure that she actually wanted answers. "How long did it go on?"

Jesse scrubbed her face with her hands before answering. "All summer."

"All sum—" Billie froze. She looked at Jesse like she was a stranger. "All summer? Are you serious? That's a relationship, not something that just happened."

"I'm sorry."

"Leah thought I was hiding something from her. Did you see her face?"

"I should've told you."

Billie started to calm down; her annoyance was replaced by hurt. Because that was really what this was all about—she was hurt Jesse hadn't told her. "Why didn't you?"

"I don't know. So many reasons, but they all seem stupid now."

"Try me."

Jesse looked up at her with scared eyes. "This is *Ellie* we're talking about, and she's a lot younger than me."

That gave Billie something to think about. "You've known her for years. She was in your class."

Jesse looked disgusted with herself. "Oh God, I know."

"But are those the only two reasons for you not to tell me?"

Jesse looked up at her. "Yeah."

"That's not good enough."

Jesse's face turned from remorse to confusion. "As the person struggling with them for months, I think it is."

"So what? Yeah, she's Ellie—my childhood best friend. Yes, she's twenty-nine, which is considerably younger than you, grandma," Billie said with a smirk, "but I'm me, and you're you. We always talk about this stuff."

"This seemed too big."

Billie rolled those words around in her mind. "Did you love her?"

Jesse's eyes went big with terror, and her throat flexed with a hard swallow. "I did."

"Did she love you?"

Jesse looked down at her clasped hands. "I think so."

Billie's ire had completely dissipated, and now she felt nothing but sympathy for Jesse, who slouched in defeat before her. "What happened?"

Jesse took a deep breath and blew it out slowly. Billie wasn't sure, but it looked like Jesse's lips trembled slightly. "Our relationship was smooth until it wasn't. Then she took the job in Baltimore and split."

Billie finally sat beside Jesse and placed her hand on her shoulder. "What do you mean?"

"I felt like I was being judged everywhere we went. I didn't want her mom to know, and I didn't want *your* mom to know." They shared a laugh. "I didn't want to be the gay teacher who was dating her student."

"She was your student over ten years ago. I hardly think anyone even remembers that."

"People in this town remember everything."

Billie thought of the car accident Mr. Phelps got into after drinking strawberry wine coolers. It had happened twenty years ago, and even though the choice of drink changed with each retelling, the story still lived on.

"Be that as it may," Billie said, trying to muster up enough confidence for both her and Jesse, "those opinions shouldn't matter."

"You know they do, especially working in education."

"You can't let that dictate your life, Jesse. You and Ellie are adults who are in control of your own happiness."

"What are you saying?"

"I'm just saying that if you want to be with Ellie, be with her, and don't be ashamed of it."

"And you're okay with it?"

"Oh, I think it's weird as fuck," Billie said with a chuckle.

Jesse's body shook with laughter. "I really wish I didn't know you two had hooked up."

"Yeah, well, today's a day of wacky surprises for all of us." Billie looked around the room as she tried to collect her thoughts. She knew Leah was likely worried about them. "We have to get back out there. Tiffany is probably torturing Leah."

"She's great. You know that, right?"

"Who? Eloise?"

"Leah."

Billie couldn't stop her broad smile even if she wanted to. Leah had that effect on her—just her name made every bit of Billie feel happy. "I know."

"I'm sorry if I added any strain to your day."

"It's fine."

"No, it's not."

"You're right, it's not. But it will be. Can I tell you something?"

"Please," Jesse said with a dramatic sigh.

"This whole day has felt a bit off. I thought introducing Leah to my family would feel more significant, but everything just feels the same."

"Maybe that's because your family is a bunch of cuckoo birds."

Billie knew Jesse was right, but something still nagged at her. "Maybe I'm more into this than Leah is. I probably need to slow down."

Jesse shifted to face Billie fully. "What do you mean?"

Billie hesitated. She hadn't voiced these feelings to anyone yet. "Leah's it for me, and having her meet everyone today was my way of seeing if she felt the same way."

"Hold up," Jesse said, pointing to the door. "You're using these people as a gauge of how much your girlfriend loves you? I thought you were the smart one."

"No, I don't mean it like that. This is a milestone for us, you know? But I don't think she really sees it that way. I think I need to slow down and let her take the wheel for a bit before I do something stupid."

"Doing that would be doing something stupid." Jesse stood and started for the door. "Come on. Let's go save Leah. Pops could be twenty minutes into a sexist rant by now."

Billie put her hand on the door to keep it closed. "He could be, but before we go out there, tell me how I'd be doing something stupid."

"Leah is madly in love with you. I see it and feel it every time you're together. She's in this for the long haul. I think you've had more than enough proof today."

"What proof?" Billie said, almost too loudly. "She wasn't even nervous about meeting my parents."

"She stayed, Billie. She's still out there. Your mother had a meltdown, your grandfather offended her several times, Tiffany has spent the entire day talking about how love is a trap, and she just believed you hid a relationship from her."

Billie went down the list and shook her head. "It certainly has been a day."

"And she's still here. That speaks a hell of a lot louder than nerves or falling all over your parents."

Billie looked at Jesse and knew she was right. "When did you get so old and wise?"

"I don't know about wise, but I got old a long time ago."

"But not *too* old," Billie said, trying to channel as much sincerity as she could into her eyes and tone. "Let's go rescue Leah."

❖

"He would get mad at me for putting his socks in the dresser wrong," Tiffany said, leaning in to Leah's shoulder. "What a stupid thing to get mad about."

Leah hummed in agreement. She watched the hallway in hopes of Billie and Jesse emerging soon. She already had her coat and bag of leftovers ready to go. She didn't want to appear too eager to leave, but Claire was already elbow deep in dishes she refused help with, and Greg was fifteen minutes into a post-turkey nap. She was left with Tiffany and Pops. *Great.*

"You're better off without him," Leah said, treading carefully.

"Yeah..." Tiffany looked down into her empty glass. "I do miss him, though." Tiffany leaned in to her more, and Leah didn't know what to do.

"That's normal. I think." She started to pat Tiffany's arm. "But everything happens for a reason."

"What's going on in here?"

Leah was too distracted by Tiffany's sulking to notice Billie's approach, but she was happy to see her. "Nothing much. I think everyone has officially started to wind down."

"We should probably get going."

Jesse clapped her hand on Billie's shoulder. "Hang around a little while longer. You know things start to get good when someone overstays their welcome."

Billie started shaking her head furiously, and Leah had to wonder what story she had yet to hear. "Let me see if my mom needs anything." Billie darted for the kitchen. Leah appreciated her eagerness.

Leah got up and walked to where the coats hung by the door. She waited for Jesse to follow. "Is everything okay between you two?"

Jesse looked over her shoulder before answering. "We're as solid as ever. What about you?"

Leah didn't bother to hide her warm smile. "I'm a little embarrassed, but I'll survive. I just hope I didn't upset Billie."

"No way," Jesse said, waving her hands and shaking her head. "She's crazy about you. You could've looked Claire in the eye and told her the turkey was dry, and Billie would still love you like a fool."

"I feel the same way about her."

"Please. Anyone with eyes can see that."

"I hope she knows it."

"It can never hurt to tell the people we love just how much they mean to us, or how thankful we are for them."

Leah was taken by how Jesse's wisdom shone in her eyes. "You're right."

Billie came jogging back into the room. "We almost forgot about the wishbone. I had it drying in the oven." Billie held the bone up to Jesse but looked at Leah. "Every year since I was little, we split the bone and see who gets to make their Thanksgiving wish."

"That is ridiculously cute."

Jesse rubbed her hands together. "Here we go," she said, gripping the other side.

"One, two, three." Billie and Jesse tugged at the same time.

The snap of the bone was audible, and a second of stillness followed. Jesse held up the bigger half triumphantly. No one said a word, but judging by the look Billie shared with Jesse, Leah figured they both knew exactly what Jesse was wishing for.

CHAPTER NINE

I don't think my dad wanted to let you go," Billie said as she turned onto the highway. "I was afraid he was making you uncomfortable."

"Greg is a great guy." Leah rested her hand on Billie's thigh. All of these touches, the smallest and most natural, were her favorite. She hoped this feeling would never fade. "Everyone was great."

Billie covered her hand. "No, they weren't."

"Billie, they were fine."

"Pops was horrible."

"I may not have won him over, but he was exactly what I expected."

"And Tiffany?"

"Is heartbroken." Leah turned slightly to look at Billie. "I really did have a wonderful Thanksgiving with you and your family." Leah felt her cheeks flush when she considered the whole day. "Except maybe the part where I had a breakdown thinking Eloise was the love of your life, and Jesse exposed their affair."

Billie started laughing. "Yeah, that was something."

"I'm really sorry about that. I'm so embarrassed." Leah smiled at the way Billie squeezed her hand.

"Don't be."

"But I am. I caused a scene. The last thing someone's girlfriend should bring to Thanksgiving dinner is drama."

Billie's jaw muscles jumped a few times, and she pulled her hand back to the steering wheel. "Can I tell you something?"

"Of course."

"I'm happy you reacted that way."

She wondered if Billie was actually there for what had happened. "You're happy I cried over Eloise?"

"Yes."

"Please explain yourself."

"I've been thinking a lot lately," Billie said with a newfound concentration for the road ahead. "I love you very much."

Leah's heart still fluttered a little every time she heard those words. "I love you, too."

Billie blurted out, "I was afraid we weren't on the same page, and I thought this holiday would tell me what I needed to know."

She had a hard time following. "Which is what exactly?"

Billie turned, her eyes sparkling in the dark. "If you love me as much as I love you."

"Of course I do."

"I love you like endgame love. Do you know what I mean?"

"Yes. I know exactly what you mean." She couldn't figure out why Billie looked so frustrated. "Are you upset with me?"

"No, it's just…"

"Just what?" she said in a panic.

"I thought this step would feel bigger than it did, but you weren't even nervous about meeting them."

Leah was done with cryptic talking. "Pull over in the next parking lot."

Billie pulled into the dark lot of a small strip mall. Lights were on in the stores, but very few cars were around. Billie turned off the headlights and unbuckled her seat belt.

Leah did the same and immediately reached for Billie's hands. She needed to touch Billie to really feel connected, like a silent communication she had grown dependent on over the months. "I need you to listen to me, okay?" Billie nodded, but Leah wasn't satisfied. "Look at me. Okay?"

Billie raised her head slowly. "Okay."

"I wasn't nervous because I knew it wouldn't change anything, and all families are crazy in their own way. And I knew Jesse would be there."

"But meeting someone's family is a big step."

"It is, and I was ready for it, but I don't need your parents' approval to love you. Meeting them has no impact on this," she said, bringing their joined hands to her chest.

The corner of Billie's mouth twitched. "What if they hated you?"

"I knew they wouldn't."

"You're quite sure of yourself."

Leah shrugged. "Once upon a time you said my confidence was sexy."

"It still is."

Despite the playful exchange, Leah still felt the tension of Billie's earlier words. "I'm sorry if I ever made you doubt how much I love you."

"I never doubted you. I just felt like I was light-years ahead of you."

"I see myself with you through everything, you know. I see our today and tomorrow, and I see a forever for us." She saw how watery Billie's eyes got after her final word. "And I absolutely love what I see."

Billie cleared her throat. "I guess now would be a good time to ask—your place or mine?"

"Let's go to your place. It's closer."

"That's not what I mean." Billie brought Leah's hand to her lips and kissed her knuckles, slowly, one by one. "We should move in together."

Leah's heart was instantly revived with a strong flutter and dip. Her cheeks hurt from smiling so wide. "My place. It's bigger."

"But mine has the big windows you love so much."

"I have a view of trees."

"I have the jacuzzi."

She fought to hide her smugness as she delivered what she knew would be the winning argument. "I have a yard big enough for a puppy."

Billie's eyes widened. "Your place it is."

Leah practically lunged forward to give Billie a solid kiss. "I'd like you there as soon as possible. Please and thank you." She pressed harder, deepening the next kiss. Billie was all greedy hands and gentle nibbles, knowing exactly what to do to drive Leah crazy. "We should probably get going," she said weakly.

"I'm pretty happy right where I am." Billie kissed the side of Leah's neck.

Leah whimpered. She struggled to get out of her coat. It was suddenly much too hot in the small car. "What if someone sees us?"

"When has that ever stopped you?" Billie took Leah's bottom lip between her teeth.

Leah shivered and focused on the sensation of goose bumps spreading across her skin. Billie made her feel more in a few kisses than any other lover ever had. The intensity and sweetness between them were a constant reminder of how perfect they were together. She tried to be graceful as she climbed over the small center console, but her knee hit the dashboard, her ass turned the radio's volume to high, and the jolt sent her head into the roof. Leah was deep into a laughing fit by the time she settled on Billie's lap and lowered the music.

"Sorry about that," she said, flipping her hair out of her face and adjusting her dress.

Billie looked up at her with pure adoration. "For what? Being perfect?"

She ground down into Billie's lap. "I love you." The words felt absolute as they fell from her lips into the quiet cabin, and she wanted to say them over and over until Billie never doubted her again. "I love you so much. Always and forever." Billie slid her hands up Leah's dress to her backside. The slight separation of her cheeks made her growing wetness impossible to ignore.

"Always and forever. I like the sound of that." Billie pulled Leah against her body roughly.

"Touch me," she said in a harsh whisper.

"Here? In the parking lot of'"—Billie looked out the window, squinting—"Donatello's Pizzeria?"

"Right here. Right now." Leah emphasized her demand by hiking the skirt of her dress even higher. Even in the dark lighting of the car, she could see Billie's excitement and hear her labored breathing. "Get me off now, and I'll rock your world when we get home." She reached into Billie's sweater vest and pulled out her tie. "Maybe I'll even make good use of this."

"Yes, ma'am." Billie kissed her again, ending any and all conversation.

Leah got exactly what she wanted, twice, and her heart felt fuller than it ever had. She knew, without a doubt, Billie was the only woman on earth for her, and she'd be thankful for their love until her dying day.

CHRISTMAS EVE: LIV AND THEO

Chapter Ten

Liquor had a magical way of clinging and trickling down the side of a glass. Not quite watery, not quite thick, but a texture all its own. "You are special," Liv said, tapping her fingertip to the glass. She watched a small droplet join the last mouthful of her honey whiskey. "You make *me* feel special." Her voice sounded loud in the empty bar.

The bartender's shadow obscured Liv's focus. "You sure have a lot to say to that drink of yours."

"Mm." Liv threw back the rest of the whiskey and handed the glass over. "I do, which means I need a refill. Otherwise, it won't have ears to listen." Liv chose to ignore the bartender's glare. "I appreciate you, Dot." Liv drummed her hands on the worn bar top as she waited for her third drink of the night. Or maybe it was her fourth? She shook away the unnecessary calculations and gave Dot her most charming grin. "Dot. Dottie. Dot-Dot," Liv said as she pointed. "Do you believe in Christmas miracles?"

Dot placed Liv's drink down on a damp napkin. "Sure."

"What about wishes come true?"

"I suppose. Anything can happen, really." Liv took a sip and nodded. Dot continued, "I think wishes are just seeds being planted. We think or say the words, and that's step one." Dot pulled her hand towel from the waist of her apron and shook it gently at Liv. "Then it's up to you whether you really do want it badly enough."

Liv sipped again as she considered Dot's words. "What's step two?"

"Doing the hard work to get whatever it is you want."

"Wow," Liv said, staring at the wall of bottles across from her. "That's deep, Dot. And not at all what I wanted to hear." She laughed at her own honest joke. Dot was not amused. "I'm sorry."

Dot leaned on the bar and offered Liv a gentle smile. "Cheer up, sober up, go home, and put in the work. It's the night before Christmas."

Liv brought the glass to her lips but paused before drinking. "And all through the house, one creature went drinking to avoid her spouse." Liv finished her drink in one long swallow. She smiled at Dot's worried look. "The spirits were warm and poured with care, by an angel named Dot with long dark hair."

"You're a poet."

Liv snorted. "Hardly."

"Am I remembering wrong? I'm pretty sure those aren't the words."

"No, no, they're not." Liv checked her empty glass, hoping for a refill but knowing better than to ask for one. "There's no children nestled in bed, and I can't quite picture what that's like in my head."

"I think it's time to call a ride."

"Do you have any kids, Dot?"

"I do."

"How many?"

"Three."

"Wow." The liquor made Liv's lips move way more slowly than they normally would. "How's that?"

Dot laughed and then blew out a long breath. Her dark eyes were sparkling in the low lighting. "Exhausting, frustrating, *exhausting*, busy, but also incredibly rewarding."

"Everyone says that."

"Because it's true. I can't even really explain it."

Liv felt a deep sense of skepticism. "How did you know you were ready for kids?" She held her head up in her hands, elbows firm on the wooden bar. The night might have been young, but Liv was tired.

"Honestly? I didn't know if I was ready when my first one came along. He was a surprise to all of us."

The cogs in Liv's brain moved slowly, but she got it. "Oh! A surprise pregnancy." But the more she thought about it, the less she understood it. "How? I thought you were—"

"Gay? Because I work here?" Dot stood up straight with her hands on her hips and a firm expression on her attractive face. Although she couldn't have been much older than Liv's thirty-six, she knew how to scold with a look. Definitely a mom.

Liv knew her face was reddening from embarrassment and mild shame, but dammit, why wouldn't she assume such a thing? "Well, yeah. *Sylvia's.* Sylvia's is a gay bar."

After a moment, Dot's face softened. "You aren't wrong, but I was married to a wonderful man for over ten years. We had two kids together. I knew I was gay the whole time, but I stayed because I thought it was best for the kids."

"What happened?"

"You sure do ask a lot of questions."

Liv shrugged. "I'm drunk."

"Call a ride, and I'll tell you what happened."

Liv considered that a fair deal and knew she couldn't get home too late. Not if she wanted a marriage to wake up to Christmas morning. "Okay." She took her phone from her coat pocket and pulled up the one person she knew wouldn't judge her or yell at her. After a few stumbles, she sent the message. "Done. Now tell me." She pushed her curls away from her face. They fell right back down.

Dot stacked the last few glasses she had dried and turned back to Liv. "Kids ask a lot of questions, and the more they asked about me, Daddy, and love," she said, waving her hands in the air as if physically weighing her next words carefully, "the more I started to learn about myself with each answer. Being unhappy isn't going to do any good for the kids."

Liv closed her eyes. Being happy, blissfully happy, was something she knew about. Until recently. "Are you happy now?"

"I mean, we all have bad days, but yeah. I go home to my family, and we hustle to make it all work, and I wouldn't change a thing about my journey. Not for nothing. Can I ask you a question now?"

"Shoot," Liv said firing finger guns at Dot.

"It's Christmas Eve. Why are you avoiding your spouse?"

She looked out the small front window of Sylvia's, and it looked much colder outside than inside the warm, quaint bar. She noticed a light sprinkling of flurries drifting through the air. Still, she didn't feel an ounce of holiday cheer. "Theo was moody, and I was a crank, and we ended up fighting over a sperm bank," she said with a voice more theatrical than needed. Liv's phone buzzed, and she checked it. "My ride will be here in five minutes. I think I'll wait outside and get some fresh air. How much is my tab?" She stood and made sure she was steady on her feet before patting her pockets for her belongings. Liv remembered she didn't leave with much, just her phone and debit card.

"It's on the house, Liv. Merry Christmas."

Liv smiled and turned toward the door. She stopped with her hand on the knob. "Why don't you stop by for dessert tomorrow? Sixteen Chancellor Drive. We'd love to have you."

Dot laughed outright. "Maybe. Be careful, poet."

Liv stepped out into the brisk evening. She hated how at barely six o'clock the sky was pitch black. The snow whipped around her dramatically, and she looked up and down the streets for a familiar car. People rushed across the road and exhaust pipes blew clouds into the air. She could hear the chiming bells from busy shops and the distant sound of Christmas music playing. She shivered.

"The cold snowy streets were alive with clatter," she said quietly, her breath the only thing giving her away. "And I can't help but think, does any of this matter?"

CHAPTER ELEVEN

"Where are you?" Jesse said as she lowered her car radio. The snow had started to pick up, and the flakes were big enough to be annoyingly distracting. "You're going to owe me more than Christmas dinner for this." She pulled her car up along the curb in front of Sylvia's. After turning on her hazards, she took the phone out of its clip on her dash. The passenger door swung open and caused her to jump. Liv fell into the seat and slammed the door, all while shivering dramatically. "Hey," Jesse said.

Liv leaned across the console and gave Jesse a loose hug, finishing with a firm pat on the arm. "I appreciate you."

"No problem." Jesse looked over Liv, quickly noticing her slightly disheveled appearance. Uncharacteristic for Liv, who wasn't prim and proper but always made sure to look finished. Her inky-black curls were frizzy, her light makeup was smudged, and she had dark circles under her glassy eyes that gave away more than she ever willingly would. "Are you okay?" Jesse said, pulling out into Christmas Eve traffic.

Liv craned forward and looked up out the windshield. "I see no moon glistening on this snow. No luster, no beauty, no midday glow."

Jesse tried her best to look at the car in front of her and the worrisome Liv beside her. "What do you mean?"

Liv gripped the dash and said in an alarmingly loud tone, "What to my wandering eyes should appear?"

Jesse stopped short, afraid she missed a pedestrian crossing or a red light. "What?"

"Nothing!" Liv said directly to Jesse. "No sleigh, no reindeer."

Jesse took a deep breath to calm herself. *She's your friend, and she's obviously going through something.* She kept repeating the thought to herself to keep anger at bay. Liv's familiar words dawned on her. "Is that the Christmas poem? The famous one you read to the kids every year?"

Liv gave Jesse a broad, wild grin. "You're the little old driver, though not as lively or quick. Quite the opposite of Old Saint Nick."

"You know, I resent that just a little, but I'll let it go because I think you've lost your mind."

"More rigid than ever, but quickly you came," Liv said, poking at Jesse's shoulder. "No need to whistle or shout, just call you by name."

"Okay, I think it's time to stop."

Liv breathed deeply and sat up straight. "Now—"

"Don't do it." Jesse didn't like Liv's wide, sparkling eyes.

"Now Jessher, now Jancer, Now Jrancer and Jexen! On Jesset, on Jupid, on Jonner, on Jitzen!"

"Stop."

"To the top of the window to the top of the walls. Now drive away, drive away, drive away all."

"Stop," Jesse said so loudly she even startled herself. She pulled over into an empty parking lot. "What the hell is going on with you? I haven't heard from you in weeks, and you send me a message out of nowhere on Christmas Eve, asking for a ride. You're a drunken mess, which is bad enough, but now you're just rambling on in iambic pentameter."

"Anapestic tetrameter."

"What?"

"It's not iambic pentameter. If it was, there'd be one unstressed syllable—"

"Whatever it is, you need to stop." She felt bad as soon as Liv sank back into her seat like a wounded puppy. Jesse pinched the bridge of her nose. "I'm sorry, but you're kind of freaking me out."

"I love that poem," Liv said in a small voice. "It's my favorite Christmas tradition, actually."

"I don't know why I'm surprised you have it memorized enough to make your own remix. How many years have you even reading it now?"

Liv took a minute to think, having a visibly hard time with the math. "How old is Sam?"

"I'm not sure, he's *your* nephew."

"However old he is. Eight or nine years." Liv leaned against the door and crossed her arms. "The kids love listening to it just as much as I love reading it. Their little faces with those big eyes, you know?"

"Yeah." Jesse didn't completely know. After all, she spent most of story time helping with cleanup whenever she went to Liv and Theo's for Christmas.

"I fucking love kids. They're funny and honest and love honestly, too. Some of them are so smart, and some of them not so much. Like Sam." Liv brought her index finger up to her lips. "Shh. I never said that."

"Wow. Okay. Drunk Liv is as honest as a child." Jesse fought back laughter.

"I'm just not eager to have my own kids. I'm not eager to give up the two or three vacations a year or the cushy bank account. The peace and quiet, ugh." Liv clasped her hands over her heart. "I love my peaceful nights."

Jesse might have been a science major, but it didn't take a psychology degree to figure out what was happening. "Theo's ready to have kids."

"She's not just ready, she's big ready."

"And you're not?"

"I'm not *eager.*"

"But you do want kids, right?"

"Of course. Always have."

"So, what's the problem?"

"I'm not—"

"Eager. Right. Got it." Jesse would guess the alcohol was no longer Liv's friend, judging by the way she was rubbing circles on her temples. "It'll be okay," Jesse said with absolutely no certainty.

"This has been the elephant in the room since your fortieth birthday bash."

"What?" Jesse said, but she sounded more like a squawking gull. "That was almost a year and a half ago." Wind whipped and whistled around the car.

"Don't I know it. I dodged it as long as I could, but a couple months ago that elephant stomped right on my marriage. Theo asked me point-blank if I was ready to start a family with her or not." Liv shrugged, and if she was going for nonchalance, she failed miserably. "I guess I took too long to answer her."

Jesse struggled with how to feel about Liv drinking again. She wanted to ask if this was the first time or not, but interrogating drunken Liv wouldn't help the situation. "Are you telling me this because you want to or because you're drunk?"

"Both, I think. I'm not happy or proud of it, which is why I haven't said anything before, but it's Christmas again and…"

Jesse knew Liv well. Thirteen years of friendship took them through many milestones and hardships, but also many celebrations. The sadness she saw on Liv's face in this moment was the darkest Jesse had ever seen. "And what, Liv?"

"I wouldn't be surprised if I found divorce papers under the tree in the morning."

Jesse shook her head. "No way. I refuse to accept this."

"You? *You* refuse to accept this? How do you think I feel? We've been married for eleven years—the best eleven years of my life—and all it took was two seconds of hesitation to ruin it." Liv wiped at her cheek but left behind a slight shimmer of a tear. "I don't know what to do. We constantly fight about it now."

"Have kids," Jesse said simply.

Liv's stare felt like a dagger. "You don't think I tried that? At least once a week I tell her we should go for it. I've tried to be sweet about it, I've been sexy about it, and I've even tried to be funny about it. Every time, every way goes over as well as a fart in church."

Jesse frowned. "I don't understand why."

"Because I'm not eager, and it shows. I can't hide anything from Theo, and I never want to try. That's one of my favorite parts of our relationship." Liv scrubbed at her face with her hands. "I guess I should go home. I'm sure storming out in the middle of Christmas Eve and coming back drunk will be the catalyst for round two."

"That's probably a good idea." Jesse reached to shift the car into drive.

"Round one was over sperm."

Jesse twisted her face in disgust. "Sounds awful."

"I tried the jump-right-in approach," Liv said. "I told her I found a great sperm bank in New York."

"That didn't make her happy?" Jesse squinted against the rapidly falling snow. Brake lights were starbursts, and she couldn't see any lines on the roads.

Liv chortled. "Not even close. She yelled at me because I was looking without her when I'm not even the one who wants kids."

"I'm sorry. I really don't know what to say."

"Nothing," Liv said, her voice heavy with sadness and defeat. "Let's just enjoy the snow."

Jesse drove the rest of the way in uncomfortable silence. She hated not being able to help her friends, and watching Liv go through something this hard on her own was breaking Jesse's heart. She knew very well what it was like to keep something to yourself, to struggle and hurt without someone to lean on. She also knew there was no one to blame but herself for that, and she'd have to accept Liv's decision for the same reason. She came to a stop in front of Liv's home.

"Thanks for picking me up. I owe you one."

"You don't," Jesse said as Liv pushed open the door. "And for what it's worth, I think it's really common for people to not be eager about having kids."

Liv offered back a hollow smile. "Leave now—before the wild snowstorm fly."

Jesse looked back out the window, seeing fewer and fewer snowflakes. "I actually think it's supposed to stop soon."

"If you meet with an obstacle, take to the sky."

"Oh, we're doing this again."

Liv climbed out of the car and bent to stick her head back in. "Walk to the doorstep I think I must do, with a chest full of anxiety and exhaustion, too. And then in a twinkling, it'll be Christmas morn. A new day with new worries sure to be born."

"Theo won't leave you. You just have to figure out a way to get through to her. Go in there, kiss your wife with everything you got, and don't give up. Okay?"

Liv stared at Jesse for a beat. "Okay. Have a good night."

"Good night, Liv. I'll see you tomorrow." The door slammed shut and Jesse drove away.

Liv hugged her puffy coat closer to her body to ward off the cold wind. She looked up at her house, cheerfully decorated with few lights on. "I draw back my head and turn back around, up the walkway I go without a sound." She spoke quietly, her whispers seeming more delicate in the thinning snow. Liv continued the short walk carefully and focused on the window cling of Santa on their front door.

"Not Santa, but jolly thanks to the booze." She brought her hand to her mouth and checked her breath. "With gum or with none, I'm sure to lose." Liv opened the front door slowly and stepped inside with the same caution a zookeeper would show in a lion's den. Just before closing the door behind her, she made the sign of the cross.

"Merry Christmas to all, and to all the will to survive."

CHAPTER TWELVE

Every step was louder than the last, and Liv started to hate the original hardwood floors she often bragged about. After four years of remodeling their Craftsman style home, everything was perfect, except for the floorboards of betrayal.

"Please be quiet," she said, tiptoeing her way to the stairs. Liv could hear Theo in the kitchen, and if the last ten Christmases told her anything, she knew Theo would be in there for a while. She just had to make it to the shower to wash away the whiskey before checking on the state of her marriage. Liv gripped the banister with her right hand and slowly, quietly started to ascend the stairs. She dodged every known squeaky spot but didn't think to look for stray cat toys. She kicked a small red bell that had a much louder chime thanks to the echo of the staircase. She clamped both eyes shut and cringed as it fell down three too many stairs. Theo must have heard it. Liv opened one eye and was greeted by the culprit himself.

"Thanks a lot, Oliver." Liv stared at the fat gray tabby, who licked his front paw, looking like a cowboy blowing the smoke from the barrel of his gun. His next motions worried Liv. He crouched his front half down to the ground and raised his back end. "Don't you dare wiggle that butt." Oliver's pupils grew larger, and he started to wiggle. "Don't—" He flew down the stairs and batted the bell the rest of the way down into the corner, making it ricochet like a pinball, and finally into the living room, causing a much bigger ruckus.

"Liv?" Theo's voice carried through the house.

Liv swallowed back all the curses she had and braced herself. "Yeah, I just got home. I'm about to get in the shower." She continued up the stairs, not looking back once even when she heard Theo talking. "Don't have to answer her if you don't hear what she said," Liv said in a whisper.

She walked straight to the linen closet for a towel, fully prepared to shed her puffy winter jacket, high boots, and multiple layers in the bathroom. She'd worry about cleaning that up later. When she turned with her favorite purple towel in hand, Theo was waiting behind her.

"Where were you?" Theo's tone was flat, which was unhelpful to Liv.

"I, uh..." Liv cleared her suddenly dry throat and held her towel up in front of her mouth to catch her breath. "I went out to cool off."

"*Where* did you go?"

Liv breathed deeply, feeling shame creep up her neck. "I went to Sylvia's to cool off. I got a ride there and a ride back."

"You've been drinking."

Busted. "Just a couple."

"You stopped drinking."

Liv looked at Theo and took in how tired she looked, the circles beneath her green eyes, and the tightness of her lips. "I'm sorry."

"You promised—"

"I said I'm sorry." Liv took a deep breath and let it out steadily. "I only had a couple."

"That's what you said last time," Theo said, looking down at her feet.

Last time. Embarrassment flooded Liv. Fourth of July margaritas that ended with her flirting with their cousin's husband in the deep end of the pool. Nothing happened, nothing would ever happen, but Liv wouldn't forget the way Theo cried about it the next day.

"I haven't been the best this year—I know it. I'm sorry." Liv's struggle went far beyond her own actions. "We haven't been the best this year either, and I don't know how to fix that. I'm not making excuses, but I feel like everything is so far out of my control, and you're not even letting me try. Tonight, I just needed—"

"A drink?"

"To stop hurting," Liv said firmly. "I'm going to get in the shower now." She stepped around Theo and didn't take another full breath until she stood behind the closed bathroom door. If anyone had told Liv that she'd grow to avoid Theo, she'd have called them crazy and slapped them square across the face. "Shit."

Liv peeled her clothes off and tossed them on the floor. She stared at the small pile and noticed a long pull in the sleeve of her sweater. It was the evergreen sweater Theo had bought her last Christmas. "It's okay, I'm unraveling, too," she said, full of remorse for the loss of her sweater and whiskey buzz.

Her shower was perhaps a little too hot, but only scalding water could create the illusion of cleansing her of her day and the murkiness drowning her. She toweled off and walked to the bedroom in search of her most comforting sweats. Liv dressed slowly, trying her best to buy a few extra minutes before she had to rejoin Theo. Their marriage might have been at its worst, but Christmas was still coming, which meant preparations aplenty.

She took the stairs slowly and yawned along the way. Discomfort and anxiety at home was exhausting. Christmas music continued to play, and she gave Theo kudos for still trying to adhere to traditions. Nothing about this holiday felt like theirs.

"What can I help with?" she said.

Theo didn't turn around when she answered, "Nothing right now. The cheesecake is out of the oven, and I'm almost done prepping the lasagna."

Liv looked at the discarded containers filling the sink and bits of red sauce splattered about. She raised her eyebrows. "I can start cleaning."

"No," Theo said quickly. "It's fine. Go sit down. I'll call you if I need you."

Liv lowered her head, knowing the sad truth that Theo wouldn't be calling for her anytime soon. "Okay," she said, opening the fridge. The neatly lined bottles of beer caught her eye. She sighed and grabbed a bottle of water. Liv took her place on the right side of the couch, and in just a short minute Oliver joined her, his purrs loud enough to be heard over "Jingle Bell Rock."

Liv ran her fingers through Oliver's fur and scratched behind his ear. She looked up and smiled. She loved the way their tree lit up the walls with colorful prismatic patterns. She stared at the ornaments centered perfectly, even the small surfboard with their surname, which her brother Todd gave them on their wedding day. He was the surfer—she never was. They still weren't sure whether he was joking or not, but they had hung it proudly every Christmas for the last eleven years. *McGowan* started to look misspelled by the time she looked away and down to the presents scattered beneath.

Her favorite holiday was always Christmas Eve because it was just for them—at least it used to be. Christmas Day was chaos and hosting and having at least one person overstay their welcome, but Christmas Eve held nothing but love and excitement up until that year.

"I think everyone will get here around noon tomorrow," Theo said from the other room.

"Except Tammy, I'm sure." She looked at the boxes labeled for her and the smaller pile she had put together for Theo.

"Tammy's late to everything. Last week she was more than twenty minutes late to work every day. I don't know how she gets away with it."

Liv picked up her bottle of water and walked back into the kitchen. If Theo was willing to have any conversation with her, Liv would happily take it. "If Tammy shows up and does her job, it's easy to overlook tardiness." She took a long sip and watched Theo fill a container with freshly baked cookies. Theo wore yoga pants, fuzzy socks, and a Santa apron over a worn sweatshirt. Liv's heart sank at this look. She struggled to remember the last time they had shared any kind of intimacy beyond a quick good morning and good night kiss.

"Easy for a hairdresser to say. Your coworkers don't affect you, but how does it feel when a client is late?" Theo threw a quick glance over her shoulder. "Okay. I think I'm done here. Everything is ready to go for tomorrow, and I already divvied up the cookies for everyone to take home. I made extra Italian cookies. The kids should be happy."

Liv flinched at the word. She knew she had to be careful with her response. "Your Christmas cookies make everyone happy."

"I only care about the kids, though."

Challenge number two, and we've only been talking for three minutes. "They'll gobble up every last crumb." She waited, holding her breath and watching Theo's reaction. Her shoulders were tight, but she continued to hum along to the music. Liv believed she was safe. For now. "Is Miranda bringing her boyfriend, what's-his-name?"

"My mother will be flying solo because *Ben* is in Florida with his golf buddies."

"Ben's loss." She finished her water and threw her bottle into the recycling bin beneath the sink. "Should I start a fire in the morning and keep it burning all day or wait until after dinner?"

"Why would you have a fire burning all day if there's going to be kids running around? That's pretty stupid if you ask me."

Liv took a deep, calming breath. *Here we go again.* Every day there was something, a dig or an argument about how kids should be treated or how they enriched lives. Liv had a hard time understanding why Theo continued this painful pattern. She wouldn't listen to what Liv had to say, but then she'd punish Liv like she'd never tried in the first place.

"I obviously wouldn't put children next to an open fire," she said, trying her best to keep a bite from her tone. "Give me a little credit here." She forced a laugh to lighten the mood. Theo turned around and clued her in to just how ineffective her chuckle was.

"Save the fire for after dinner when we're all around. Did you get the papers together for our wishes?" Theo's eyes were everywhere but on Liv.

"I did."

"And the calligraphy markers?"

"Yes."

"Then I think we're set," Theo said, taking off her apron and tossing it onto the counter. She turned off the music mid "Silent Night" and said, "I think it's my turn to shower."

She stepped back and let Theo pass. They didn't say another word, and Theo didn't spare a second glance as she walked away. Liv didn't feel safe enough to move until she heard the bathroom door shut. She looked at their collection of sparkling long-stemmed wineglasses and the highball and old-fashioned glasses lined up on the counter in preparation for guests. They had a brilliant brandy ready for sharing, but Liv fought off the temptation and grabbed another water instead. She turned off every light except the Christmas tree and returned to the sofa.

They had been so happy together. Liv loved Theo, and Theo always claimed to love her more. Wives, passionate lovers, and partners in crime—that's how Liv always described them. But ever since Theo woke up with baby fever, each descriptor became less true. They were wives on paper, being lovers was a thing of the past, and partners tackled life together, which surely was no longer the case for them. Liv drank her water and watched as Oliver reached between neatly wrapped gifts for something beneath the tree.

"Don't mess up the skirt," she said to Oliver, like he understood or cared. "That tree may be the only perfect thing about tomorrow." Liv's tone matched her dry spirit. She accepted her fate so easily, maybe *too* easily. She tightened her grip on the bottle. Oliver jumped at the sound of crushing plastic.

Guilt had weakened Liv into submission, and she'd let Theo take control and call every shot in hopes of making the days a little more peaceful. All because she didn't jump at the chance of having kids. *Ridiculous.* What kind of home would this be for a child anyway? Liv chugged the rest of her water.

She left the Christmas tree lit and walked up the stairs. Liv could hear the running water, louder and louder with each step she took. She walked into their master bedroom and looked at the closed bathroom door. Once upon a time that door remained open. Even their friends called them weird when they heard they never closed the bathroom door. Liv just saw it as another example of how close she and Theo were. She placed her hand on the doorknob but hesitated. Barging in on Theo could come across more aggressive than she intended, and nothing good would come of that. Liv heard the shower stop, so she backed away. She took a seat on the edge of their bed and waited. And waited.

Liv had been wildly attracted to Theo since day one, and a good portion of her physical attraction came from how Theo put herself together. Theo took time to care for herself, pamper herself, and target any part of her appearance that was becoming problematic. Theo spent her days as an accountant, and her polished professionalism was incredibly sexy. The quality of care she put into her looks and her long thick hair meant Theo took more than a few minutes to groom herself. But Liv loved the results.

Now, Liv listened to the blow-dryer turn on and off while the faucet did the same. It was still early, but Liv felt her eyes start to droop by the time the bathroom door opened. She jolted awake.

Theo looked at her oddly. "Why are you just sitting there?"

"I, uh…" Liv said, struggling to clear the sleep from her throat. "I was waiting for you."

Theo's eyes never left Liv as she slid her robe off, revealing a red camisole and Christmas tree pants. "Is everything off downstairs?"

"I left the tree on."

"Why?" Theo sighed. "I'll turn it off." She started for the door, but Liv reached out to grab her hand.

"Just leave it. I want to talk. We *need* to talk." For the first time in a long time, Liv saw a fearful reaction flash across Theo's face. "Please sit down."

Theo sat beside Liv on the bed but left space between them. She folded her hands on her lap and rolled her shoulders. "What do you want to talk about?"

Liv looked Theo up and down, noticing her tense posture and tight mouth. "This," she said, waving between them. "Aren't you tired of this? Of not being us anymore?"

"What do you mean?"

"We barely talk."

"We talk plenty."

"Small talk," Liv said quickly. "And we hardly ever touch each other."

"I held your hand yesterday in the grocery store."

"Why?"

"Why what?"

Liv clenched her jaw to fight back angry tears. "Why did you hold my hand?" She knew Theo wasn't going to answer by the way she bit her lower lip. "Because I asked you to. Did you even feel anything besides skin and bone when you held it?" She lifted her left hand, the sad memory of their stiff interaction fresh in her mind.

"We're just going through a rough patch."

Liv could tell Theo didn't even believe herself. "A rough patch with no end in sight." Liv inhaled deeply and prepared herself. Her next words, her confession, terrified her. "I don't think I can keep doing this."

"You're done," Theo said, so matter-of-fact, like she'd been expecting it.

"I'm not done." Liv stood and started to pace. A storm of warring emotions kept her from looking at Theo. "This is me coming to you and saying something has to change. This is me trying." She swallowed hard. "I know we're breaking, Theo, but I refuse to give up hope that we haven't broken completely."

Theo looked down and picked at her cuticles.

"Are we broken?" Liv said.

Theo wiped a tear from her cheek and said in a surprisingly steady voice, "Why are you doing this tonight? We have so many guests coming tomorrow."

Liv started to crack. "Because the thought of faking a holly jolly Christmas is more brutal to me than any consequence that could come of this conversation." Liv knelt in front of Theo. "Because watching you dote on guests and wondering if you care more for them than your own wife…" Liv sucked in a breath at the pain brought on by the hypothetical situation. "I'd rather die."

"Don't say that."

"What? That you'd care about everyone else more than me, or that I'd rather die?"

Theo looked at her with red eyes. "I don't know how to fix this."

Liv shook her head. "Listen when I try to talk to you. Act like this is what you want."

"I do listen."

"You listen, but you don't hear what I'm saying."

"That makes no sense."

"I want to have a baby with you." Liv reached to hold Theo's face in her hands when Theo tried to move away. She forced Theo to look her in the eyes, hoping her sincerity was plain to see. "I'm ready to start a family with you."

A fat tear fell from Theo's right eye when she smiled sadly. "I'll never forget the look on your face when I first mentioned kids. You looked terrified—horrified, even. I can't shake that sickening feeling I had."

Liv traced Theo's cheekbones with her thumbs, and she looked at her glistening, plump lips. "I don't know how else to tell you I'm ready, and I don't know what I can do to convince you, but what I *do* know is I can't fight for us to become parents when you're not even fighting for our marriage." Liv weakened at how perfectly Theo's jaw fit against her palms. She hadn't touched Theo like this in months, and the familiar feel brought both pleasure and pain. "Do you still love me?" she said in a voice so small the words nearly disappeared between them.

"Liv..." Theo's chin quivered against Liv's hand.

Liv started to cry, too, fully expecting a no, and pressed her forehead against Theo's. "Please tell me."

"I still love you."

"Are you in love with me?" Liv closed her eyes and braced herself. She didn't realize how firmly she was pressing herself into Theo until she pulled back to watch Theo respond.

Theo clamped her eyes shut and started shaking her head. Her cheeks were flushed and wet with unrelenting tears. She sobbed loudly.

"It's okay, baby." Liv wrapped Theo in a tight embrace and held her as she cried. Liv fought against her desire to break down, to let the wave of nausea take over, and chose to comfort Theo instead. Her meltdown could wait.

Theo spoke again after her crying subsided. "I'm pretty sure I fell in love with you on our first date, the moment you told me about your childhood with a dollop of spaghetti sauce on your chin." Theo's breath was hot against Liv's neck. "I've only fallen more in love with you every day since."

Liv swallowed her sadness and the unexpected arousal she felt at having Theo against her sensitive skin. "When did you stop?"

Theo pulled back and looked at Liv through long, wet lashes. "I never stopped." Theo placed her hand on Liv's chest between her breasts. "I'll never stop, and that's what makes this so hard. I love you, but the future I want isn't what you want."

"But you still love me," Liv said, smiling and crying at the same time, "which means I still have a chance to prove our future will always be together." She pulled Theo up into a hug, this time squeezing tightly enough to communicate her relief and overwhelming love. "I love you," she said, kissing Theo's forehead. "I love you, I love you, I love you." She repeated it over and over as she kissed Theo's face, her closed eyes, her nose. She kissed Theo's temples and along the slope of her jaw. After kissing Theo's chin and the corner of her mouth, Liv lingered. She ran her eager lips over Theo's, reveling in the way their soft skin touched and caressed. She was meant to kiss Theo, every day forever. Liv chased after Theo's lips as she pulled away.

Theo licked her lips and looked at Liv through hooded eyes. "But how could you still want me after all this?"

CHAPTER THIRTEEN

They stood together in a loose embrace at the center of their bedroom, swaying only slightly. Theo ignored her mild embarrassment over sounding pathetic. It had been so long since they were last intimate. Theo's body yearned for Liv's touch, and after an onslaught of intense emotions, her body was drained of everything but carnal need. Every wall she'd built up started to crumble away, one by one. A busy life and a feeling of disconnect had squashed her libido as of late, but now she was ready. Ready to kiss, touch, and *feel*.

"Do you still want me?" she said again, worried by Liv's delayed reaction. But Theo's anxieties were instantly eased by the look of desire on Liv's face.

"I want to be offended you're even asking," Liv said, taking Theo's hand in hers, "but I understand why you are." Liv ran her fingertips along Theo's palm to her inner wrist. "I love you, and I want you just as much as I always have."

"I didn't think you did." Theo weakened at Liv's gentle stroking. She stood within inches of Liv, surrounded by her light, fresh scent. Liv was tempting every one of her senses.

"How could I not?" Liv kissed Theo's knuckles one by one.

She sucked in a breath. "I'm not the same woman I was when we met."

"Neither am I." Liv looked up through her long lashes. "And you're even more stunning today. You turn me on even when you're not trying."

She wanted to believe Liv's words so badly, but how could they possibly be true? "Remind me?"

"Of?"

Theo felt so silly, but she needed to ask. "Why you're still attracted to me."

Liv smiled, an indulgent and delicious grin. "Let me count the ways." Liv stepped back and looked at Theo's body. Theo felt her nipples tighten in response and knew they were visible through her thin tank. "Your skin is incredible," Liv said, running her hands along Theo's forearms. "I still don't know how you're this soft." Liv's hands continued up to Theo's bare shoulders and into her hair. Theo closed her eyes as Liv scratched at her scalp lightly. "Your hair, no matter how you style it, is so sexy. Your eyes and your mouth…" Liv ran her thumb along Theo's bottom lip.

Theo, as if possessed, couldn't refrain from licking Liv's fingertip.

Liv moaned. "Jesus."

Theo felt the mood in the moment shift. Everything became clear. This was how they connected and reconnected over the years. Theo was never the most patient, and Liv struggled with her words, but they both knew how to communicate through physical touch. When they made love, they poured their apologies into every kiss and caress. In this specific moment, Theo wanted to put her whole heart into showing Liv how much she still loved her. No matter the hurdles, she hadn't given up. She sat and pulled herself up to lie back on the bed.

"Come here," she said, her voice husky with desire.

Liv moved slowly, kneeling on the bed before crawling up Theo's body. She settled between Theo's spread legs. "Is this where you want me?"

"Mmm." Theo bit her lip. The feeling of Liv's weight atop her stoked the flames, filling her insides. "You feel so good," she said as Liv kissed along the side of her neck. Her control started to unravel when Liv started moving her hips. "Oh God."

"I've missed you," Liv said into her ear. "I've missed the feel of you and the way you taste. I've missed hearing you." She pushed harder into Theo's center, drawing out a long moan. "But most of all, I missed this." Liv pulled back enough to look into Theo's eyes. "I've missed this," Liv said before leaning down to kiss Theo slowly, deeply.

Theo kissed back with fervor, drinking up every ounce of building passion. Liv was the best kisser, and Theo swore every kiss felt like the first with her.

Theo filled her hands with Liv's hair and pulled her closer and closer still until any movement felt impossible. "Make love to me."

Liv smirked and started to kiss her way down Theo's throat to her chest.

"No," Theo said. She gripped Liv's hair again and tugged her until their open mouths could meet. "I want you to stay here." She swallowed hard. "I want you to fuck me."

The sparkle in Liv's eyes matched the tree downstairs.

"I want to feel you everywhere," Theo said.

Theo kissed Liv back with the same urgency then. She could see and feel Liv's building desire in her actions and the heat emanating from her skin. Theo wondered if Liv, too, had started to believe this kind of crackling passion had disappeared from between them forever, and if Liv was just as relieved to feel ignited once more.

Theo spread her legs farther apart and focused on the many sensations taking over her body. This, the physical, was all that mattered. Her palms felt hot against the bare skin of Liv's neck, her clit pulsed, and Liv's mouth tasted the same as it had during their first heated kiss years ago. She pulled at Liv's top to remove it, rewarded with a simple floral bra that cradled Liv's small breasts wonderfully. She ran her hands down Liv's chest, along the subtle swell of flesh.

Liv pressed her lips to Theo's ear. "Take it off."

Theo shivered at the low timbre of Liv's demand. She removed Liv's bra quickly and tossed it aside. Liv's nipples were dark and erect, practically begging for Theo's attention. She palmed both of Liv's breasts and kissed her deeply. Her body felt alive. She could no longer keep her hands in one place, the buzzing energy building within becoming too strong. She needed to reacquaint herself with Liv's body, gripping her hips, feeling the muscles flex along her sides, and scratching her way up Liv's lithe back. Theo worked these parts of Liv's body over and over like a circuit until the need building within herself overwhelmed her. She reached lower and started to inch her fingertips beneath the waistband of Liv's pants.

"Wait," Liv said, placing her hand over Theo's. Liv's lips were still touching Theo's, and she made no move to put more space between them.

"What? What is it?" Theo swallowed hard, just now realizing how dry her mouth had become from breathing heavily. She scanned

Liv's face, looking for any indication of what Liv was thinking. Was she regretting this? Was Liv just now discovering she wasn't really attracted to Theo anymore? Maybe it was the extra weight she'd put on since spring. Maybe it was her attitude. Maybe there was someone else. Theo felt nauseous. Could she really blame Liv for developing feelings for someone else?

"Theo?"

Theo jumped when Liv touched her cheek. "Yeah?" she said, her throat too tight to manage more than a whisper.

"I love you. You know that, right?"

Words which should be sweet filled Theo with foreboding. "But…?"

Liv frowned. "But nothing. I need you to know that, and I want to make sure you're okay."

Theo wished she could fight back her tears, but her vision started to blur despite her efforts. "I'm okay." She kissed Liv for a distraction. "I love you, too."

Liv looked in Theo's eyes before kissing her neck, then her chest, and then removing every bit of clothing between them. Liv settled back between her legs and smiled softly.

Theo had so much more she wanted to say and so much reassurance to ask for, but right now was for action. No more words. The bristly hairs on Liv's mound tickled her most sensitive skin. Theo canted her hips, encouraging Liv to start moving. The slow back and forth, the grind between bodies, reignited Theo. With no control, Theo drove her tongue into Liv's mouth, hungry for the taste of passion and connection. She moaned when Liv surged forward suddenly with bruising pressure. She matched Liv's frantic movements. She always preferred this position because she could kiss Liv, touch Liv, and really *feel* Liv, all while experiencing intense pleasure.

Liv dipped her head to take one of Theo's nipples between her lips. Theo's left breast had always been bigger and more sensitive, a fact Liv learned early on and used to her advantage as often as possible. Liv tongued the stiff peak, making tight circles and alternating with firm laps.

Theo knew what was coming next but still gasped as the pleasurable pain of being bitten shocked her body. She tugged at Liv's hair to bring their lips together again. She felt an orgasm approaching quickly. They hadn't been intimate in so long—Theo's body was a hair trigger ready to fire.

"I'm going to come so fast," Theo said. She clamped her eyes shut and tensed her jaw.

Liv reached between their bodies and started rubbing firm circles with three fingers over Theo's throbbing clit. "You're so wet."

"I've been waiting for you."

Liv opened her eyes, and the connection took Theo's breath away. Liv entered her bit by bit, until her palm was firmly against Theo's clit.

Theo started moving her hips faster, feeling possessed, and driven by the need for more pressure, more speed, more Liv. More, more, more, until all of Theo's pieces fell back together.

"Please..." One word said it all.

Liv started using the force of her own thrusts to fill Theo harder, deeper, and faster.

Theo's face started to heat up, and she began to shake. She wrapped her arms and legs around Liv and held her so tightly. She dug her nails into Liv's back and called out as she climaxed. Spasm after spasm, wave after wave of pleasure crashed through her body. She let her arms and legs fall lifeless to the bed and began to cry. Release and relief came pouring from her eyes.

Liv kissed along Theo's neck, up her jaw, her eyebrows, her nose, before finally settling on her lips. After a gentle kiss, she pulled back to look down at Theo. Liv's eyes were wet but her mouth was spread into a beautiful grin. "I still got it," she said.

Theo's cries turned to laughter, and she felt an overwhelming sense of gratitude for Liv. "Yeah, you do."

"So do you," Liv said, moving to bring Theo's thigh between her legs. Liv started moving against her. "Shit."

Theo tensed her thigh, trying to add to Liv's pleasure. She felt the wet slick of Liv's center and knew no other feeling would arouse her in the same way. She noticed the change in Liv's breathing first, and then the tremor in her strong arms and legs. Theo gripped Liv's ass firmly and dug her nails in.

"Fuck, fuck, fuck."

"You feel so good," Theo whispered. "Let go, baby, let go."

Liv choked out a quiet moan into Theo's ear and bit the side of her neck, causing a shiver down her spine and between her legs. Liv went limp atop Theo.

Theo welcomed her comforting weight. She felt secure being held in place, and she felt strong in the way she held on to Liv as she recovered. An addictive dynamic. She kissed Liv's head, smiling into the curly hair that tickled her nose and cheeks.

Once Liv finally came back to life, she rolled to the side of Theo and took her hand. She had a dazed happiness in her eyes. "You're incredible."

"No," Theo said, shaking her head and fighting back another onslaught of tears. Nothing could be further from the truth. All of her harshest, most unkind moments flashed in her mind like a highlight reel. "I've been so cold and cruel."

"*We* haven't been at our best."

Her next words came out broken with emotion. "There are some days I'm convinced our marriage won't make it to dinnertime, and other days where I believe we'll survive anything. And then there's nights like tonight…"

Liv tightened her grip on Theo's hands. "I'm sorry."

"You drank because of me."

"I drank because—" Liv shook her head.

"Because I hurt you."

"It's so much more than that."

Theo fought her desire to get defensive and yell or, worse, get up and run away. She placed her hand against Liv's cheek and let the soft warmth ground her. "Tell me."

Liv stared at her hard and long before even breathing again. "Weakness. It's easier for me to drink and dilute my problems than face them head-on. It was easier for me to cool down after we argued by numbing the pain. None of that is your fault."

"But if I had been kinder—"

"Then I would've drunk because we were happy." Liv placed her hand over Theo's and turned to kiss her palm. "You made me face the truth that I had a problem not because I was drinking too much when I was sad, but because I was drinking too much. Period." Liv kissed Theo. "I'm just thankful you told me while I could still control it."

She burrowed her face into Liv's neck and dared to want the impossible. "Maybe we can just go to sleep, and we'll wake up feeling like the first three-quarters of this day never happened." She closed her eyes as Liv kissed her forehead.

"It'll be Christmas morning. Anything is possible."

Chapter Fourteen

Christmas morning was beautiful. Uncharacteristically warm for a New Jersey December, but just chilly enough for a holly jolly season. Liv peered out the bathroom window and watched a bare tree sway in the breeze. Her body was pleasantly sore and tender, but her heart still felt heavy. Theo had woken up before her and slipped out of bed unnoticed. Liv shouldn't have been surprised to find the bed empty beside her, and now she felt a bit foolish for believing one good night would change everything.

After taking the time to pamper herself and enjoy these moments before her house was full, Liv checked her appearance one last time in the mirror. Her chin-length black curls were perfect, but the heavy bags beneath her eyes marred her otherwise pleasant look. Her very merry red and green sweater dress came past her hips and over her yoga pants. Sure, the pants were a staple piece in her everyday attire, but when you hosted the holiday, you could be as comfortable as you wanted. She gave herself a quick pep talk full of reminders of the day. *Be kind. Be patient. Count your blessings. Love your wife unconditionally.*

She opened the bathroom door and heard the clattering of dishes. Theo was as quiet as a mouse when getting out of bed, but she might as well have been a rhinoceros in the kitchen. With a deep breath, she steeled herself for the day ahead. Guests were on their way, dinner was filling the house with savory aromas, and the sweet smell of baked desserts still lingered in the air. And more than enough worry sat in her stomach, keeping her from truly enjoying any of it.

She walked the long hallway that led to the stairs. One step after the next, Christmas music got louder, and she felt herself start to fill with cheer. Liv took a deep breath and smiled at the mistletoe hanging above the front door when she stepped off the bottom stair. She was in charge of her day, her mood, and what she gained from it. Mindfulness went a long way. She took another breath and closed her eyes. She imagined welcoming positivity and exhaling negativity.

She entered the kitchen, smiling and ready for cheer. "Hey, babe. I didn't hear you get out of bed." She kissed the back of Theo's neck, noting her light perfume and warmth. She let her lips linger and said, "Merry Christmas."

Theo leaned back into her body slightly. "Merry Christmas, love."

The pet name eased any lingering tension. "Everything smells wonderful, you included." She turned Theo around by her elbow and kissed her. Their kiss was slow and deep, a hello and an I love you wrapped up in the meeting of lips. She pulled back and reveled in the way her body responded to Theo again and again. "We have about a half hour before everyone gets here if you want to fool around…"

Theo ran her hands up Liv's arms, chills following in their wake. "The last time we tried that, Sheila almost caught us."

"My mom has learned to ring the bell like everyone else."

"Because your father almost had a heart attack."

"He was fine."

"He wouldn't make eye contact with me until New Year's."

Liv laughed at the memory. "I guess catching me on your lap was a bit jarring."

"And I was topless."

The imagery made her warm. "You most definitely were." She looked at Theo's simple burgundy button up and smirked. "This could be off and on in no time."

"Not happening."

She pouted and said, "Keep it on, then. I can work around it." Liv wrapped her arm around Theo's neck. "Just a little taste?"

Theo's wavering resolve could be seen in her green eyes. "We shouldn't…"

"Oh, but we should," Liv said with a nod. She started to lean in, pressing her breasts firmly into Theo's ample chest. "Last night just made me want you more."

The oven timer went off. Theo pulled back with a sigh. "Later."

"Is that a promise?"

"Yes."

"You're not allowed to break a Christmas promise."

Theo pulled two pans of mini quiches from the oven and evaluated them with a critical glance. "I hope there's enough food."

Mood gone. "There's always more than enough. Todd and Terri will leave with so much food, they'll feed the family for a week."

"I know you're right. Then why doesn't it feel like enough?"

"Because you're Italian. It's in your blood to feed one hundred people or more."

Theo's full lips turned up into the most attractive, smug smile. "I do know how to fill a table."

"And it's perfect every single time." Liv kissed Theo's cheek before leaving the kitchen. "I'm going to set things up and light some candles." She looked at the pile of presents again. "Are you sure you don't want to exchange now instead of waiting?"

"No," Theo said firmly, her voice carrying from the kitchen. "I like waiting until everyone leaves and the dust settles."

She felt the same as Theo, but that didn't mean she wasn't impatient to exchange. She always was. "You're really all about making me wait this year."

"You love it."

"I do. And I love you." She heard Theo murmur a similar sentiment and went about lighting evergreen-scented candles. The Christmas spirit was alive and well after all.

She made sure everything was perfect and in place. No matter how many years of hosting they had under their belts, Liv still felt excited every time. The pillows on the couches were fluffed, wood was stacked and set perfectly for their evening fire, and small bowls of treats were scattered throughout the downstairs. Ready, set, Christmas.

"Did I tell you Rich called?"

Liv stopped dead in her tracks, and all joy drained from her body. "Rich called you?"

"Yeah, a couple of days ago."

This Christmas really would be one for the books. "What did he have to say?" Liv said, standing just outside the kitchen.

"He just asked about the family and what my plans were for the holidays. He wanted to know if we'd be interested in going to a New Year's Eve party in the city."

"Mm-hmm." Liv breathed deeply to calm herself before talking. "Did he actually invite both of us or just you?"

Theo turned and tilted her head, giving Liv an unamused look. "I obviously declined."

"Well, thank goodness for that."

"Don't be like that."

"Like what?"

Theo sighed. "Don't be weird about Rich."

"Don't be weird about Rich?" Liv said, scratching her chin. "Don't be weird about the guy who continues to hit on you even though you're both married? The guy who ignores me every time I'm around?"

Theo chortled. "No, he doesn't."

"He called me Liz the last time we were all together."

"He was just being—"

"A jerk! He was being a jerk, and I don't get why you're defending him right now." Liv crossed her arms over her chest. Theo chewed at her bottom lip. Liv raised her right eyebrow.

"I'm not," Theo said weakly before fiddling with a nearby pile of napkins. Theo looked at Liv and smiled. "I love that dress on you."

"Theodora." She never used Theo's full name, and the accompanying tone made Theo's smile fall flat. "What are you not telling me?"

"Rich is coming here for dessert."

Liv went into a full body sweat. "What?"

"I'm sorry." Theo's eyes were genuinely apologetic, but that mattered very little to Liv.

"Why?"

"My mom invited him."

Liv pressed her palms together and brought them to her mouth, ready to beg Theo to tell her this was all a joke. "Why would she do that?"

"Because Rich is a family friend."

"But this isn't her house to invite anyone to, friend or foe, or in this case both, for any occasion. Why would you let her do this?"

"What was I supposed to say?"

"No. You were supposed to say no."

"She'd ask why," Theo said as if she had won the argument right then and there.

Liv tried her best to crack her tense neck. "Tell her the truth." Her ire rose when Theo made a sound in the back of her throat, like her suggestion was ridiculous. "You tell her that her golden boy Rich is actually a creep who makes your wife incredibly uncomfortable, and now she'll have to deal with that in her own home, after everything else. Thank you very much."

Theo was silent as she basted the turkey. She closed the oven and turned back to Liv. Her face was stiff again, the look Liv had hoped to erase for good after they had talked. "It'll be fine."

The familiar aching sadness was back. All she wanted, all she *needed*, was to feel like the priority, but instead she just felt defeated. "Fine." She started to walk away but got called back.

"Don't be like this all day. You'll ruin Christmas."

"If Christmas is ruined, I can assure you it's not my fault."

"I really am sorry."

Liv looked Theo in the eye for a moment. The apology did nothing, but a phone call to cancel would solve everything. Clearly, Theo had no intention of doing that. "I have to get our extra guest a folding chair from the attic." She walked away quickly enough to avoid being called back again.

Liv breathed in the gust of cold air coming from the attic. Her face was heated with anger, and her cute sweater dress felt more like a vise grip of flames. How dare her in-laws? How dare Theo allow it? And above it all, what truly astounded Liv was how Theo was okay with doing something that'd clearly upset Liv when they already weren't at their best. Was she being malicious, or were Theo's sights set so far from Liv and their marriage that she was basically blind? Liv tossed a bag of clothes aside with a satisfying amount of force. Maybe it was time to quit yoga and take up boxing. At least she could let out this constant stream of frustrations.

She shuffled, awkward and bent, to the back corner and grabbed a chair snugged behind a tall stack of boxes. Each box was labeled and relabeled so many times, she still wasn't sure what was in any of them. "Dammit," she said while struggling to free the chair and maintain her balance. "Come on, you piece of—" Suddenly the chair came free and swung around to hit a lone, stained box. The top flap opened slightly, and Liv laughed at the way the universe worked. The contents, now visible, were her and Theo's wedding and honeymoon photo albums.

Liv had an idea. Rich wouldn't be able to ignore their marriage anymore.

Chapter Fifteen

Theo sipped her wine and stared at the photo of her and Liv on the mantel. She didn't remember putting it there, nor did she remember seeing it recently. The kids played on the floor around her feet and distracted her with the sound of their giggles. Sam was eight and very gentle with Julia. He knew she was younger and smaller and needed a little extra care. Every day she imagined her own children in the same place, playing the same way, and loving every second of it.

"Aunt T?" Sam said from his place on the carpet.

"Yes, sweetheart?"

"Can I have a cookie?" His eyes were big and blue, and his cherub's cheeks punctuated his sweetness.

"No can do. We're going to eat soon, and your dad always gets mad at me when I give you treats."

"Sure, blame me," Todd said, putting his hand on Theo's shoulder. "You have to eat dinner first, bud, then you can have cookies."

"Promise?"

She was ready to promise Sam anything he wanted. "Yes."

"If you're good at the table." Todd's voice was loud enough to overpower Theo's. "You can't be such a softie, sis. Your kids will walk all over you."

Theo bristled at the mention of her nonexistent children. She really wanted to believe Liv, but the nagging voice in the back of her mind kept screaming it couldn't be true. "I think I'll be okay with that." She cleared her throat and tried to act natural, but Todd had been able to detect her bullshit since they were kids.

"What was that about?"

"What?" Theo took another sip of wine, trying her best to hide behind the glass.

"Nice try," Todd said, effortlessly stopping Julia from running away from the group at the same time. "What's going on?"

She spotted Liv across the great room, greeting their best friend, Jesse. "Now's not really the time."

Todd looked over his shoulder and then back to Theo. "Trouble in paradise?"

She rolled her eyes. He always made comments about how jealous he was of her marriage. She tried to explain how the understanding between two women couldn't be beaten, but he didn't understand it or believe it. "Not necessarily. It's just—" She stopped talking as Sheila walked by. Her mother-in-law didn't need to know about their problems. When she was in the clear, she continued, "I'm ready to start a family, and Liv seems, I don't know, hesitant? I brought it up a couple of months ago, and she didn't have much to say. The more I mentioned it…" Theo allowed Todd to fill in the blanks instead of mentioning Liv's drinking. "Now she talks about being ready, but I don't know if I believe her."

"Kids are a lot to handle, sis. They change your entire life in the blink of an eye. I can't blame Liv for not being ready."

"Whose side are you on?" Theo said in a near squawk. She saw Jesse approaching them and forced a smile. "Hey, Jesse, it's so good to see you." She leaned in and gave Jesse a long hug.

"Merry Christmas," Jesse said, shaking Todd's hand and turning back to Theo. "I really appreciate you inviting me."

"Please. You know you're invited every year." Theo gently slapped Jesse's shoulder. "I was hoping we'd see you for Thanksgiving." She meant it, too. Jesse was one of their oldest friends, and having her around brought them so much joy. "And every day in between, for that matter. Where have you been?"

Jesse scratched the back of her neck. "I've been lying low. Just trying to get through to Christmas break. I swear these kids get worse and worse each year. Who decided social media was a good idea?" Her words were stiff, and her demeanor seemed closed off, which was unusual. Normally, she was warm and eloquent.

"Julia, lower your dress. For Christ's sake," Todd said under his breath. "I'm never allowing her on social media. That's for sure."

Ignoring Todd, Theo kept her eyes on Jesse. "What are your students doing exactly?" Theo said, rolling her wineglass between her palms.

Jesse closed her eyes and shook her head. "I've had six students so far messaging me and trying to follow me on Instagram."

Theo laughed lightly, not at all surprised. "You're always a favorite teacher."

"Yeah, so give me an extra apple—don't try to comment on a picture of me from the apple harvest we went to three years ago."

Theo pulled a face. "That's not good."

"Everything is private now, and I'm this close to deleting it all," Jesse said, holding her thumb and forefinger millimeters apart.

"You would never," Theo said, getting distracted by the doorbell. "That's probably straight Tammy. Excuse me." Theo walked to the door, touching Liv's lower back gently along the way. She smelled Liv's faint perfume and smiled as she opened the door. "Tammy. How are you?" She hugged Tammy gently.

"Better now that I got here. Traffic is fucking horrendous." Tammy removed her jacket, her long, dark hair unruly as she flipped it around. "Oh shit, the kids are here already. Sorry."

Theo could feel how wide her eyes were. Tammy's tendency to curse nonstop wasn't usually a problem around the office, but young ears were rarely around to hear her colorful speech. "It's okay, just leave it at the door."

"You got it," Tammy said with a wink.

Theo hoped the wink meant she *actually* understood. "Everyone's almost here. I have a charcuterie board set up in the kitchen and a bunch of drinks to choose from." She laughed as Tammy made a beeline for the kitchen. Theo was proud of her reputation for putting out the best spread from first course to finish.

She stood by the front door and looked at her family and friends gathered together. She was still waiting on a few arrivals, but her heart grew at the smiling faces in front of her. Having her loved ones in the same place, especially the kids, made her so happy.

"Your famous spinach dip is almost gone. These people are

beasts." Liv took Theo's nearly empty wineglass from her. "My mom tried to get the recipe from me again. She doesn't believe I don't know it."

"No one knows it."

"That's what I told her. Again. Would you like a refill?"

"No. Thank you," she said. Theo wished Liv would remember she had cut back on alcohol to support her, and just in case they tried to conceive. She wouldn't remind her because Liv seemed happier than earlier. "I'm glad you're over the Rich stuff."

Liv sipped her sparkling water and shook her head. "Oh, I'm not. I'm just focusing on being a good host right now."

Theo tried to read Liv's face, but she couldn't quite decode the expression she had never seen before. Which made her think of Jesse. "Does Jesse seem okay to you?"

Liv looked over her shoulder. "I haven't really talked to her yet, but she's having a good time with Todd."

Theo watched Jesse laugh and chat, appearing normal and at ease. But she couldn't explain it. Something felt off from the moment they talked. Maybe Theo was projecting her own uneasiness on others, or perhaps more happened the previous night than Liv let on. She wouldn't meet Liv's eyes. "Did anything happen last night? Did you two talk about anything?"

Liv puckered her lips and made a show of thinking, an exaggerated show. "Not really. I was pretty embarrassing."

"Did she say anything about you drinking?"

"No," Liv said quickly. "She was shocked for sure but didn't say anything."

"Okay." Theo didn't know what to believe, but if Liv wouldn't tell her anything and Jesse wouldn't open up, there was very little Theo could do.

"I'm going to bring this into the kitchen," Liv said, holding her glass up, "and I'll talk to her. If you're sensing something, you're probably right. You usually are."

Now Theo was smiling. "I usually am."

"Don't I know it," Liv said with a wink and walked off to the kitchen.

Theo felt guilt tug at her heart. She should believe Liv and allow them to move on, but they'd always been on the same page since they started dating, which made this odd disconnect all the more alarming.

"What's wrong with you?" Miranda said.

"Nothing," Theo said a little more spicily than she intended. "I'm sorry. It's just everyone keeps asking me that."

"That's because it's obvious."

"I'm fine, really. Just a little stressed about the holidays. I'm looking forward to them being over."

"I think that's a common theme this year. It all came on too quickly. No one was really ready."

Theo looked across the room at Liv, who chased Julia around in a circle. Liv stood up and feigned being dizzy, or maybe she wasn't faking at all. She laughed as Liv took a deep steadying breath. "I'll be right back, Mom." She walked over and put her hand on Liv's shoulder. "Aren't you supposed to be the centered, more balanced one?"

"Spinning around isn't really our most popular yoga move."

"Maybe it should be," she said, kissing Liv's cheek softly. "I'm going to start putting the food out on the table. I think everyone will be here by the time I'm done." She walked off toward the kitchen.

❖

Liv watched Theo curiously. They had been together for so many years, and she still had a hard time predicting Theo's moods. The morning started out great, but now she felt shaky. What an odd Christmas. She noticed Miranda staring at her and raised her glass. Miranda's eyes looked the opposite of cheery, more like mean daggers and fire.

Jesse approached her and looked around. "Hey, bud, can we talk for a minute?"

"Yeah!" Liv coughed to mask her eagerness. She noticed how worried Jesse looked, but that didn't curb her concern over Miranda's odd expression. "Are you also scared by the look my mother-in-law is giving me?"

"What?" Jesse looked at Miranda, and her eyes widened. "Yikes. What did you do?"

"I'm not sure." She sipped at her water.

"Anyway, sorry to make this about me but," Jesse said, pausing to look around again, "Eloise is back."

Liv marveled at how Miranda blinked so infrequently. "Yeah, I know. Ow!" She grabbed her bicep where Jesse had just slapped her.

"You knew?"

"Yeah, I knew."

"And you didn't think to tell me?"

"Why would I think to tell you?"

Jesse wouldn't answer.

Everything hit Liv at once. "I fucking knew it," she said, regretting the words immediately when the kids turned their heads at the no-no word. "Garage. Now." She urged Jesse to lead the way and kept nudging her shoulder when she'd start to slow. She closed the garage door behind them and turned to stare at Jesse. "Well?"

"I, um, it—I didn't—so it was just…" Jesse stumbled and stuttered but finally stopped to just breathe. "I figured you knew."

"You *assumed* I knew and used that as an excuse to avoid telling your best friend you were hooking up with Eloise Grant."

"That is not true."

"The hell it isn't. We all know assuming and knowing are two very different things."

"I didn't know how to tell you."

"The same way you told me about Julie in college or Carole a few years ago. You just say, *Hey, I'm dating this girl.* Simple as that." Liv knew she was getting more and more animated, but Jesse was always the cool constant in her life. This situation took her by surprise. She waved her hands in the air. "Or the same way I opened up to you last night. You just say it."

"Drunkenly or within a holiday poem?"

Liv waved her off. "Openly and honestly."

"Over a year later. And I thought you stopped drinking."

Liv's skin crawled at her own actions. "This is about you, and we always tell each other everything. Always. Everything," she said, punctuating each word. They both turned to the door when the faint sound of the doorbell could be heard. "I have to get that." She walked into the house and got halfway to the front door before realizing what was about to happen. "You may want to stay here."

"What? Why?"

Liv opened her mouth to explain herself, but she heard a commotion that stopped her. "Our next guests are here. Theo invited Lena and Eloise."

Jesse's face went white. "Eloise is here for Christmas dinner? Like, as in staying here and sitting at the table with all of us?"

Liv winced. "Yes. That was what the invitation was for."

"Since when do you invite Lena and Eloise to Christmas dinner?"

She felt her defenses go up. Jesse was her best friend, but she didn't owe her an explanation. "Since Lena had knee surgery and hasn't been able to cook."

"This is a disaster."

"A disaster that could have been easily avoided if you had told me about your relationship with Eloise."

"So this is my fault?"

"Yes!"

Theo rounded the corner into the hallway and stopped short when she saw them. "What are you two doing back here?" Theo looked pointedly at Liv. "And not answering the door like you were supposed to. My mom just let our guests in."

"Great," Liv said under her breath. "We'll be right out." She watched Theo roll her eyes and walk away.

Jesse elbowed her. "She's mad at you, bro."

"What else is new?" She started to walk but Jesse held her back by the shoulder.

"Still the kid thing?"

Liv considered the simplicity of the question, and the complexity of the answer. "Yeah, but we don't have time to get into it now. Plus, the latest episode of your secret soap opera is about to play out live in my dining room. I want to make sure I get a front-row seat."

"You're a jerk, but I'm not mad at you because I know you're using humor to cope and deflect."

Liv shook her head. "You really need to stick to chemistry and leave the psychology to the pros."

"Will do, yoga master, will do." Jesse took a deep breath.

Liv did the same. "I shouldn't pick on you because my episode is up next. Rich is coming for dessert." She took two more deep breaths, one for herself and one for Jesse.

"Oh shit."

"Time for dinner."

They walked to the crowded dining room like two soldiers headed to the front line.

CHAPTER SIXTEEN

"You are looking wonderful," Theo said as she hugged Lena. She stood back and held her at arm's length. "What's different about you?"

"Well, I did lose a bit of weight, and I'm not in constant agonizing pain anymore."

Theo hesitated to believe it. "Really? Even though you're only a few weeks post-op?"

"I'm serious. The pain after surgery was nothing compared to the daily aches and the shooting pains I'd feel bending into the counters at the bakery."

"That sounds awful." Theo felt terrible for not checking in on Lena sooner. "No one would've ever guessed you were in that kind of pain."

"Eh." Lena shrugged with the same casualness she always gave off. "What's the point of complaining?"

Theo took Lena's jacket and smiled at Eloise, who stood just behind. "I'm so happy you both could make it."

"Thank you again for inviting us. There was no way I'd be able to manage the bakery and throw together a nice Christmas, too." Eloise's smile looked shy and maybe even a little guilty.

"Our pleasure," Liv said, appearing out of nowhere. "Theo, can I talk to you for a minute?"

Theo fought to keep the smile on her face. "One minute. I'm welcoming our guests."

Liv's eyes looked wide and panicked. "Eloise, you and Lena can head right in. There's wine, cheese, and some spinach dip scraps in the kitchen. Please excuse us." Liv grabbed Theo by the elbow and all but dragged her farther into the house and into a half bath.

"What are you doing, you maniac?" Theo adjusted her sweater.

"We have to rearrange the seating."

"No way," Theo said, shaking her head quickly. "We struggled to put everyone in a good place or, more importantly, Tammy away from anyone who'll get her in trouble. Remember last year when I served clams casino, and she made a lesbian joke every single time you or I ate one?"

Liv started to laugh but quickly sobered up. "This is a little more serious." She paused, and Theo wondered if she'd have to shake it out of Liv. "I want to make sure Jesse isn't next to or across from Eloise."

Theo didn't understand. "We went over this already. They're next to each other because they know each other enough to chat without feeling obligated to make small talk." Frustration started to mount, and Theo's cheeks warmed. She turned to open the door and spoke over her shoulder. "Is this because of the Rich thing? You want to make sure we don't sit near each other."

"No. Babe, please," Liv said, her tone uncharacteristically serious. Theo looked at her. "Jesse just told me she and Eloise were seeing each other."

A positively gleeful feeling took over. Theo couldn't contain her smile or surprise. "This is great! Wait." She frowned. "Why can't they sit next to each other?"

Liv smiled sadly and crossed her arms. "They *were* seeing each other. Apparently, the secret breakup at the end of the secret relationship wasn't pretty."

Theo read Liv's body language loud and clear. "I'm sorry Jesse kept this from you, from us," she said, smoothing her hands over Liv's arms. "Do you know what happened?"

"No idea." Liv leaned back against the sparkling white sink. "She just told me, then nearly pooped her pants when she heard Eloise would be here. That bit was a little funny."

Theo pressed her thumb between her eyes. The headache was supposed to come at the end of dinner, not before everyone was seated. "Jesse has always been the easiest guest. Why would she do this to me?" She knew her dramatics were flaring, but she didn't care. "Why is being a good guest so hard?" Theo whined as she stomped her foot.

"Okay, okay." Liv grabbed Theo's left hand and rubbed it between hers. "Let's put Jesse next to me, Lena next to her, and then Eloise. The only way they'll really get a good look at each other is if they break their necks."

Theo pictured the layout of the table and imagined each guest in turn. "That would work." She opened the door swiftly, feeling rejuvenated with determination. She just barely made out Liv's voice behind her.

"That's why we're a good team."

She threw a quick thumbs-up over her shoulder before rounding the corner into the kitchen. Theo jumped when she nearly ran into her mother. "Mom," she said loudly and placed her hand on her chest. "Why are you in here and not mingling?"

"I thought I smelled something burning."

Theo felt her heart rate rise. "Was it the lasagna?" She ran over to the oven and opened the door. Everything appeared to be just fine. She closed the oven and lifted the lid from a stovetop pot. "The gravy?"

"It must've been my imagination. What can I do?"

Every year without fail, Theo had to remind her mother of her role. "Nothing. Just relax and enjoy the company."

"Surely there's something you need help with." And every year her mother would remind Theo she doubted her capabilities.

Theo tensed her jaw twice before speaking in hopes of feigning a calm she most definitely did not feel. "Everything is ready to head to the table, including the guests. And you're one of the guests."

Her mother's shoulders fell slightly, and her smile seemed small for her big personality. "I'm sorry, sweetheart. You know I'm still not over the Christmas debacle of 1995."

Theo chuckled, even though she knew the story like the back of her hand. Traditions weren't just recipes and actions. Sometimes a story could carry just as much comfort and sentiment. "I'm still convinced that's why Uncle Andy refuses to come to our holidays."

"Oh, are we telling *the* story?" Liv said as she reentered the kitchen, Jesse hot on her heels.

Jesse raised her hand just a little. "What story?"

"I'm not sure if my mom wants—"

"It was Christmas Day, 1995. Theo was only ten at the time."

Theo shook her head and sighed. "Eleven."

"That's what I said." Her mom brushed her off.

Theo leaned back against the counter and watched as her mother commanded the attention in the room. Liv had heard the story nearly as many times as Theo, but it didn't matter.

"This was the first Christmas her father and I had hosted. God bless that man's soul," her mom said to the sky before blowing a kiss to the heavens above. "He put it off for as long as he could, but by then we had moved into a new house with plenty of room for parties."

"My father loved silence and peaceful nights at home," Theo said.

Her mom held her hands up. "I love having a good time and inviting people over so they can have a good time, too."

"The only thing he loved more than peace at home was you," Theo said directly to her mom. She missed her father, but beyond that she missed seeing the sparkle he'd put in her mother's eyes.

"We had a long table"—her mother spread her arms apart—"the longest we could afford at the time, and it just about took up the entire dining room. The skinniest in the family had to sit against the wall because no one else would fit." She chuckled deeply. "We went above and beyond with the menu. We had a turkey, a ham, lasagna, and all the sides, plus we forgot to tell our guests not to bring anything. Needless to say, we had enough food to feed the neighborhood, but no table space for our own plates."

Jesse whispered to Liv. "Is she exaggerating?"

"No, this is all true. Even the kiddie table had very little room for kiddies."

"It never occurred to us that so much food would weigh a lot, or that bargain tables were a bargain for a reason."

Theo bit the inside of her cheek at the sound of Jesse's audible gasp.

"Saying grace did us in," her mother said, lowering her head. "Everyone must've leaned a little too much of their weight on the table, and boom." She clapped her hands. By now, everyone had joined them in the kitchen. A chorus of *no way* and *oh my God* filled the room. Jesse's mouth hung open. "We blessed the food as it slid right to the floor. Poor Paul was buried in all the main courses."

"For real?" Jesse said. She had a smile of disbelief on her face. "This really happened?"

Theo's mom crossed her heart. "Paul built us our very own table for the following Christmas. It took him seven months, but he did it."

"And now we host every Christmas at that same table." Theo took Liv's hand. They were a family.

"I love that table," Liv said.

Theo's mom turned to Liv. "You'd better."

Theo's hand hurt as Liv tightened her grip. "Let's all head into the dining room. I'll be out in a minute with the lasagna." She didn't let go of Liv's hand to ensure she'd stay behind. "You too, Mom." Her mother narrowed her eyes at her, and she narrowed her eyes back until her mom finally exited the room.

"I can never tell if your mom hates me or actually likes me."

"We can worry about that later." Theo grabbed Liv's shoulders and turned her so they could face each other. "While I get this together, you go out there and take control of the seating. Can you do that?"

"Yeah."

"Yeah?"

"Yes. Jesse to my left, Lena to my right, and Eloise out of sight. I love you." Liv kissed Theo quickly and rushed off to the dining room. Theo smiled and felt the softness of Liv's lips lingering even after they were far apart.

Just a few more hours to go, Theo reminded herself. Everything would be okay.

CHAPTER SEVENTEEN

Liv's lower back started to hurt from the constant back and forth of trying to shield Jesse from Eloise. Eloise was very quiet, only chiming in when Lena spoke of her recovery and the bakery. Tension was at a minimum, and when any silence stretched on for too long, Liv filled the lull with compliments.

"Babe, this lasagna is really incredible. The turkey is perfect, too, but the lasagna has to be my favorite part of the meal. Hands down." She winked at Theo across the table. As much as she'd wanted to sit next to Theo, survival was more important this Christmas.

"Thank you. I think about you saying that every time I prepare it, actually."

"Aw, how gross," Todd said. He shot them both a playful smile.

"My boyfriend, Lee, is a vegetarian, and he's been introducing me to a whole bunch of meat alternatives." Tammy poured more gravy over a thick slice of turkey butting up against a nearly finished meatball. "I am so glad he had to work tonight." The table erupted in laughter.

"What does he do for a living?"

"Graphic design," Tammy said around a mouthful of potatoes. She swallowed and wiped her mouth. "But he's been selling his art on the side, hoping he can get some traction."

"Very cool." Liv placed her fork and knife down to show genuine interest. "What kind of art is it?"

Tammy shoved an olive in her mouth and said, "Hyper-realistic sculptures of vaginas." Silence followed. Long, painful, awkward silence. Liv fought to swallow. "I'm just kidding." Tammy guffawed. "You should've seen all your faces." Tammy pointed at each person with her fork.

Theo leaned forward. "Tammy—"

"Don't yell at me," Tammy said with a raised hand. "He's a painter. Mostly landscapes but kind of abstract. It's all really neat."

"I was called to the scene of a car wreck a couple months ago," Eloise said, getting everyone's attention. She hadn't said one word until now. "One driver was transporting $100,000 worth of paintings in an unmarked van."

Eloise continued when Todd in particular showed interest. "This guy was in a complete panic when we arrived. I was sure he was on drugs. He was red and sweating, more concerned with getting back on the road and avoiding the police."

"If he was innocent, why avoid the police?" Lena said.

"That's exactly what I was thinking. The police opened the van, expecting to find worse than art. The driver explained he had to be at the gallery in less than an hour. He didn't have time and just wanted to be on his way."

"Was he injured?" Jesse asked.

"A couple bruises we could see." Eloise shook her head, obviously picturing the scene. "I'm convinced he had a shoulder injury, but he wouldn't let us evaluate him. All he cared about was his job. I'll never understand people like that."

Jesse snorted.

Liv swallowed. Time to change the subject. "Terri, do you and Todd have any trips planned with the kids?"

Terri nodded as she finished chewing. "Now that Julia's four, we think it's finally time to take that trip to *D-I-S-N-E-Y*."

Liv looked at Sam, knowing he was old enough to spell, but he still didn't catch on. "That's fun and exciting."

"There's nothing wrong with caring about your job," Jesse said.

Liv turned to Jesse. "I don't think that's what Eloise meant."

"He put his job before his own health, and he didn't even care about the other people involved," Eloise said, defending herself quickly. "He didn't care if he hurt anyone."

Liv locked her gaze on Theo's worried eyes. She needed to tamp down this growing fire. "Regardless of his actions, $100,000 of art is a lot."

"He could've lost his job for being late." Jesse wouldn't let it go. "Maybe his entire reputation was on the line. Hell, for all you know, he was the artist himself, and this was his big break."

Eloise crossed her arms and sat back. "He was just a runner for the gallery."

In a panic, Liv said the only thing that came to mind. "At least the accident wasn't terrible, and he could still make his Van Gogh." Several groans sounded out around the table, followed by pained laughter. But the terrible joke worked, and the focus shifted from Eloise and Jesse. Liv shrugged. "Sorry not sorry."

"You should be ashamed of that one, babe." Theo smirked.

Liv winked. "You loved it."

"Your home is beautiful," Lena said. She had finished her third glass of red wine and was noticeably relaxed. "Spacious but still warm."

Theo beamed with pride. "Thank you, Lena. We took our time finding a home. We were very particular, and we couldn't be happier."

Todd laughed. "They were painful."

"Oh. Did you help them?" Lena said.

"I was their real estate agent. I showed them more houses than any other client, and they ended up completely remodeling this one anyway."

Miranda chimed in. "Liv was mostly to blame."

Liv was taken aback. "I was not."

Miranda nodded and placed her napkin on the table. "You insisted you needed the perfect space for that yoga nonsense."

"It's *not* nonsense, Mom," Theo said firmly. "Liv has a huge following at the studio, and it's nice for her to have her own private space to find peace at home."

Liv softened at the way Theo defended her, even if she couldn't help but think about how peace had been a little too hard to find recently.

Lena touched Liv's shoulder. "I thought you did hair."

"I do, three days a week, and then three nights a week, I teach yoga at a studio in town. I've always been very interested in the practice of yoga, and once I took it up, I couldn't stop. I knew it was my calling." Liv then noticed how flat Lena's hair was falling. "You should come down to the salon someday soon while you're still taking it easy at the bakery. I'll freshen up your color and give you a whole new look for the new year."

"New knee, new look, new year." Eloise raised her glass, and everyone but Jesse joined in for a jovial toast. "And then maybe a new man." Eloise covered her smirk with her glass and sipped her wine slowly.

Liv chuckled at the way Lena looked at Eloise with an expression only a mother could make. Her thoughts led to wondering about parenting with Theo. Which of them would be the notorious bad cop? Would either of them be capable of The Look?

"Liv?"

She started slightly before looking at Tammy with a small smile. "Sorry, I must've zoned out."

Tammy snorted. "I'd say."

Eloise leaned toward Liv. "We were talking about setting my mother up with someone from Todd's office."

Liv shook her head. "I don't believe in setups."

"We were a setup." Theo twisted her mouth. "I think we worked out pretty well."

Liv wanted to smile at how cute Theo was, but Miranda decided to chime in.

"Do you disagree, Liv?" Miranda said.

Tread carefully. "Of course I agree, but lightning doesn't strike twice."

Liv's mother, who had been otherwise engaged in quiet conversation at the other end of the table, held up her glass. "No other love story could compare to yours. Just look at those smiling faces," she said, pointing to a perfectly placed wedding picture on the hutch.

Liv's cheeks warmed. "Thanks, Ma."

Theo looked at Liv curiously. "Did you put that there?"

Liv was ready with a phony denial but her dad cleared his throat to speak. "Does that put us in second place, honey?"

Her mom placed her hand on his shoulder. "Yes, dear."

"Are we a measly third?" Todd said to Terri.

Terri laughed. "They're hosting, so just let them win."

"Yeah, just let us win, Todd," Theo said and stuck her tongue out.

"Plus, we have at least two eligible women at the table who still stand a chance to beat us all," Terri said with a playful tone. "Let's give them some hope."

"I'll be lucky if I can get this one to leave my side long enough to go on even one date," Lena said, nudging Eloise.

"Mom, I'm fine."

Terri's face lit up. "So…"

Liv needed to intercept. "I think—"

"We actually have three eligible women at this table." Terri looked between Eloise, Lena, and Jesse. "I think I just came up with a New Year's resolution."

Lena waved off the attention. "Don't worry about me, dear."

"No, thank you," Jesse and Eloise said simultaneously.

"Too bad you're old, Jesse. I'd say you should just date Eloise." Tammy started laughing at herself. Liv could hear crickets beside her. "Two broads, one stone."

"Ha ha, you're funny, Tammy, but that's actually a very offensive term nowadays." Jesse said, sounding more artificial than the evergreen decorations.

"How old are you, Jesse?" Lena said.

Liv looked at Theo, internally screaming for something to be done. Theo must've been in tune because she stood abruptly.

"Let's clean up so we can get some desserts on the table and open that bottle of brandy." Theo grabbed her own empty plate and reached for Tammy's with the other hand, only to be swatted away.

"I'm not done yet."

"I'm stuffed," Liv said, turning to Jesse. "I just remembered I need more firewood. Want to come out back and help me? It'll make it go so much faster."

Jesse turned to look out the sliding glass doors that made up one wall of the dining room. "It's freezing out there."

"Exactly why I need help." Liv stood and resisted the urge to tug Jesse from her chair. "Hurry. We can't be late for dessert." She made sure to keep angling her body between Jesse and Eloise. "You don't mind, do you, babe?"

Theo waved her off. "We can't run out of firewood. Just be quick."

Liv didn't say another word. She stayed focused on getting Jesse out the door into the cold, crisp air. She slid the door shut with such force it nearly bounced back. "Wood is just by the shed."

"Jeez. You couldn't let me grab my jacket at least? It must be twenty degrees colder than before."

Liv waited until they were in the far corner of the yard before talking. Their breath filled the air with pillowy clouds. "Because it is suffocating inside. Are you okay?"

"No." Jesse's word carried such force that it echoed in the evening air. "None of this is okay. I think I should just leave. No one will really notice."

"I will," Liv said earnestly. "I feel awful we even put you in this position." Her throat hurt as she took a deep frigid breath and coughed it back out. "I'm sorry. That's very selfish of me. If you want to leave, I'll cover for you." Liv sobered completely. "It's the least I can do after last night."

Jesse stared at her for what felt like minutes instead of seconds. She was clearly thinking about it. "No. I'm too old for this. I'm not running away from my Christmas with my friends because of an ex."

"*Secret* ex."

"Really? Right now?"

"Sorry."

"It's not fair, you know? We tried a relationship, and it didn't work. Big deal. We're both adults, and we can sit around a table and have a meal."

"And we're halfway done. Dessert's coming out as we speak."

"Yeah." Jesse kicked at the ground. "I just wish she didn't look like that."

Liv's shoulders fell. "I'm sorry."

"She's perfect. She'll always be perfect." Jesse hugged herself tighter and smiled a grin full of heartache. "Just not perfect for me, and that's fine."

Liv's heart broke for Jesse. This was the first time she had ever seen someone affect Jesse so deeply. Carole had been an exception, but not in a good way. Their relationship had carried on for too long, and then Carole broke Jesse's heart. Jesse had never been the same, and Liv had been convinced she'd never let someone in again. But Eloise broke through. Liv wished she could've witnessed the good and the joy Eloise had brought into Jesse's life. Their relationship must've been grand for it to have shattered so explosively.

"Come on," Liv said, punching Jesse's bicep lightly. "Let's grab a few logs and head back in to start a roaring fire."

"You're not going to recite the poem again, are you?"

"Yes, but only the original." Liv laughed and Jesse groaned.

Chapter Eighteen

Theo felt good. Actually, Theo felt great. The guests had settled back at the table without another mention of eligible women. Sure, the quiet one-minute lecture she gave Tammy for meddling probably had something to do with it, and maybe Liv chiming in to control every conversation helped, but did the details really matter? Jesse was talking comfortably with Terri about teaching and the state of their current school systems, while Eloise and Lena described the process of controlling the quality of their baked goods while feeding the holiday rush.

"Breads and rolls are the worst. They can be so"—Lena rubbed her thumb and forefinger together—"finicky. Very testy."

Eloise clarified, "It's the proofing process. Too much humidity or five minutes too long?" Eloise dragged her thumb across her throat. "No one likes a dense loaf, and anything doughy is an embarrassment."

Theo was completely intrigued by Eloise. She hadn't spent much time with her, but being in her presence now helped her see why Jesse was drawn to her in the first place. "Eloise, I want to ask you something, but I'm afraid it'll come off as a bit nosy." A noticeable hint of apprehension flashed in Eloise's hazel eyes.

Eloise sat back. "Hit me."

"Why nursing? You obviously have a knack for this, and you work well with your mother. Why not work in the family business?"

Eloise smiled graciously. "I actually—"

"Two reasons," Lena said firmly and raised one finger. "I told her no."

"You told her no?" Theo said to Lena.

Lena gripped Eloise's forearm. "She played nurse since she was in diapers."

"I played baker then." Eloise wouldn't look at Theo but kept a broad smile on her face. "I was out of diapers when I started tending to my stuffed animals' injuries."

Lena looked at Eloise incredulously. "My apologies."

"Nursing is a kind of calling. You know instinctively whether or not you're built for it, and I thought I was when I was working on Mr. Bear."

"I believe that," Liv said, jumping into the conversation. "You have a very calming presence. I bet you're great with patients."

Eloise's cheeks colored, and she lowered her head, no doubt trying to hide behind her long dirty-blond hair. "Thank you for the compliment."

Sheila was glued to the conversation. "What's the other reason?"

Lena didn't answer and instead reached for a cannoli from the tray of goodies they brought from the bakery. "What's your favorite pastry? I always loved cannoli."

The question caught Theo off-guard. "Um, I'd say sfogliatella or a good cream puff like the ones you brought."

Tammy joined the conversation. "I love eclairs, and just recently I've gotten into macarons. Not macaroons. I had no idea they weren't the same thing."

Lena held up the cannoli. "Imagine making dozens of your favorite treats every single day. They're not as magical as they used to be." Lena punctuated her point by taking a big bite of her dessert, and Eloise looked at her mother with a gentle smile.

Theo looked longingly at the rest of the pastry tray. She'd indulged all day, which meant one more cream puff wouldn't kill her, but she was trying to keep herself in good health. Just in case. She snapped to attention when she heard Sam's voice.

"When are we opening presents, Aunt T?" Sam's face was pale from powdered sugar, and smears of chocolate still clung to the corners of his mouth.

She pulled him close and planted a big smooch on his forehead. "Soon, love. We're just finishing up dessert."

"And talking," he said with the biggest over-the-top pout.

Theo's heart swelled at Sam's overwhelming cuteness. "I'm sorry, sweetheart." She just couldn't handle the sight of his big sad eyes. "I tell you what," she said, leaning in. "I'll try to get them to stop, but I can't be rude. Okay?"

"Okay."

"Go tickle your Aunt Liv—she looks bored." Theo chuckled as Sam took off in the direction of Liv. He reached Liv and started poking at her sides rapidly. Liv made a show of squirming and laughing. Theo's insides ached. Everything about children just stoked her yearning, but watching Liv act effortlessly with the children in their family turned Theo's yearning into sadness. She watched Liv ruffle Sam's hair and continue to give him her undivided attention. Liv's smile was beaming, a grin Theo knew was authentic.

"I think it's time for us to go," Eloise said. Lena nodded.

"You can't go yet," Theo said, truly appalled by such an idea. "If you come to our house for Christmas dinner, you stay and make a Christmas wish."

"We don't want to overstay our welcome," said Lena.

Theo appreciated Lena's and Eloise's manners, but she wasn't having it. "This is our tradition, and you both are part of it this year. And that's final."

"Okay." Eloise held up her delicate hands. "Tell me about these wishes."

"We started the tradition the year we moved in. Liv and I wanted something of our own to add to the magic of Christmas, and I remembered hearing about a wishing tree."

Lena raised her hand. "I've heard of this. You write down your wish and hang it on the tree."

Theo pointed at Lena and smiled. "You got it. These trees are usually in public places, but there's no rules. We decided we wanted to start one with our family, so every year after dinner we gather around the tree, in front of the fire, and we each write down a wish. The important thing is to make it a good one," she said, winking at Liv. "After you write it down, you roll it up, tie a ribbon around it, and then hang it on the tree."

"And the love in the room, combined with a little Christmas magic, helps make your wishes come true," Liv said, picking right up where Theo left off.

Satisfied, Theo looked back to Eloise to see if she had any

questions, but Eloise's eyes were down. "Let's head into the living room and we'll show you."

Like a disorganized gaggle of geese, everyone made it into the living room eventually and found a place to sit. Theo sat on the arm of the chair Liv occupied, like she did every year, looking over the rest of the guests. Everyone looked comfortable except Jesse, who had no place else to sit but beside Eloise.

"Okay, everyone," Theo said loudly enough to be heard over the chatter in the room. "I want you all to grab a slip of paper and a pen."

"We know the drill," Tammy said. "You just explained it."

She took a deep, calming breath. "Write one wish you have for this season or next year, and we're going to hang them on our tree."

Sam held his paper up high. "I wish for more cars."

Todd shook his head. "You can't tell us your wish, kiddo, otherwise it won't come true."

"My wish for a Chippendales dancer under my tree didn't come true last year." Tammy snorted at herself. "You know what they say..."

"We don't need to know what they say," Liv said.

"If at first you don't succeed, try and try and try again." Tammy made a show of mock-licking the tip of her pen and scribbling on her paper.

Theo locked eyes with Liv and shook her head. "Keep your wishes to yourself, Tammy." She held her own slip of blank paper in her hands and thought carefully about her wish. She knew what she wanted more than anything in the world, but did she have the courage to put it in writing and continue to torture herself by believing she could make it come true? Theo felt silly when her hands started to tremble slightly. She wrote carefully, making sure each letter was crisp and clear, as if the spirit of Christmas had bad eyesight.

Believe.

She looked at the word in bold black ink and smiled, hopefulness filling her chest while the small voice of fear kept at it in the back of her mind. What if Liv was lying? Why set herself up for even more pain?

"Want me to hang yours up?" Liv said. "Hey, did I scare you?"

Theo didn't even notice she'd jumped until she felt her heart racing. "Yeah. Sorry. I must've gotten lost in my wish." She rolled up her wish quickly and carefully, making sure Liv wouldn't be able to read it, and tied a gold ribbon around it. She handed it to Liv like it was the most important piece of paper on the planet, because that's how it felt. She needed this wish to come true.

"I'll hang ours right next to each other, so they can help each other come true." Liv kissed Theo's forehead after taking the small scroll.

Theo's eyes started to burn, a telltale sign of impending tears. She paused and took in the moment before her. Family and friends surrounded her in the home she'd built with the most amazing woman she had ever met. Love was abundant, and for that, Theo was grateful. The heaviness she had been carrying for too many months came to the surface, and instead of becoming a painful or angry thought, it simply vanished. Theo took a long, deep breath and exhaled slowly. She trusted Liv, she trusted the universe, and she believed in their path. Everything in life felt like it was headed in the right direction.

The doorbell rang. Theo shared a look with Liv as Theo's mom leaped to her feet and insisted on getting the door. She tried to mouth an apology to Liv, but Liv turned back to Jesse, who seemed very reluctant to write down a wish.

Maybe life had a few more bumps to get over on its way to perfection.

CHAPTER NINETEEN

M iranda held on to Rich's broad shoulders and then held his broad jawline in her hands. Liv wanted to gag.

"I am so glad you could make it, Richard," Miranda said before pulling him back into another long hug.

Liv watched in horror from the couch as Miranda made a show of kissing Rich's cheek beneath the mistletoe. Mistletoe she'd insisted on hanging. "Barf."

Miranda's ridiculous smile had to be painful. "It wouldn't have felt like Christmas without you."

Liv knew her face reflected just how disgusted she felt. "Double barf."

Jesse leaned in. "Is that the guy? The ex?"

"He's not an ex. They were never a thing despite Miranda's twisted version of history."

"Maybe Theo never told you about it because she knows how much of a Jealous Judy you are. Let's just hope they stay away from the mistletoe."

Liv turned very slowly to look at Jesse. She cocked her head. "I know you're used to drama," she said, shifting her eyes briefly to a distracted Eloise, "but that's not how we roll in this house."

Jesse lowered her head, properly scolded. "I'm sorry, but you have to admit it feels like an ex situation."

Liv followed Jesse's eyes and watched Rich hold Theo a bit too long for her liking. "Now I'm really going to barf."

"Hey, everyone," Rich said, addressing the room. No one really seemed all that interested in his arrival, much to Liv's satisfaction. "What are we up to?"

"There's still some desserts on the table and coffee in the percolator. If you're hungry, I can put a plate together for you." Theo stepped away before she continued talking. "What can I get you?"

Liv understood Theo had to be a polite hostess, and she also reminded herself Miranda was to blame for this uncomfortable situation. Thankfully, she was prepared. "Can I get you something to drink, Rick?"

"Rich," Miranda and Rich both said, correcting her simultaneously.

Liv smiled internally. "We have wine, beer, water, and soda. Where's your wife?"

"We split," Rich said to Theo. "A few months ago." Jesse started coughing and had to step away.

Theo tilted her head in sympathy. "I'm so sorry."

Liv felt that backfire like a punch to her face. "Wine, beer, or soda?"

"Or brandy," Miranda said.

"Not the brandy." If Liv couldn't drink the brandy, neither could Rich.

"Speaking of," Rich said, ignoring Liv completely, "this is for you. I know you love a good cabernet." He handed Theo a red and green plaid bag.

Theo took the gift and looked directly at Liv. She walked away from Rich and stood next to Liv. "You didn't have to do that, but we appreciate it."

"Come on, Theo. You know it wouldn't be polite for me to show up empty-handed." Rich's eyes held far too much adoration.

Liv cleared her throat. "You're right. Never show up uninvited or empty-handed. How about that drink?"

Rich didn't look away from Theo. "I'll take a beer. Thanks."

Liv walked to the kitchen, breathing in and out rhythmically to keep calm. She grabbed a beer from the fridge and gave it a small shake before bringing it to Rich. She was only mildly satisfied as suds sputtered on his hand upon opening. "Sorry about that. I always tell this one we can't store beer on its side. Napkins are on the coffee table." Rich grabbed a couple of poinsettia-decorated napkins from a pile carefully placed beside a photo album. "Please be careful not to drip. I'll never be able to replace those memories."

"Is that our wedding album?" Theo's breath was warm against Liv's ear as she whispered. "Did you put that there?"

"He won't forget my name this time."

"I love you."

Liv turned to Theo, mildly surprised she wasn't being reprimanded for acting immaturely. "And I love you."

Tammy started waving her hand. "Rich, come over here. We were just making our annual Christmas wishes. Write one down, tie it up, and hang it on the tree."

"Oh, I don't really think I should."

Liv didn't hate him for one second.

"Go on," Miranda said, shooing him toward the tree. "I'm sure there's a wish in that big heart of yours."

His smile was goofy. "Okay. Sure. Why not?" He walked over and took the pen Tammy was holding out to him. He placed his beer down on the photo album and stared at Theo before scribbling on a piece of paper.

Liv couldn't take any more. "Is he aware of how obvious he is? And how disrespectful he is?" Liv said perhaps a bit too loudly. She didn't care because she was in her own home with her own family and felt like she had zero control. "I want him out as quickly as possible."

Theo looked at her, horrified. "I can't kick him out."

"Then talk to your mother and have her do it. She's the one who invited him without our permission in the first place."

"It's fine, Liv. There's nothing to worry about."

"It's not about being worried." Liv realized she needed to calm down when Jesse looked at her with raised eyebrows. She lowered her voice. "This is our house, and I shouldn't be treated this way or made to feel this way. Why do his feelings matter more? Why do your mother's?"

"I want to be a good host."

"I don't understand how any of this is okay to you. Are you seriously telling me right now that you don't see what's very wrong with this situation?" Liv looked at Theo expectantly. She wasn't willing to sit and accept this discomfort. "I want him out."

"Babe, it's just for a little longer."

Liv's words and patience were exhausted. "Okay. Then I'm out. Call me when it's over." She stepped around Theo, grabbed her jacket from the hook by the front door, and left the house.

❖

Theo stood in shock. How could Liv have just left? In the middle of Christmas. The room grew quiet. Caught between embarrassment and worry, Theo didn't know what to say. "I, um…" She looked over the small crowd of concerned faces. Nervous laughter bubbled up awkwardly. "It's fine," she said unconvincingly and waved everyone off. "How traditional would the holidays be without a little drama?" The room was still. Painfully quiet. No one even laughed along. Theo rushed away to the solitude of the kitchen. She didn't know whether to cry or panic or chase after Liv. Crying seemed the most appropriate.

"Sweetheart?" Her mother inched into the room. "What on earth is going on?"

Theo steeled herself against the counter with her back to her mother. The last person she wanted to talk to was her. "It's fine, Mom. Go back out to the living room." She tried to sniffle as quietly as she could.

"I don't know who you're trying to fool, but—"

"Please," she said firmly, "go back into the living room."

"What did Liv do this time?"

Theo went from blue to red in an instant. "Liv? What did *Liv* do? This is all your fault."

Her mom stepped back, aghast. "Excuse me? I've barely spoken to Liv."

"Sometimes it's not what you say, but what you do. And because I'm an emphatic people pleaser, I just let you make the rules."

"Theodora, I am having a hard time following. I've done nothing to cause waves, and that includes *making rules*," she said, using air quotes. "And I most certainly do not appreciate you talking to me like this."

"I most certainly do not appreciate *your* guest being invited before you ask us. Not me, us. This is our home."

Her mother rolled her eyes. "My guest?"

Theo hated being scoffed at. "Yes. Your guest. I would have never invited Rich."

"He's a family friend."

"No, Mom, he's not. He's your friend's son, and you seem to have this obsession with pushing him into my presence."

"He likes you," she said, as if that was an okay excuse.

Theo blinked. How could her mother be so dense? Confused, she tried to determine whether her mother woke up one day and suddenly decided Theo would be better off with a man, or if she had lost her mind altogether. Or both. "Do..." She shook the jumble of thoughts around in her head. "Do you hear yourself?"

Her mother stood firm with her arms folded across the chest of her ugly Christmas sweater. "I do."

"He is disrespectful to my wife and to my marriage, but out of respect for you I never say anything about it." Theo swatted heavy, angry tears from her face.

Her mom softened. "Theo, please calm down." She shrugged off her mother's attempts to comfort her. "This was not at all the outcome I was hoping for."

Theo's tears stopped. "What?"

"Nothing."

"Mom. What do you mean this isn't the outcome you wanted?"

"Exactly what I said."

Theo was well aware of her mother's little tells when she was keeping the whole truth to herself. Or when every word out of her mouth was a lie. "I swear to God, I am barely hanging on by a thread right now, so if you don't tell me what you're up to, I will lose—"

"I know you and Liv have been fighting, okay?" Her mom showed her palms in a surrendering gesture. "I've seen and felt the tension. You don't talk to me like you used to, so I don't know what problems you're having, but I know there's been problems. Call it a mother's intuition."

"Or you have eyes."

"Curb the sarcasm, will you? I may have pissed you off, but I'm still your mother."

Theo stood in defiance, neither apologizing nor adding another sarcastic quip. "And?"

"Rich is kind and a fun person to be around, and he obviously has a crush on you. I clearly see *that*."

Choosing to ignore her mother's dig, Theo said, "A kind man doesn't flirt with a married woman in front of her wife. Actually, a kind man should never flirt with a woman if he knows she's gay."

"Eh," her mom said, shrugging, "I said he's kind, but he's not smart."

"Okay, fine, so…what? What does this matter?"

"I like to, um…" Her mother shifted and looked out the kitchen window.

"Spit it out."

"I invite Rich around when I know you and Liv are going through a rough patch."

"Mom!"

"*Because* I know jealousy can reignite a relationship. It's my way of reminding Liv of how lucky she is to have you and how people are still lined up for you."

Theo sighed and rubbed small circles on her temples. At this rate, her headache would never go away. Actually, her head was more likely to explode. "While your heart was in the right place, oddly, I do hope you see how terrible an idea it was."

"It worked the first few times."

"But it blew up on Christmas Day in front of my friends and family." Theo would not allow her mother's need to be right win this argument. "You need to fix this," she said, pointing at her mom. "You and only you." Her mother choked out a sound that reminded Theo of a turkey. "Go."

Her mom stomped off with a grumble.

Theo closed her eyes and hung her head. "Play stupid games, win stupid prizes."

CHAPTER TWENTY

Liv sat in her freezing car, not having the heart to let it idle. All she'd hear in her head was Theo's voice, *You're killing the Earth.* She didn't need to add guilt to the laundry list of feelings she was experiencing. In spite of the cold, she sat wallowing and fighting with the many scenarios flipping through her imagination. Some were ugly, others were sad, but every single one involved Theo defending other people once again. Maybe the past year was nothing more than one long sign. She and Theo weren't as strong as she'd thought, and Liv would never come first. The had struggled over several chasms over and over, unable to bridge any for good. She laughed bitterly. "Good thing we didn't have kids yet." She jolted when the passenger door swung open and Miranda fell into the car.

"It took me ten minutes to find you," Miranda said, blowing into her clasped hands. "Why the hell isn't this thing on?"

Liv started the ignition without a second of hesitation. "I didn't exactly want to be found."

"I was ordered."

Liv couldn't believe it. "So Theo sent you instead of coming out here herself?"

Miranda checked her red manicure. "Not exactly."

Liv sighed. She was exhausted. "Look, I appreciate you trying, but if Theo wants me to come back inside, she should be the one asking."

"I agree. However, Theo felt it was important for me to…" She bobbed her head side to side as she thought. "Disclose a few things."

Liv studied Miranda in the dim light. "Like what?"

"First of all, I sent Rich home. I realized he has no place here."

Liv knew her skepticism was radiating from her pinched face. "Uh-huh. All of a sudden?"

"You storming out brought some things to light." Evasion was never Miranda's strong suit, yet she always tried.

"Like…?"

"You are a good match for my daughter. You've kept her happy, you've grown with her, and you've allowed her to flourish."

"Thanks."

"She also loves you very much."

Liv was in the mood to argue that point until she was blue in the face, but Miranda had more to say.

"Lately, I've noticed the two of you were not at your best, and I tried to help."

Liv scratched her head, trying to think of any moment recently where she had even interacted with Miranda, never mind a moment where Miranda seemed helpful. "Help how?"

"I invite Rich around when I know you and Theo aren't at your best in an effort to save your marriage. Now can we please go inside where it's warm and there's coffee? Or do I need to freeze to death?"

Liv needed a minute to process what Miranda had just confessed to, and she was kind of impressed with how Miranda never took a breath. "That's insane. Why would you do that?"

"Theo will fill you in on the rest. I did my duty." Miranda got out of the car, slammed the door, and rushed back to the house.

Liv watched in shock. She sat back and laid her head against the seat.

"I'm sorry this turned out to be such a crazy day. I'm sure you were hoping for a much more relaxed Christmas." Theo gave Eloise a quick hug.

Eloise stepped back and smiled politely. "We had a wonderful time. The food was delicious, the conversation was great, and best of all we got away from the bakery for a while." They shared a laugh. "Really, we appreciate you and Liv being so welcoming and look forward to repaying you."

Theo placed her hands on her stomach. "You repaid us plenty already with the desserts."

"Oh, please. You're our friends."

Theo's breath caught at the genuineness in Eloise's eyes. She looked at Jesse, who lingered by the fireplace, seemingly lost. Eloise looked, too, and the kindness that once shone in her eyes was replaced by a forlorn expression much too heavy for someone like Eloise. Theo opened her mouth to speak but caught herself. This was not her place, nor should she concern herself with any relationship other than her own at the moment.

"I hope to see you again soon, Eloise." Theo turned to Lena next. "I'm sure it'll be sooner than my thighs need, but your muffins call to me on my way to the office."

"I'll make sure Eloise has a blueberry, lightly toasted, ready for you Monday morning." Lena offered a polite hug before Eloise led her out the door.

Liv stepped around the outgoing guests awkwardly and mumbled a good-bye. Her eyes were sadder than Theo had ever seen them, but she also saw confusion. "Is everyone leaving?" Liv said, tucking her hands into her back pockets.

"Yeah. Todd and Terri are doing the final bathroom runs with the kids." Theo felt the weight of everything unspoken hanging between them, but the festivities had to be over before they could talk. "You may want to check on Jesse while I say good-bye." Theo wanted to give Liv an out. Facing a crowd after storming out would be less than fun.

Liv nodded. "Tell them I said bye."

"I will. Okay." Theo left Liv and went to find Todd. She didn't want to rush anyone, but desperate times and all. "Todd?"

Todd appeared in the hallway. "We're just about done. Terri's getting them bundled up. That's a beautiful wedding portrait in the bathroom. Interesting choice for placement."

"Liv put it there," Theo said with her hand to her forehead.

"I'm sorry for how today turned out for you."

"Nothing to apologize for."

Todd looked at her with concern. "What exactly did Mom do? You gotta tell me."

"And I will, just not tonight." She grabbed Todd's arm and gave it a squeeze. She was exhausted, and the hardest part of the evening was far from over. "But please let me know what version she tells you."

"You mean the story that'll be added to her saintly biography?"

Theo laughed and felt a little less tense. "I do know she means well."

"Well enough."

"Aunt T," Sam shouted, running down the hallway in a puffy coat and hat. He latched on to Theo's legs. "Can I come over again soon?"

"Of course you can, sweet pea. Anytime." She hugged him back the best she could, given the position. "And who knows, maybe you'll have a little cousin to play with soon." Theo couldn't believe she let herself say it out loud.

"Really?" Terri said, approaching them. "I'm so happy for you two." Theo put a finger to her lips, and Terri mouthed an apology.

Todd grinned. "Does this mean Liv really is ready?"

"It means I'm ready to trust the universe."

Terri chuckled. "You sound more and more like Liv every day."

She considered that for a moment. Liv was wise and calm, calculated yet free-spirited compared to many. Liv had an outlook unlike anyone Theo had ever met, and a hunger for life she hoped to one day achieve. While Liv might not be perfect, she was perfect for Theo. "I don't think that's the worst thing."

"Not at all." Todd planted a kiss on Theo's temple, an uncharacteristic move, but after the Christmas she'd had, the affection went a long way.

"Let me know you got home safe."

"Will do. Please tell Liv we said good night, and we missed the poem this year." He looked around. "Where's Julia?" Todd said, looking around. They looked down, and there Julia was, with her dress pulled up over her face. "I hope you have a girl, so we can commiserate."

Theo pushed Todd down the hall playfully and wished the rest of the family good night. The only person left in the living room was Tammy, who was always the last person standing. She looked around for Liv, not surprised in the slightest to hear her milling about in the kitchen. Liv was always quick to clean up after company left, especially if it meant avoiding Tammy.

Tammy took a deep breath and put her hands on her hips. "Another successful Christmas for the books."

Theo wondered if they'd been at the same Christmas. "Uh, something like that, I guess."

"That spinach dip was fucking phenomenal as usual. The lasagna, too."

Kiddie gloves are officially off. "Thank you."

"Do you have any meatballs left? Lee won't leave Vermont until tomorrow afternoon. I plan on sleeping forever, rolling out of bed whenever I feel like it, and stuffing my face with meat. And then stuffing my face with more meat when he gets home, if you know what I'm saying."

Theo would continue to invite Tammy to holidays for this very reason. Tammy might be brash, colorful, and a bit inappropriate, but she was authentically herself. And that brought a smile to her face.

"I'm sure I have something I can send you home with." She turned to the kitchen, but Tammy stopped her.

"I hope you know I'm always here if you want to talk."

"I know."

Tammy pulled Theo into a bone-crushing hug and said into her ear, "I'll take as much meat as you're willing to give."

"Okay." Theo pulled back and walked to the kitchen, stretching the aches from her muscles along the way. Much to her chagrin, Liv wasn't in the kitchen.

Theo packed up an ungodly amount of leftovers for Tammy and sent her on her way. She locked the front door and paused to take in the peaceful silence of the house. She just wished her feelings inside matched.

Chapter Twenty-one

Hey," Theo said with her most gentle voice the moment Liv entered the room. "How was your shower?"

Liv pulled at the sash of her terry cloth robe. "Good. Nice. I'm sorry I disappeared like that. I tried to clean up as much as I could."

"I finished everything in a breeze thanks to the head start you gave me."

Liv stepped farther into the room but wouldn't join Theo on the couch. Theo thought it was like getting a kitten to trust you before petting it. "I just needed a minute, and I had a raging headache."

"I understand. I really do. And I would've waited here all night for you to be ready to come down and talk." Theo placed her hand on the cushion beside her in invitation. "There's a gift under the tree with your name on it."

Liv smirked and looked at Theo, the Christmas lights twinkling in her eyes. "There's actually three."

"Someone's been poking around."

"I like presents," Liv said with a small shrug.

Theo held out her hand. "Come here and sit with me." Liv took her hand instantly and sat with no space between them. A good sign. "I'm jealous you're so cozy."

"Go get changed."

"No," Theo said, grasping Liv's hand in both her own. "I want to talk first, then presents." Theo noticed the challenge in Liv's eyes, but thankfully Liv kept quiet. "I'm sorry."

Liv hitched her eyebrow. "For what?"

"The entire day. You were right—I should always put us and your feelings first. Always. And by not doing so, I'm disrespecting you. I never, ever want to do that."

Liv's face grew painfully serious as she listened. Her pause made Theo worry she'd never be forgiven. "I appreciate that. I know your mother is tough—"

"More of a pain, but go on."

"*But* that shouldn't mean she'll always win. We wake up together and tackle the day, you and I. Nobody else should be making our rules."

"I agree, and I will do better from here on out. It may take me a little time, but I can promise nothing like today will ever happen again."

"Promise?"

"Promise."

"Okay, with that said, please tell me what the hell happened today?" Liv said with an airy chuckle.

Theo still couldn't wrap her head around the day's events and decided a summary would be better than any long-winded explanation. "Long story short, because I'd like to get to presents *before* next Christmas, my mother likes to use Rich as a device to strengthen our marriage."

Liv's face twisted, and she looked at the ceiling. "Huh. That's almost exactly how she explained it before telling me she was going to freeze to death and running away."

"Apparently, she has a sort of radar and can detect when you and I are going through a rough patch. Somehow, someway, it makes total sense to her that jealousy will fix whatever problem we may be dealing with."

"If only she knew what we were actually going through and how terrible her timing was."

Theo nodded. "She believes it's a reality check for you and makes you realize how lucky you are, and poof, all problems solved."

"That's pretty twisted." Liv still looked like she was trying to figure it all out. "But kind of sweet, too."

"I know, right?" Theo laughed, sharing in the disbelief of it all.

"Her plan backfired today," Liv said. She reached up and traced Theo's jaw. "I don't need Rich to realize how lucky I am—I know it. Every single day I'm aware of my luck and feel incredibly grateful to be loved by you."

Theo held Liv's hand against her cheek and soaked up the warmth from her palm. "I feel the same way," she said, kissing Liv's hand. "And I'd like you to know I basically told my mother to send Rich back to where he came from. For good."

The corner of Liv's mouth twitched. "Thank you."

"My pleasure."

"You won't miss his attention?"

"Oh God, no." Theo wiggled her eyebrows. "But you'll have to give me more attention to make up for the loss."

Liv stood abruptly and grabbed a box from beneath the tree. She sat back next to Theo and said, "I'm not sure if I'll be able to do that. Open this."

Theo took the box hesitantly. "I don't understand."

"Open it." Liv shifted anxiously, which made Theo nervous.

She ran her fingertip beneath the folded edge of the red and green paper, opening the package delicately. The box beneath was plain and gave no hint as to what was inside. Every side was taped down. She rolled her eyes. "Easier said than done." She pulled the box apart, and cottony green material peeked out. A shirt? Theo pulled at the material, and three silver snaps caught her eye, causing her to move faster and pull the gift out completely. It was a baby's mint-green onesie with a simple print on the front.

Namaste up all night and cry.

"When I tried to think of the perfect Christmas gift for you, I couldn't come up with one piece of jewelry or concert or sentimental tchotchke, but there was one article of clothing I knew would be right."

Theo stared at the tiny outfit in awe, even when her vision blurred with happy tears. "It's perfect."

"I'm ready, and I'm scared," Liv said, laughing, "but I am definitely ready for the next chapter of our life. I want to raise a family with you. I want a mini-me and a mini-you, but not a mini-Todd."

Theo laughed so hard it echoed through the house. "I love you."

"Yeah?"

Theo nodded. "With everything I am."

"Does that mean you believe me?"

Theo dried her eyes before answering. She couldn't even remember why she was hesitant to believe Liv in the first place. "I do believe you."

Liv's eyes lit up. "So we're going to start a family?"

Theo's cheeks hurt from grinning so widely. "We're going to start a family."

"We should call first thing Monday morning."

Theo pursed her lips. "Or wait until March."

"What? Why?"

Theo walked over to the tree and came back with a small wrapped package. Instead of taking the spot next to Liv, she straddled Liv's lap. "Open this one first."

Liv did as she was told the best she could, considering the scant space between them. Slowly, she drew out a brochure. Her eyes went wide. "Aruba?"

"Two weeks all inclusive, just you and me. The last week of January into February." She kissed the side of Liv's neck and trailed her lips along the soft skin. "The hot sun, sand, and a king-size bed."

"How did you pull this off without me knowing?"

"One thing I've learned about you over the years is you become a little..." Theo paused to find the right, softer word. "Oblivious to a lot around you when things aren't good between us."

"That's not true." Liv shook her head.

"It's endearing because I know your sole focus is our marriage. Plus," Theo said and grabbed the brochure, "this kind of proves my point." Theo yelped and found herself on her back in an instant.

Liv lay atop her. "Be nice to me. It's Christmas and your mom attacked me."

Theo laughed heartily at the crazy truth behind Liv's exaggeration and goofy pout. "I am nice to you. I just gave you a trip to Aruba."

"You sort of gifted it to yourself, too."

"That's the point," she said, kissing Liv quickly. "I wanted us to get away and reconnect. We weren't at our best, and I knew this would help. We can turn off our phones and just disappear for two whole weeks." She kissed Liv again but much slower this time. Liv's breathing had changed by the time she was done with her. "But now, instead of a trip to help our marriage, it'll be our final hurrah before starting the journey to becoming parents." Theo's heart skipped a beat at the thought.

"Gulp," Liv said.

Theo gave her arm a swat. "Hey that's not—" Liv cut her off with a long, deep kiss. She was positive her toes couldn't curl any more. Theo ran her hands inside Liv's robe and scratched Liv's side.

"Wait."

"No."

Liv smiled against Theo's lips. "You opened a onesie, and I got a trip to Aruba."

Theo looked up into Liv's shining eyes and felt more love in that moment than she had in her entire life. "You gave me everything I could ever want." They breathed long, slow breaths accompanied by soft smiles. After soaking up the moment, Liv broke the silence.

"So I should return the earrings I have hidden in the tree?"

Theo gawked. "There's earrings in the tree?" She tried her best to wiggle out from beneath Liv, but Liv wouldn't budge.

"They'll still be there in the morning. I'm ready for bed."

"I guess I shouldn't put on new jewelry just to sleep in."

"Oh, we're not sleeping."

"No?"

"Nope," Liv said right against her lips. "Your mother made today very stressful, and I think you should make it up to me."

"Is that so?" Theo grabbed Liv's ass. "And how do you propose I do that?"

"You get naked, and then we get in bed and have a holly jolly Christmas," Liv said with a shimmy of her shoulders.

Theo felt Liv's backside, up to her breasts, and then held Liv's face in her hands. "I love you, Liv, even if our days have been rough, and this Christmas was absurd."

"Every Christmas with you is the best, even the ones where your mother purposely makes me uncomfortable and jealous."

"You're never gonna let me live it down, are you?"

"No. Maybe. Probably. We'll see." Liv pecked at Theo's lips. "Let's go." Liv stood and pulled Theo up with her.

They made quick work of the lights in the house and walked hand in hand to the stairs. Theo stood at the threshold of their bedroom and gave herself a few seconds to simply absorb the moment, the night, and the life she was grateful to be living. Liv's voice was loud in her head when she thought, *Merry Christmas to all, and to all a good night.*

New Year's Eve: April and Gemma

CHAPTER TWENTY-TWO

W hy wouldn't you go to the liquor store *before* the second most drunken holiday of the year?" April adjusted her grip on the case of Blue Moon she had been holding for way, way too long. "Why would I let you convince me to tag along?"

"Because I promised you I'd let you pick out anything you wanted for being so good," Jesse said mockingly.

April shot Jesse the best lethal glare she could muster. "Why am I even friends with you?" Her harsh tone lacked authority, and her smile gave her away. She had met Jesse at the start of the school year, her first year as a counselor with the high school. They had hit it off immediately when they met up to work on ideas for the LGBTQI Youth Group.

"Because like all wild children, you needed a good mentor in your life." Jesse started placing her items on the counter. She took the beer from April.

April squeezed her numb fingertips. "You know, just for that I'm adding a few things." She waited for the cashier to look at her. "Can we also get that bottle of Fireball and the Southern Comfort above it," she said, pointing to the wall of bottles behind the older gentleman.

Jesse huffed. "It's like I'm in college all over again with you."

"You can actually remember college?"

"I need to see some ID," the cashier said. April looked at his name tag. *Charles.* "For both of you." Jesse laughed as she pulled out her wallet.

April was a bit less amused. "I'm twenty-six."

"And I'm twenty-nine if I want to be," Charles said with no change to his expression. "ID please."

April dug into her pocket and pulled out her phone. She slid her driver's license from the attached wallet and held it up for Charles to read. He looked back and forth between their identifications. With no follow-up, he turned and grabbed the two bottles.

"You look quite pleased with yourself," April said, shaking her head at Jesse's grin.

"I haven't been carded in years."

"It must be too dark in here to see all your gray." She watched Jesse's smile become even more gleeful as Charles scanned each bottle. "Weirdo."

"Maybe if you stopped wearing these," Jesse said, flicking the brim of her backward cap, "people would think you're an adult."

"And maybe if you stopped dressing like this," April said, tugging at the collar of Jesse's oxford shirt beneath her sweater, "you'd get laid more." Jesse pushed her hand away, adjusted her wool peacoat, and shot Charles an uncomfortable look. April started laughing. "You know I'm right."

Jesse wouldn't look at her as she paid and gathered the full bags.

Jesse spoke again once they were out in the brisk cold. "Those hats get you laid?"

"Bro, you wouldn't believe it. And the number of students who crush on me? Insane." April knew she sounded cocky, but facts were facts.

"Huh."

She waited for Jesse to open the back of her black Subaru Outback and started to load up the bags. "What's the huh for?"

"Nothing."

"Yeah, right." She closed the trunk. "You have the ten-minute drive to talk."

They got in the car and Jesse started the engine. "I just can't imagine being comfortable knowing any student has a crush on me."

"Students do have crushes on you, even with that wardrobe."

"Leave my clothes out of this."

April raised her hands in a peacekeeping gesture. "Sorry. But we work with a bunch of hormonal teenagers. They have crushes. You are one."

"It's gross."

She didn't recognize Jesse's tone. Something was off. "*Okaaay*," she said.

Jesse adjusted her grip on the steering wheel. "Do you think you could ever be friends with a past student?"

"Oh yeah. For sure. After they graduate, they become regular people."

Jesse nodded, nearly moving in tune to the music on the radio. "True, true. Good point."

She studied Jesse's tense profile. "Why do you ask?"

"No reason, really," Jesse said, shifting in her seat. "I was having a conversation about social media with Theo the other day. A lot of students reach out, and I don't really know where to draw the line."

"Easy. Pre- and post-graduation, like I just said. If you felt like there was a connection with a student who could be a genuine friend, go for it."

"But I'm old."

"Only as old as you act." She waited for Jesse to look at her before smirking. "Which is geriatric."

"Now I'm wondering why I'm friends with you."

"Because I keep you young." April unbuckled her seat belt as they pulled into Jesse's driveway. "Who all's coming tonight?"

"Some of my friends you haven't met yet, Billie and her girlfriend Leah, and a good number of teachers." Jesse got out of the car and April followed. "Oh, and the girl I want to introduce you to."

April rolled her eyes. She did not need anyone's help hooking up. "And who do *you* have your eye on?"

"What do you mean?"

April took the lightest bag from the back and left the rest for Jesse to carry. "Throwing a New Year's Eve party usually means you're going to invite the person you want to kiss at midnight."

Jesse locked her car, the beep sounding loud in her quiet neighborhood. "I throw a party every year, and I don't create the guest list like that."

"Why not? You're literally in charge of your New Year's destiny." April hopped and shivered, waiting for Jesse to open her door. "You didn't invite anyone to hook up with?" April sighed at Jesse's silence. "Have I taught you nothing?"

Jesse walked into her house and started flipping on the lights, paying zero attention to April. "Bring all the booze into the kitchen."

April knew the conversation was over, but that didn't mean she wouldn't be scoping out the attendees for Jesse's potential smooch as they arrived. For the first time that night, she was grateful Jesse asked her to stop by early to help. "What else needs to be done? Don't tell me I have to prep food." She looked around the large open kitchen. April loved Jesse's house for its simplicity and openness. The kitchen was part of the great room, with a small den set toward the back of the house, and three large, comfortable bedrooms.

"No," Jesse said, placing bottles of champagne in the fridge. "Everything is all ready." She turned and pointed to a stack of plastic bowls on the kitchen counter, and an assortment of bags lined up next to it. "Just fill those bowls with those snacks."

"Did you get any kettle cooked—"

"And *don't* eat them as you go." Jesse walked out of the kitchen.

"Okay, Mom."

"I heard that."

April stuck out her tongue and got to work. She wasn't much of a pretzel fan, but the chips and Cheez Doodles passed inspection, and all bowls were full by the time Jesse reentered the kitchen. She clapped and said, "Done."

Jesse checked her phone. "Perfect. Everyone should start getting here in fifteen minutes." Jesse looked nervous, almost jumpy.

"Can I ask you a question?" April said.

"Yeah. Of course." Jesse tugged at the collar of her shirt.

"Why did you ask me to come by early to help? You have a bunch of friends, and I know for a fact you're much closer to a few of them." April noticed Jesse's look of panic. "I'm not upset or anything. I'm happy you asked me, and I'm happy to help. I just thought it was odd."

Jesse's shoulders relaxed. "Honestly? I've had a hell of a few weeks and just wanted to have fun tonight without being asked a million questions."

April absolutely wanted to ask a million questions now, but she'd get the info out of Jesse another time. "You think I'm fun?"

"I think you're the only friend I have who's too self-absorbed to worry about me."

"Ouch." April wasn't hurt. She knew the way Jesse deflected and chose to defend herself. "Anyway," she said, scratching her chin, "who am I going to kiss at midnight?"

"No one." Jesse shifted a stack of plastic cups to the side and leaned on the counter. She pointed at stiff finger at April. "I'm introducing you to someone tonight, and I don't want you messing it up right out of the gate."

She squinted at Jesse. "Why would you try to set me up on New Year's Eve? It's a terrible plan. I'm going to drink too much, forget her name, and not pay any attention to her," she said, ticking off each point on her fingers. "And I'll probably kiss someone else right in front of her."

Jesse held up her hands and approached April. "Hear me out." Jesse placed her hands on April's shoulders. "You could not do any of those things, and just trust me that this woman is good for you."

April took it personally, like a slap to her ego. "Now hear *me* out," she said, covering Jesse's hands with hers. "I don't need help meeting women." She patted Jesse's hands and walked away.

"Never said you did."

"Good. I'm glad that's settled. Now tell this chick I couldn't make it, or I'm already dating someone, or something. I really don't need a clinger tonight."

"This *chick's* name is—" Jesse stopped at the sound of the doorbell. "Look at that, your complaining took up all our quality time. Darn." Jesse rushed off toward the door.

"Oh yeah, real grade A stuff." April grabbed another handful of Cheez Doodles and went in search of her Fireball.

Chapter Twenty-three

Jesse hugged Billie tightly and wouldn't let go until Billie started to complain. "I'm just so happy to see you," she said, turning to Leah. "Both of you. How have you been since our most wonderful Thanksgiving together?"

Billie perked up right away. "Great, actually. We had Christmas with Leah's family, and they were normal in comparison, so at least I know half of my holidays will be pleasant."

"You say normal." Leah wrapped her arm around Billie's waist. "I still think my vegan sister with pigeons for pets is a bit much."

Jesse shrugged. "Sounds like a walk in the park to me." They laughed.

"How was Christmas with Liv and Theo? Same amazing spread as usual?" Billie talked as she took Leah's jacket, and they made their way deeper into the house. "I'm still not over Theo's baked eggplant from last year."

Jesse wanted to tell Billie how her Christmas really went, with surprise guests and more drama than a Bravo series. Instead, she placed her hand over her stomach. "So much food, and just like every other year, I'm disappointed I didn't eat enough." Jesse smiled at the way Leah held Billie's arm and tugged slightly to get her attention. She missed simple intimate touches like that.

"I know you've told me about Liv and Theo, but I forget. Are they family?"

"Might as well be," Billie said.

Jesse agreed. "I've known Liv..." She blew out a breath, causing her lips to flap. "A really freaking long time," she said with a laugh.

"We've always been close, and we formed this little unit when Theo came along. I've gone to their house almost every year for Christmas."

Leah's grin was blindingly genuine. "I love groups like that."

"Good," Jesse said, reaching out to touch Leah's arm. "Because you're part of one now." She winked at Billie and excused herself. More guests were arriving, and she hadn't even put on music yet.

She felt jumpy, like something was crawling beneath her skin and itching to be released. Jesse hadn't told anyone, mostly because she couldn't believe it herself. Ten minutes alone with Eloise after Christmas dinner changed the course of Jesse's plans for good.

Jesse stared at the fire, counting the seconds until Lena returned from the bathroom. If she left her spot next to the couch, it would look like she was running from something she shouldn't be scared of, but she was terrified. Out of the corner of her eye, she could see Eloise playing with the rim of her wineglass, delicate fingers against delicate glass. Jesse took a deep breath and hoped Liv would come back inside or someone else would cause a scene.

"I'm sorry."

Jesse heard the two simple words, even as they were spoken no louder than the crackle of flames. She lowered her head and contemplated her next move. Ignore or engage? Walk away or tempt fate?

"You have nothing to be sorry for," she said, finishing her drink in one long swallow. An empty glass was the perfect excuse to escape. As she started to walk away, she heard Eloise speak again.

"Jesse, please..."

She froze. Hearing Eloise utter her name cut like a knife. As if the deep, unsealing wound from months ago wasn't enough. "What?" Jesse couldn't look at Eloise, but she wouldn't be rude and walk away, either.

"I should've warned you I'd be here."

Jesse wanted to agree, but her main goal was to get through this interaction as quickly as possible. "It's fine."

"My mom was invited, and she wouldn't come without me. You know how she can be. I knew it would be better for her to be off her knee and socialize a bit. Liv and Theo are such wonderful people."

"They are. I'm going to get another drink. Do—"

"Why won't you talk to me?"

"I am talking to you."

"Why won't you look at me?"

Jesse sucked in a breath. What answer could she give that wouldn't sound childish? She turned slowly, her anxiety surging with every move. Jesse finally looked at Eloise. She had seen her face so many times, in so many different states, and it still affected her deeply. Jesse felt dizzy. "It's better not to," she said.

Eloise adjusted her sweater. One shoulder was left bare by the slouchy style. Jesse chose to focus on the small exposed patch, but she remembered sinking her teeth into the tattooed skin. She swallowed hard and pointed to Eloise's empty glass. "Do you want a refill?"

"I want you to talk to me like you used to," Eloise said, her voice so earnest it cracked.

Jesse's heartbreak surfaced and continued to splinter into more pieces. "You know I can't, and I wouldn't even know how to anyway." Jesse resisted the urge to step back when Eloise started to come closer.

Eloise looked up at her with her innocent hazel eyes. "You could start with Merry Christmas."

Jesse let herself smile slightly and relaxed her back. She'd always considered Eloise's eyes a tranquilizer, and a drug on the more dangerous days. "Merry Christmas, Eloise."

"Merry Christmas, Jesse. How have your holidays been?"

Sad. Lonely. Empty. "They've been good. Yours?" Jesse really wished she had gotten that refill. Her mouth grew drier with each word in this oddly mundane conversation with the secret ex-love of her life.

"Busy with the bakery and everything." Eloise slid aside to make way for Julia and Sam, who were chasing each other. "Oh, to have that energy again."

Jesse chortled. "I don't think I ever did."

"What are your plans for New Year's?"

"My party," Jesse said, bending forward to avoid Sam's sugar-covered hands as he ran by again.

"You're throwing a party?"

"I do every year."

"Okay, that's enough," Todd said loudly, his dad voice sounding authoritative and practiced. "Come here." He caught Sam midstampede and lifted him from the ground. Todd should've told Sam to lower his *arms because as he went up into the air his hand smacked the side of Jesse's head.*

"Ow." Sugar and crumbs stuck to her face and her hair and were scattered on her shoulders. "That's some right hook you got there, Sam." Jesse wiped her face and tried to identify what exactly was smeared on her. Jam? What had jam in it?

Todd looked back, cringing. "I'm sorry."

"It's okay." She waved him off. "It's just really sticky," she said under her breath.

Eloise covered her mouth but didn't bother to stifle her laughter. "I'm sorry."

"No, you're not." Jesse picked a crumb from her eyebrow. "I don't even know what this is."

"Come here," Eloise said, stepping into Jesse's space and running her hand over the side of her head.

Jesse stopped breathing and stood still. She watched as Eloise concentrated on removing the mess from her short hair. Jesse's hair was always haphazardly styled, being too thick and full of cowlicks to really hold a set style. She kept it buzzed on the sides and very short on top, apparently the perfect texture for food debris to get lost in.

Eloise gripped Jesse's jaw and encouraged her to tilt her head. "Wow. He even managed to get some in your ear. There you go." With a few more strokes and a pat on the shoulder, Eloise stepped back.

"Thanks."

"No problem."

Lost in the closeness or maybe the magic of Christmas, Jesse spoke without thinking. "You should stop by."

Eloise was shocked. "When?"

Jesse realized how her vague invitation sounded and stuttered. "New Year's. You should stop by my party. On New Year's Eve."

Eloise's smile shone in her eyes. "I'd like that."

Jesse flinched when cold fingertips probed her neck. "What the hell?"

"Sorry," April said, holding up her hands. "I was just checking you had a pulse. You were seriously spaced out there."

"Oh. Yeah." Jesse cleared her throat. "I was just going over the checklist in my head and making sure I didn't forget anything." Jesse hated lying because she knew she was terrible at it. She scratched the back of her neck. "Can't have a party without having everything you need, you know."

"Yeah..." April looked at her like she had not only sprouted a second head, but that head was ugly. "I don't know what's going on with you, bro, but this is going to be a great night for the both of us." April took off her cap to fix her long, pin-straight hair. She had great hair but covered it up with that backward cap. April tilted her head as a knock sounded at the door. "I'll get that."

Jesse remembered asking for April's help setting up, not hosting, but she let April do whatever she wanted if it meant avoiding the third degree. She went to the fridge and grabbed a beer, hoping to warm up before Eloise arrived. But maybe Eloise wouldn't show up. Why would she? Christmas dinner had been painfully awkward and bogged down with passive-aggressive conversation. Why would anyone willingly put themselves in the same situation again?

She walked out of the kitchen into the living room, where the party had started to come together. A few coworkers from school were milling about and catching up with each other. Christmas break always felt like a blink and an eternity for teachers. No one ever rushed to get back to school, but Jesse missed her friends and the routine of it all. She noticed Lori near the corner of the room all by herself.

She walked up to Lori and smirked. "I almost didn't recognize you in real clothes."

Lori raised her hand and shook her head. "I don't want to hear it. You academics pick on us gym teachers when you're all actually jealous that we get to dress in lounge clothes every day."

Jesse laughed. "How are you? Can I get you a drink?"

"Actually," Lori said, looking over Jesse's shoulder, "Hannah is getting me a drink."

Jesse looked back and forth so fast her neck hurt. "Hannah? You brought her?" Lori nodded with a telltale bright grin. "So you guys are, like, *official* official?"

"Mm-hmm. I almost didn't because I don't want to be looked at as the stereotypical lesbian gym teacher, but then I realized fuck anyone who looks twice."

"Cheers to that," Jesse said with feigned confidence. She wished she could hold as much conviction when it came to not caring what anyone else thought. Jesse noticed Lori's smile became softer. Jesse recognized that smile as the one only lovers share.

Hannah stepped in to form a small circle with Lori and Jesse. "Here you go, babe," Hannah said, handing Lori her drink. Their fingers touched and lingered. Jesse practically saw the sparks.

"Hannah, this is Jesse, the chemistry teacher I told you about and the reason why we have such a great LGBTQI group for our students."

Hannah extended her hand and said, "Our host."

Jesse shook Hannah's hand and nodded. "I'm so happy the two of you could make it."

"Jesse is actually fighting with the board to allow our health curriculum to include same-sex education."

"It was just a few phone calls." Jesse's face started to warm, and she ducked away from the praise. "Such a big change is far beyond my solo capabilities."

"A few phone calls and two meetings," Lori said, shoving Jesse's shoulder. "Don't downplay what you've put in motion."

Jesse crossed her fingers. "Hopefully, we'll make it happen."

"I used to work for Planned Parenthood," Hannah said. "I still have a few connections if you need resources or just a group of people to back you in any way."

"That's great," Jesse said. "I'll probably cash in on that offer sooner than you'd think."

"Teresa's here." Lori kissed Hannah's cheek. "I'm going to get her to come over here. Be right back."

Jesse was more than happy to focus her attention on somebody new because it meant she didn't have to focus on anyone from her past at all. "What do you do now, Hannah?"

Hannah took a long swig from her beer. "Social work. You know, I used to think she had a crush on you."

Jesse was so surprised by this sudden turn that she knew her eyes couldn't possibly open wider. "Me? No way." She shook her head vigorously, happily risking a brain injury to avoid this conversation. "We've always been friends."

Hannah tilted her head. "She talks nonstop about you and all the amazing things you do for the students and the school."

"I just want what's best for the community."

"I believe that one hundred percent, but you also charm the pants right off women while you do it."

Jesse's mental strength drained away. "Hannah, I swear, there never was or will be something between me and Lori. We're solid friends."

Hannah took another drink. "I believe that now after meeting you. You're not her type."

Jesse shook off the irrational indignation and looked Hannah over. Her femininity was fiercely on display, the perfect complement to Lori's tomboy appearance. "No, I'm not," Jesse said and checked to see if Lori was coming back anytime soon.

"I also think she looks up to you, like a mentor or trailblazer in the high school. Having someone older than you taking risks and being yourself means a lot for our generation. Oh," she said, raising her hand, "Lori's waving me over. We'll talk later."

Jesse couldn't comprehend how an introduction to her friend's girlfriend made her feel equal parts scolded and incredibly old, but she needed another drink.

Chapter Twenty-four

April didn't normally like hummus, but the simple dip always looked so alluring when it was part of a large spread. She dipped a baby carrot, another food she never wanted unless offered at a party, into the dollop of hummus on her plate. She crunched and chewed, studying the carrot between her fingers before each bite. None of it made sense, but she was ready to devour at least fifteen more.

"Excuse me."

She followed the voice to her right and was pleased to see a cute woman looking at her expectantly. "Yes?" April tried to smile charmingly, but knew the hummus on her fingertips probably worked against her.

The woman raised her eyebrows and giggled. She had red hair, definitely from a bottle but with the kind of dimension that told April a professional applied it regularly. "I was hoping you'd share the vegetables with me."

"Oh my God. Yes," April said with an embarrassed laugh. She picked up her beer and a few napkins from the buffet table and moved aside. "I'm sorry. I didn't realize I was monopolizing the crudités." Internally, April gave herself a high five for remembering the classy term.

"It's okay. I actually felt bad interrupting you. You seem really into those carrots."

April smirked. "It's funny you should say that—I was thinking about how I rarely eat carrots or celery or hummus. Anything super healthy actually, unless it's like this."

"Free?"

April gasped. Who was this woman, and who did she think she was to poke fun at someone she just met? Whoever this person was, she might be her midnight date. "Only a holier-than-thou vegetarian would speak to someone like that."

"Vegan, actually."

She choked. "Ugh. The worst." April moved back farther. "Let me really get out of the way, then. I'd hate to come between a vegan and her vegetation. I'll go find some real food," she said, pointing her thumb over her shoulder.

The other woman studied April for a silent minute. "I'm Gemma."

"April," she said, extending her left hand. "There's no hummus on this hand. Promise."

Gemma laughed. "Nice to meet you, April."

"Gemma," April said, noting the way the syllables fell from her tongue. "That's a great name. You don't hear it often." April tried her best to be casual as she checked Gemma out. Gemma wore colorful patterns unabashedly. Her skirt was floor length with a large paisley print swirling all around, the colors of an autumn sunset. She paired it with a teal tank and a thick, chunky knit cardigan over it. Everything about Gemma caught April's attention. "The name fits you."

"Oh yeah?" Gemma said with a tilt of her head. "Is that what you're going with?" Gemma started laughing harder.

April flinched at the retort. "Wow. You're spicier than the salsa. Is this how you always get to know new people? Do you even have any friends?" she said, trying to keep her tone light for fear of scaring Gemma away. She hadn't been this intrigued by anyone recently. Gemma grimaced and covered her eyes with her hands. April felt the loss immediately. She hadn't even figured out what color they were yet. Gray or blue, maybe?

"I'm sorry. Jeez, that's embarrassing. I'm just used to people running with my name and using it as a pickup line."

April couldn't help but tease Gemma further. "Must be tough to deal with."

"Yeah."

"Getting hit on so much, I mean. Poor you." April grinned.

"Who's spicy now?"

April pointed at herself. "Me? No way. You're salsa—I'm hummus."

"This is, by far, the strangest meeting I've ever had at a party before."

"Me, too." April popped the last bite of carrot into her mouth and chewed slowly. Silence stretched on. April thought of a dozen more insults and quips but didn't want to press her luck. She bobbed her head from side to side briefly. "Well, Salsa, I'll let you get to your limited meal of grains and greens. Maybe I'll stand in your way again sometime."

"Maybe, Hummus. Maybe." Gemma looked up through her long lashes. Her eyes were definitely gray, and her eyelids looked just heavy enough to tell April the interest wasn't one-sided.

"Okay. Yeah." Her exit was far from smooth as she grabbed a piece of pepperoni bread and three slices of pepper jack cheese along the way. April shoved the cheese into her mouth and walked directly into the living room in search of Jesse, who was MIA. Fortunately, Billie was there. April marched right over and tried to speak through her mouthful of food.

Billie cringed. "Please swallow before I throw up."

April forced down the cheese as quickly as possible, needing help from a large swig of her beer. "Dude, I just met the hottest chick, and it was so weird. I think she's into me." She sipped her beer again and nodded to Leah. "Hey."

Billie stared at her, expressionless. "I'm not even sure which part of that sentence needs attention first."

"The hot part. For sure. She's got red hair, which I know you can appreciate," she said with a wink and nudge to Billie's elbow.

"That's true." Billie cast a sideways glance at Leah, who giggled. "But what was weird about it?"

"We kept zinging each other. From the moment we started talking, we ripped on one another. But it was nice. I think. Isn't that weird?"

Leah nodded while Billie appeared thoughtful. "I think it's weird," Leah said. "Babe," Leah said, placing her hand on Billie's stomach, "if you'd been anything but kind to me when we first met, I probably wouldn't have talked to you again."

April ate the pepperoni bread as she watched the exchange. "Ouch."

"But I *was* kind," Billie said, shooting April a stern look. "Because ultimately, that's what people are looking for."

"I don't know, dude. She seemed into it." April wasn't dumb when it came to women. She listened to spoken and silent cues. She knew flirting, and she knew what body language was doing the talking. April also knew attraction. "For real."

"So what happened? You guys made fun of each other and then you came running to us to show off how much cheese you can eat?"

April nearly stomped her foot as she shot Billie an incredulous look. "No."

Leah shifted her gaze between the two of them. "You two are worse than siblings. April, what makes you think she was into you? Seriously."

April smiled a cheesy grin. "She took as easily as she dished, which *clearly* means the initial lack of kindness didn't bother her. Also, she assumed I was hitting on her, and even though she laughed at my line, she didn't give me any hint she wanted me to stop. She's into it."

"One last question." Leah tapped her nail on the side of her glass. "Why are you here? If you two hit it off, and you're certain she's into you, why are you telling us about it instead of getting to know her better?"

"Yeah," Billie said.

"I…" *Fuck me.* "I don't know. It just felt like I needed to play it cool." Both Billie and Leah were shaking their heads now, and April hung hers. "Play hard to get or whatever you call it."

"Do you date often?" Leah said.

"Yeah, I hook up."

Billie looked pained. "Dating and hooking up are not the same."

Leah looped her hand into Billie's arm. "If you really believe she was into you, you should probably go find her," Leah said. "Because running off with a handful of cheese may make her think you're not interested."

"You know what? I think you're right. You guys enjoy the party." April rushed off in search of Gemma.

❖

Billie watched April make her way around the clusters of people throughout Jesse's home. "Oh, to be young again."

"First, you're sounding more like Jesse every day, and I don't mean that in a good way, grandma. Second, how old is April?"

"Twenty-seven going on fourteen, I think. The hat makes her look eleven, though."

"I think the hat works for her. She has that tomboy skater appeal."

Billie tilted her head slowly and looked at Leah with a raised eyebrow. "Appeal? Did you just say April is appealing?"

"You know I didn't." Leah grabbed Billie's long silver chain and the pendant of a bird she had gifted Billie for Christmas, a nod to her favorite Emily Dickinson poem. "But your jealousy is very cute."

"I'm not jealous." Billie was absolutely jealous but couldn't bring herself to admit it outright. "It was just an interesting choice of words."

"April has a certain kind of appeal, while you appeal to *me*. There's a big difference."

Billie already started melting, but she needed to hear more. "And how exactly do I appeal to you?"

"Well…" Leah followed the silver chain up to the bare skin at the base of Billie's throat. "Right here, right now, I'm really loving the way you look." Billie looked down at her simple outfit of a black Henley sweater and dark-washed jeans. "I love when I can see your skin. You're usually very buttoned-up. Unless you're naked, of course," Leah said, tracing her fingertip down Billie's sternum.

Billie shivered. "I'll buy one of these sweaters in every color," she said.

Leah laughed. "Your hair is much better, too," she said, scratching along Billie's hairline on the back of her neck, knowing better than to muss her carefully sculpted short hair.

"I love you," Billie said, resisting the urge to add *forever*.

"I love you, too." Leah leaned in to kiss Billie.

Billie happily accepted the sweet kiss and deepened it the moment Leah was ready to pull away.

"Save some of that for midnight," Leah teased.

Billie would save the best kiss and then some for midnight.

Chapter Twenty-five

Two hours until midnight. Jesse checked her phone for the tenth time since nine o'clock, unsure if she was rushing the night or counting the minutes until she could confidently believe Eloise wasn't going to show. Either way, Jesse finished her third drink of the night, barely feeling the relaxing buzz she needed. She smiled to a few people as she went back to the kitchen in search of the bottle of bourbon. Beer wasn't cutting it anymore.

After her refill, she walked toward the back of the house into her den where the music was coming from. Not many people stayed in the den, but Jesse was happy to find a small group dancing. Seeing her friends laugh and chat, dance, and just enjoy themselves as the year came to a close was the reason she did this. She tried to remind herself of that every time she regretted taking on party duties.

"Are you going to get in here?" Erica said, shimmying from side to side.

Jesse met Erica years ago through Liv and Theo. There had always been a simmering attraction between them, but timing was never on their side. Needing a distraction, Jesse walked up to Erica and started to move to the rhythm.

Jesse leaned in close to be heard clearly. "Have you seen Liv and Theo yet?"

Erica rolled her eyes. "They're here. Probably sitting someplace, being boring."

She laughed. "At least they show up."

"I know. I'm just jealous."

She studied Erica's face, whenever her wavy brown hair wasn't in the way. "Jealous of what?"

Erica's moves fell out of beat slightly. "It's just nice, having someone to grow boring with. Imagine liking someone so much you don't mind sitting and talking to them when you're out at a party."

An image of Eloise flashed in Jesse's head, sitting at a bar and giving her a reason to not care about anyone else in the room. "Sounds nice." Erica stepped in to Jesse and looked up at her. As if Erica's broad mouth and long lashes weren't enticing enough, their height difference drove Jesse's imagination into dangerous territory.

"You didn't have that with Stacy?"

Jesse thought of how Stacy always dictated which parties they were allowed to attend. "No," she said. "We were anything but calm and relaxed."

"Then why were the two of you together for so long?" Erica's tone, although muddled by the music, was unmistakably full of chagrin.

Because she wouldn't let me leave. Jesse took another long drink. "We fit together in a lot of other ways, and eventually our lives just melded together."

"You were another couple staying together out of convenience."

"I don't know if I'd put it that way." *Fear is more like it.*

"It's okay," Erica said, placing her hand on Jesse's forearm. "I think we all do that at some point. That's exactly what I did with Tee."

Jesse couldn't even stop herself from quirking an eyebrow at this new information. Erica and Tee were together for three years, and she thought they were happy. But then again, everyone thought she was happy with Stacy, too. "Oh?" She wanted to kick herself for not coming up with a more articulate response.

Erica nodded and licked her lips. "We were great together in a lot of ways, but the things we did lack were big." They were no longer dancing.

Jesse knew she should mind her own business and carefully chose her next words. She shouldn't ask Erica a question she wouldn't want to answer herself. "Like what?"

"We got together because we had a lot of mutual friends and plenty in common. But we never had *that*," she said, making a grabbing motion with her hands. "You know?"

Jesse tried to come up with a good guess, but charades were never her strong suit. "No," she said, laughing. "I have no idea."

"Passion," Erica said simply and sadly. "We were great for all the practical reasons, but we didn't have that burning desire necessary to want to be around the other person all the time."

Without warning, Eloise popped into Jesse's mind again. She thought about their endless days and simple pleasures like strolling the beach or shopping for dinner ingredients. They were together as the sun rose, and they fell asleep in each other's arms almost every night for months. The only time they'd go their separate ways was for work, which gave Jesse the perfect amount of time to socialize with those who didn't know about her relationship with Eloise. Which was everyone.

"Jesse?" Erica looked at her expectantly. "You okay?"

"Yeah. I, um..." She looked around the room. "Sorry. I keep spacing out tonight. Too many things on my mind, I guess."

"Like what?" Erica said, looking soft, caring, and enticing. The hairs on the back of Jesse's neck twitched, but not from Erica's intense eyes.

Jesse knew Eloise had arrived. She could tell by the way the energy in the house shifted, the same way clouds parted to let the sunshine through. She turned slowly, not quite ready to see her again but knowing one quick glance would give her a taste of what she had been longing for. Tonight was a spontaneous invitation driven by the need to share a space one more time. *Just one more time.*

"I keep feeling like I should check the snacks and drinks and see if anyone new arrived. All the important host duties," she said distractedly. She wanted to see where Eloise was, or if something in her had finally snapped and she was imagining the unshakable gut feeling.

"Or..." Erica started dancing again. "You could stay here with me and actually enjoy your own party."

Jesse should've been quick to agree. Erica was a good fit for her, and their relationship couldn't be much easier. But Jesse couldn't jump in. She saw a motion out of the corner of her eye.

Eloise stood shyly in the doorway, wearing her long burgundy coat. Eloise knew where she could hang her jacket, but she looked around instead of moving. Jesse held her breath until their eyes met, and in that second, she was transported back to the bar on that fateful night, when they were acquaintances suddenly colliding in an unexpected way.

Eloise's small wave made her smile. She waved back but didn't move. Jesse second-guessed what to do next because, much like that first night in the bar, she'd talk to Eloise and be drawn in by her sweetness and her laugh. Jesse knew one look at her smile would cause her to completely come undone. Erica's laugh brought her back to earth.

She looked at Erica quizzically. "What's so funny?" When she tried to find Eloise again, she was gone. Jesse frowned.

"Nothing. I just..." Erica pushed the hair from her face and shook her head. "Maybe one day the time will be right for us. Go check on your guest."

"I'll be back," she said, a blatant lie. She left the den and scanned the room. She might have spotted the back of Eloise turning the corner into the living room.

Jesse jumped and turned to find Billie looking at her with wide, worried eyes. "Hey."

"I came to tell you Eloise is here, but it looks like you already noticed that."

"Yes, Billie, I noticed." She lowered her head before saying more to Billie. "It's fine. I invited her, which means I'm just going to have to handle it."

"You could talk to her."

"No," she said. Billie had just saved her from making that mistake. She could avoid Eloise for the next hour and forty minutes. Easy.

"It's not a bad idea."

"It is a bad idea. A terrible idea, actually."

"Why invite her, then?" Billie looked truly perplexed. "To stare at her?"

"Shut up." Jesse nudged Billie's shoulder. She wanted Billie to stop asking questions she didn't want to answer, but she also wanted Billie to tell her what to do. She took a long swallow of her bourbon, the burn offering a momentary distraction. "I don't know why I invited her. We were talking at Liv's, and it just slipped out."

"You invited her to your party just to ignore her? I think you've officially snapped."

"Have you seen April anywhere?" she said, wanting the subject changed immediately. "I want to introduce her to someone."

Billie snorted. "I saw her a little bit ago. She'd already set her sights on someone, though. I'm afraid your matchmaking plan may be delayed."

"The hell it is," Jesse said with a huff. "This is all I have right now to help keep my head on straight." She finished her bourbon and slammed the glass on a nearby table. "I'm going to find her. I need you to keep Eloise from finding me."

"What the hell?"

"You don't have to track her or anything crazy like that. Just text me a heads-up when she's nearby."

"You live in a three-bedroom ranch. Where the fuck do you plan on hiding?"

Jesse waved Billie off. "Not hide, evade. There's a difference. You should know that. You're the English teacher, after all." She patted Billie's shoulder and walked away. Everything would work out just fine.

It had to.

CHAPTER TWENTY-SIX

"Woo!" April tossed the plastic shot glass over her shoulder into the sink. That second shot of Fireball would likely loosen her up enough to get back to the party. Cinnamon whiskey was like a magic elixir. She broke into a few erratic dance moves before wandering back toward the living room.

Times like these highlighted how much of a lone wolf she really was. While she got along with everyone, she didn't really fit in anywhere. There were small groups of teachers, mostly sticking together by subject. Billie turned away from her fellow English teachers and raised her glass to April. Still, April didn't approach. Then there were groups of Jesse's personal friends like Liv and Theo, who were always kind enough to invite her to barbecues but struggled to hold conversations with her.

April was the youngest friend Jesse had, and she wasn't an academic who could talk about lesson plans and homework for hours. As one of the school's guidance counselors, April's role in their students' lives was different. April was different. A familiar voice caught April's attention from behind.

"I thought only college students drank that stuff."

April smiled at Gemma. "I was looking for you."

"Oh?" Gemma said, looking genuinely surprised.

"I wanted to make sure you weren't feeling faint from just eating a leaf." April heard Billie's voice in her head, chastising her for being a sarcastic butthead. "And maybe I wanted to talk some more."

"Is that so?"

April nodded. Gemma's hair seemed darker now in the living

room lighting, with a lighter copper color around her face. She had round, vibrant eyes and a freckled button nose with a faint scar next to her right eye. Gemma was beautiful.

"I'll tell you what, April," Gemma said, tapping her nail on her cup, "you stay here, and I'm going to get a refill and tell my friend I'm floating around."

April's hopes fell. "Friend? Like a boyfriend or girlfriend?" She held her breath.

"Like a friend. I'll be right back."

April watched Gemma walk away, unable to tame the smile on her face. She waited and waited. And waited. Five minutes turned into ten, and April started to get too antsy for her own good. She needed to talk off her nervous energy, but she didn't want to stray too far. She spotted Jesse coming right for her.

"Bro, your party is a hit as usual."

"April," Jesse said, laying her hand on April's shoulder, "I've been looking all over for you."

"Really? I never leave the food or the booze."

"If you keep hiding, I won't be able to introduce you—"

"Are you okay? You're acting really weird right now," she said, looking at Jesse in concern. "You're all shifty and shady."

Jesse looked over her shoulder.

"Who are you looking for?"

"Um..."

"Hey, if this is about your little setup, just let it go. I already have my eye on someone tonight, and you clearly need to relax. I'm good. For real. Please forget about it, and go hang out with your friends, or check the chips again." April thought of the handfuls she'd eaten. "You may be running low."

"The chips are fine. Why are you fighting me so hard on this? Just meet her. It's not difficult. I'm not asking you to change your whole life or grow up."

"Whoa." April did not like any of Jesse's implications. "I'm glad you're not asking me to change my life or grow up because I don't have to. Just because I'm not sitting at home with my sweaters feeling sorry for myself doesn't mean I'm doing something wrong."

Jesse lowered her head. "I'm sorry." She took a deep breath and rolled her shoulders. "I don't really believe you have to grow up." Jesse looked up at her and smirked. "I know you're more mature than your hat lets on."

April laughed in spite of herself. "Are you okay? You've been off all night."

"I'm fine," Jesse said. "I do think I've lost my ability to avoid myself, though. That's a bummer."

April knew by the way Jesse shifted that this had something to do with her ex. The holidays were always hard for people who weren't used to being single. "Hey, it's almost a new year. Which means you'll have nothing but new possibilities ahead."

"You're right. I'll go check on those chips now."

"Especially the kettle cooked," April said guiltily.

"You know, April," Jesse said over her shoulder, "I'm still going to try to set you up." She walked away before April could say anything to defend herself.

She laughed under her breath. "Jerk." But time was up for Gemma. April went on a search for her but didn't have to go too far. Gemma was in the corner of the den, having a serious conversation with a woman April vaguely recognized as a tenured coworker who rarely spoke to her. April hesitated between interrupting and walking away. Her hesitance worked in her favor, however, because Gemma looked over and spotted her.

Gemma excused herself and walked over to April. "I'm sorry I left you waiting."

"It's okay. I was getting hungry, but then I remembered you told me not to move. I didn't want you to lose me, so I came to find you."

"Do you want to get more to eat?"

"Nah," she said, waving her hand. "I heard they're running low on chips anyway. And leaves."

Gemma shook her head. "You're not going to let me live down my veganism, are you?"

"Absolutely not. It's how I charm women—find out one thing about them and then mention it until I kill it. Is it working?"

Gemma's eyes sparkled. "You're funny."

"And cute," April said with a wink. Gemma laughed loudly, and April couldn't get enough. "Do you want to dance?"

"Actually, if you wouldn't mind, I'd like to find someplace quiet to talk and sit. I'm really tired of standing," Gemma said, lifting her right foot and flexing the ankle.

April loved the ballet flats Gemma wore. Something about Gemma screamed simplicity, but her aura said there was much more than met the eye. "I know where we can go." She put out her hand, palm up, and smiled when Gemma took it instantly.

April hadn't been in Jesse's house many times, but her visits were frequent enough to recall the simple floor plan. And if memory served her right, there was a guest bedroom off the kitchen, down the hallway, and right before the garage entrance.

She swung the door open. "Bingo."

"How did you know this was here?"

April understood Gemma's question and the several unspoken questions, too. "Jesse and I have hung out a bit. I used to work odd computer and IT jobs to pay my way through college. Now that Jesse is near retirement, she doesn't understand technology the way she used to, and she asks for my help from time to time."

"Jesse's not—"

"I know," she said with a chuckle. "But I refuse to say anything behind my friend's back that I wouldn't say to her face." April sat on the crisply made queen bed and motioned to the spot next to her.

Gemma sat, keeping a good distance between them. "I wouldn't have pinned you as someone who works IT."

"Because I'm not. Computers bore the heck out of me." She could see Gemma's confusion. "I have a knack," she said with a shrug.

"What is it you do, then?"

"I'm a guidance counselor at the high school, and I work with Jesse on the LGBTQI group."

"Wow." Gemma turned shy and looked at her hands. "You're so young."

April was very used to that reaction by now. "I'm twenty-six. And before you even ask, I busted my ass to get through college on time."

"I wasn't going to…"

She wondered where the zesty spunk Gemma carried earlier had gone. "What do you do?"

"We don't have to talk about that."

Curious. "I showed you mine—now you show me yours," April said lightly.

"I work the floral department at Wegmans," she said after hesitating a little.

"That's really cool."

Gemma brightened up. "Really?"

"Heck yeah. Is that something you're really into? Floral stuff?" April angled herself to get a better look at Gemma as the spoke, but she honored the boundaries Gemma set when she chose to sit.

"Kind of, but not really. I sort of fell into it after dropping out of art school."

April nodded. Gemma would be an art student. "I have a few questions, but I don't want to overstep."

"I won't answer if I don't want to."

"That's fair."

"And I get to ask questions back."

"Of course. It'd be a real shame if you didn't get to know me." Lucky for April, Gemma looked amused. "Aren't most art schools pretty hard to get into?"

"Yes, for the most part. If you think there's even a chance you'll want to pursue an art degree, you have start building your portfolio as a high school freshman. That includes in-school projects and hours of work on your own at home."

"Yikes. Is art even fun anymore at that point?"

"No," Gemma said with a sigh.

"What made you drop out?"

"See last question." Gemma twisted and finally they were looking at one another fully. "My dad wanted it more than I did, anyway. I wanted to be an artist, a true gritty artist. My dad…"

April knew the story all too well, listening to high school juniors and seniors struggling to pick a career they wanted while their parents beat a different path into them. "Your dad didn't think it counted unless you had a degree."

Gemma raised her thumb and smiled stiffly. "Bingo."

She felt genuinely sad for Gemma, the Gemma of the past and the one in front of her. "I hope it didn't make you stop creating art. What's your favorite?"

"Depends on my mood, the weather, and even the seasons. I love painting, but I get the urge to carve and build when it's colder out. Oftentimes I lean into sculpting for comfort. What about you? Are you artsy?"

"Oh God, no," she said with a self-deprecating laugh. "I appreciate art and envy anyone with an artistic bone in their body. I lack it all. The most I can do is match colors."

"An important adult skill for sure." Gemma picked at a small pull in her cardigan, and April wondered if she was nervous. "What made you want to be a guidance counselor? Teenagers can be awful."

"They are absolute monsters." They laughed. "But for all the reasons you can guess. I could've used someone like me in high school, not only when I was figuring out my path and my career options, but when I was figuring myself out, too."

"Being gay?"

April gasped dramatically. "You think I'm gay?" She had never felt more accomplished as she did when Gemma snorted. "Yeah, gay. I was lucky to have Jesse as a teacher. Seeing someone like me be open and fearless gave me hope."

"That's how you got into helping with the LGBTQI group."

April nodded. "How do you know Jesse?"

"I don't," Gemma said with a small grimace. "Not really anyway. I probably shouldn't even be here, but I was kind of dragged."

"By your friend?" April tried again to rack her brain for who that woman was.

"Will you think poorly of me if I told you I lied? She's not my friend, she's my sister-in-law." Gemma just kept getting more and more interesting.

"And she knows Jesse?"

"I'm surprised you don't know her, too. She's a science teacher. Mrs. Reynolds."

April finally placed her. "I knew she looked familiar. But wait, why lie?"

"It doesn't exactly sound cool to say you were forced to go to a party at a virtual stranger's house all because she felt sorry for you."

April knew her smile was smug. "You wanted to be cool for me."

"Shut up," Gemma said, pushing at April's shoulder.

April caught Gemma's hand and froze. That simple contact, even self-initiated, took April by surprise. She breathed deeply and tried to quell her desire for more contact. Normally by now April would be voicing her wants and making her moves, but something about Gemma switched April's thoughts to a more caring track.

Was April getting into way more than she bargained for?

Chapter Twenty-seven

Eloise pinched the bridge of her nose and counted to ten.

"Nurses are very busy on New Year's Eve. Like, isn't this one of those holidays where people get hurt a lot?" he said, swaying slightly from side to side. "You should be at work."

"Alcohol poisoning."

He leaned in closer and yelled, "What did you say?"

She shuddered at the alcohol coming off him. "Alcohol poisoning and car accidents," Eloise said, taking a step back to regain some space. She had no idea who this guy was or how she'd ended up listening to him talk about what nurses did. She was more than ready to excuse herself when an irate woman came up and claimed the sloppy mess of a man who'd probably end up in the ER himself at this rate.

"I am really sorry about him," she said to Eloise. "He doesn't get out much."

"Couldn't tell." Eloise tried to be nice, but her sweetness was wearing thin. She had been at Jesse's party for over an hour. Midnight crept closer, and she was still being shunned by the host. But that was no one else's problem but her own. "It's okay, but he should probably start drinking some water now, or he'll never make it to midnight."

The other woman shook her head. "Sadly, I'll probably have to dress it up as a mixed drink in order to get him to drink it."

"Shots," Eloise said. "Something about shots get drunk people excited. Make it a competition, and he probably won't even realize it's water until he's four or five in."

The woman lit up. "Thank you. Come on, Stephen, I have some

shots for you in the kitchen." Stephen perked right up and followed her.

"Works every time," Eloise said to herself. She looked up to see Leah and Billie staring at her. They waved her over, and relief flowed through her.

"Ellie!" Billie's grin couldn't be more genuine. "I am so happy to see you." Billie opened her arms, and Eloise fell right into them. Just like old times, old comforts.

"It's nice to see you again," Leah said, making Eloise feel equally welcome.

Eloise stepped back and placed a hand on each of their shoulders. "I'm so happy to see the two of you together." She gave a squeeze for good measure and directed her next words to Leah. "I'm sorry if I was weird at the bakery."

Leah waved her off. "Oh no, you were fine."

"I was creepy," she said with a laugh. "Who outwardly admits they recognize a stranger from social media?"

"You would, Ellie, you definitely would." Billie pulled her in for another quick hug. "I can't believe you're back."

Eloise grew mildly uncomfortable and suspicious. She and Billie hadn't been close for some time, which meant if Billie knew anything about her social life, her mother was to blame. Or maybe...

"How long have you been back?" Leah's practical question snapped Eloise back.

"Almost two and a half months now, and I've been busy every minute."

"Have you been working, too? Like, aside from helping your mom with the bakery?" Leah said.

She shook her head. "I've had my hands full with mom's surgery and the bakery, but I've talked to my old boss at Monmouth Medical, and they agreed to meet with me if I decided to continue with nursing."

Billie's eyes widened. "If?"

Eloise weighed whether or not she wanted to get into her whole life path with Billie on New Year's Eve in Jesse's living room. "I'm taking this break to figure a few things out. My career in nursing is a top thing."

"It's not easy," Leah said to her drink, not to Eloise.

"I'm not looking for easy," she said with more bite than she intended.

"No, I'm sorry. That's not what I meant. I see firsthand what our nurses do every day, and I don't even know how…" Leah took a deep breath. "It's something I could never handle."

"What is it that you do again?"

"I'm an EMT."

"So you *do* get it." Eloise stared at Leah and knew by her solemn nod that she really did understand. Not wanting to bring the mood down, Eloise cracked a smile and said, "How many favors did you have to cash in to get the holidays off?"

Leah laughed out loud. "I will not have another holiday off for a long time."

"I guess as a teacher I should stay out of this one," Billie said. Eloise and Leah shot her twin glares.

Leah ran her hand up Billie's arm and wrapped her fingers around the back of Billie's neck. "You're lucky you're cute. Otherwise, I'd be telling you where you can shove your winter break." Eloise choked on a laugh.

"I love you, too," Billie said, leaning in for a kiss. Leah melted right into Billie.

Eloise was truly happy for Billie and Leah, but she definitely felt awkward standing by as they kissed one another. At the forefront of her mind was the thought that she'd known a love like that not too long ago. That sadness was too much. She didn't know whether she should walk away or stay put. Thankfully, they pulled apart before things grew too uncomfortable.

Leah pinched Billie's earlobe. "I'm running to the restroom. I'll be right back."

Eloise stood with Billie. She swirled the same drink she had been nursing for nearly an hour and watched the small pieces of ice dance.

Billie broke the silence. "I'm not gonna lie. I'm surprised you came."

Fearful, Eloise looked at Billie. "What do you mean?"

Billie's small smile was the same as it was fifteen years ago, charming and very telling. "Ellie…"

She covered her face and groaned. "I don't know what I'm doing, Billie."

"Hey," Billie said, placing her hand on Eloise's forearm and encouraging her to look at her. "It's okay. For what it's worth, I don't think Jesse knows what she's doing either."

Eloise could tell Billie wouldn't betray Jesse's trust by saying more. Eloise swallowed hard, suddenly very hot and fidgety. She was on the brink of an anxiety attack and needed to get her bearings. "I need some fresh air." She stepped around Billie, ignoring her questions, and walked straight out the front door.

She looked up at the clear night sky and studied the stars. Taking one deep breath after another, Eloise began to calm her racing heart. Anxiety attacks—another new development in her life. Although the night was biting and frigid, the cold felt good against her heated, pulsing skin. Eloise didn't understand what was happening to her. Before Jesse, she was sure and confident and remained cool no matter the circumstances. Then her heart broke and everything changed.

And what did Billie mean? Jesse had obviously told Billie about their relationship, but how much? And which version? Did Jesse spare details to make herself look better, or did she spill the whole truth? Eloise's head began to spin.

She should leave. Eloise could see her car, inviting and ready beneath the amber streetlights. All she had to do was go back in the house to get her coat, and she'd be gone without a trace. She laughed sardonically. *Gone without a trace.* She'd tried that before by fleeing to Baltimore for a big-city job and women who were nothing like Jesse. Women who were available and looking to be permanent. Women who wanted everything Eloise had to offer, which wasn't much. Because every single one of those women lacked one important quality. They weren't Jesse.

Eloise took a deep, frigid breath. "This is stupid," she said to herself, shivering. Clearly she was a glutton for punishment, but that stopped here. Resolute and spurred by freezing, Eloise marched back into the house and headed straight for the coat closet. She didn't notice anyone or anything. Her sole focus was on escaping. Much to her dismay, her coat was no longer where she had hung it. If this was some sort of prank, Eloise was not in the mood. She turned to a group of three mingling by the closet door.

"Did you see anyone take my coat?" she said, expecting more than the odd looks she received. "Long burgundy puffer with a fur-lined hood?" Still, she received no response. She growled, "Never mind." She traveled farther into the house with heavy-footed steps and grew more annoyed with each passing second.

Could this night get any worse?

CHAPTER TWENTY-EIGHT

I am completely serious."

Gemma continued to shake her head. "I don't believe you. I can tell you're the type of person to fib to people."

"Fib to people?" April said, aghast. "You think I fib to people?"

"Yes. You seem like someone who'd prey on gullible people and play pranks on them."

She wanted to defend herself, but aside from being a fibber, April was also very honest. "Okay, fine. I like to joke around, but I really am serious about this. Up until last Super Bowl, I had no clue Wisconsin was known for their cheese. Blew my mind because I knew Packers fans were called Cheeseheads."

Gemma looked contemplative as she regarded April. "Tell me you at least knew Idaho was known for potatoes."

"Wait. What?"

Gemma's mouth fell open. "No way."

"That one was a joke. Of course I do. I actually considered moving to Idaho for that reason." April laughed. "Do you know what Jersey is known for?"

Gemma thought for a minute. "I can't really say I'm an expert on the history since I moved here when I was fifteen, but I'd guess tomatoes? Pork roll?"

April waited a beat for dramatic effect. "Road rage and sarcasm."

"I can't stand you." Gemma's laughter completely negated her words. "I can't believe I'm choosing to sit here and listen to terrible jokes instead of enjoying the party."

April was trying to decide whether or not Gemma was serious. Her gut told her if she wanted to make a move, now was the time. What did she have to lose? She slid closer to Gemma on the bed until their thighs touched.

"I just got out of a really long relationship, and I'm not taking it very well," Gemma blurted out. April slid back an inch and remained quiet, not really knowing where to go from *there*. "I'm sorry," Gemma said, covering her red face with her hands. "I'm an idiot. I should've warned you that I also embarrass myself all the time."

She reached out and grabbed Gemma's hands, gently encouraging her to lower them. She smiled when Gemma opened one eye to look at her. "Hi."

Gemma opened her other eye. "Hi."

She turned Gemma's hand over and ran her fingertips over Gemma's palm. "Can I tell you a secret?"

Gemma didn't hesitate. "Of course."

"I've never just sat with anyone and talked during a party. Ever. Normally I'm drinking too much and eating as much as possible all while looking for a potential hookup."

"Oh…"

"And I'm really, really enjoying this change of pace."

Gemma looked at her with a small smile and hopeful eyes. "Yeah?"

"Yeah, and I am more than happy if we sit here guessing what each state is known for until midnight."

Gemma surged forward and kissed April.

April didn't move. She didn't even lean in, searching for a deeper kiss. April let Gemma take whatever she felt most comfortable with because soaking up the softness of Gemma's mouth was a treat in and of itself. Gemma pulled back, looking bashful, but she didn't go far. April still felt the warmth of Gemma's lips.

April didn't know what to do or say. She didn't want to scare Gemma away or put too much focus on the kiss. The last thing she wanted was for Gemma to feel pressured or pushed. "That was nice," she said dumbly.

Gemma winced. "Nice?"

"Yeah, I mean *really* nice. You have great lips." April struggled for more safe things to say. "I wouldn't mind kissing again if that's what you'd like to do at some point tonight. Or not." She cleared her throat. "It's your call. I'm happy either way."

"Am I making you nervous?"

"No," she said, not even convincing herself. "Yes. But only because I want to make sure you're comfortable and enjoying yourself." April's breath stuttered when Gemma took her hand and played gently with her fingers.

"Then I think I'd like to kiss some more."

April couldn't confuse that green light. She leaned forward and captured Gemma's lips again, this time allowing herself to control and indulge. But every time she tried to gain the upper hand, Gemma would push and take the power back, a dynamic April had never experienced. She carefully placed her hand on Gemma's thigh and closed the distance between their bodies again, all while remaining connected.

Gemma was the first to open up. She traced April's upper lip delicately with her tongue until April invited her in. Gemma was a slow, sensually deep kisser, as if she wanted to get to know your soul before your mouths parted. April had to pull back to catch her breath. She had never been left light-headed from a kiss before.

"Are you okay?" Gemma said, genuinely concerned. April nodded. Gemma smirked. "Still very nice?"

If April hadn't been turned-on already, seeing Gemma's confidence would've completely done her in. "Very, very." She leaned in slowly, aiming her lips lower and lower, watching Gemma for any indication to stop. She went straight for Gemma's neck. Gemma was intoxicating. She smelled of the earth with a hint of sweetness. April's lips buzzed with excitement as she explored Gemma's incredibly soft, smooth skin. Gemma's pulse point was like a beckoning bull's-eye for April's teeth. Gemma yelped and moaned as she bit her and licked her reddening skin.

Abruptly, April stood and pulled Gemma to her feet. Gemma looked up at her with confused eyes. "What?"

April smirked and started leading Gemma, who followed April's subtle direction to sit atop a nearby dresser. She pushed Gemma's long skirt up to her hips and switched to a softer, sweeter touch next, hoping she would enjoy the sudden change. She ran the tip of her nose along the column of Gemma's neck, up the side, and to her earlobe. She whispered a kiss behind Gemma's ear before returning to her mouth.

April kissed Gemma slowly now, relishing the feel of her skin and smooth tongue. It had been too long since she simply kissed someone. Her every craving was satisfied. Well, almost every craving. She ran her hands up the outside of Gemma's thighs. Gemma responded by tightening her legs around April's waist.

They separated, their deep breathing filling the silence between them. Gemma rested her forehead against April's.

"I don't normally do this," Gemma said.

April pulled back and looked into Gemma's heavy eyes. "I can't tell if you're serious or if that's a line."

"I'm serious," Gemma said, pushing her red hair away from her face and taking a deep breath. "I'm known for monogamy and long-term relationships, not hooking up with a stranger in a spare bedroom at a party." Gemma sounded hesitant as she explained herself. April tried to step away, but Gemma wouldn't let her. "I'm not saying I don't want this."

"Look," April said, pulling Gemma's hands away. "Wanting it now doesn't mean you won't regret it later." She felt unsettled by even the thought. "I can't be a part of that."

Gemma grabbed the front of April's plaid button-up and held her close. "I'm here because I want to end this horrible fucking year feeling happy."

April traced Gemma's cheek with the pad of her thumb, along the bone and down to where she faintly remembered a dimple being only minutes before. "What happened?" she said, not wanting to pry but unable to stop herself from asking. "Who did this to you?" She licked her lips.

"Wrong person at the wrong time, but you don't want to hear about that. This is supposed to be fun, right?" Gemma reached back and dug her hands into the back pockets of April's jeans. She pulled April in to her. "Remind me what fun feels like."

April's body was on fire. She couldn't remember the last time she had reacted this way to someone, and it felt fucking fantastic. "I'm going to ask one more time," she said in a low voice, one she knew drove women crazy. She kissed Gemma's cheek dangerously close to the corner of her mouth. "Are you sure this is what you want?"

Gemma tilted her head and leaned in to chase April's lips. "I'm absolutely sure."

"And you won't regret it tomorrow?" She exhaled against Gemma's mouth. "You won't regret me?"

Gemma's grip tightened on her ass. "I won't regret any of this," she said in a loud, crackling whisper.

April pushed her hips forward and swallowed Gemma's responding whimper. She kissed Gemma deeply and ran her hands up under Gemma's cardigan, over the plane of her back, memorizing the slight jump of muscles through her thin tank. When she pulled her mouth away, she leaned in to Gemma's ear. "I want to feel your skin."

Gemma slid her cardigan from her shoulders and tilted her head back. "Please…"

She touched Gemma's sides, just past the opening of her cardigan, and continued until she reached the sliver of bare skin on Gemma's lower back. She ran her fingertips along it before daring to move upward, listening to the way Gemma's breathing changed with each new touch. She teased slightly before feeling the edge of Gemma's rib cage and noticing she was ticklish. April smiled against Gemma's mouth as she giggled.

"I like making you laugh," April said without removing her hands but not progressing either. She kissed Gemma's cheek and then her ear. She waited until Gemma's giggles faded into controlled breathing. She kissed the angle of her jaw and started moving her hands again. "I'd like to find out what other noises you make." In a swift motion she cupped Gemma's breasts.

Gemma's responding gasp was everything April needed to continue.

Her next kiss was harder, laced with passion and intent. She wanted Gemma, and that want burned beneath her skin. "What do you like?" she said, trailing her lips to the tiny notch where Gemma's jaw met her ear. "What do you *want*?"

Gemma pushed her back and hopped down onto her feet. She swayed slightly, which made April smile smugly. "I'd like to go back to the bed."

"Oh."

"I liked this, I really did," Gemma said, squeezing April's shoulders.

"I just thought it'd be hot, and we wouldn't have to worry about making the bed again."

"Totally." Gemma bobbed her head for a silent moment. "But all I keep thinking about is whether to not this dresser is going to break. Very hard to stay in the moment."

"Yeah, okay," April said, stepping back and allowing Gemma to lead the way back to the bed. She tried her best to hide the mild embarrassment she felt, even if it was silly, but one thing April was known for was not being able to keep her mouth shut. "I'm sorry. That was stupid." She felt oddly jittery with nerves now. What was happening?

Gemma stopped herself from lying back and sat up. She tilted her head at April. "Nothing stupid about it. If it was my dresser at home, I wouldn't have thought twice about staying put and seeing what that furniture could handle."

April was surprised again by a sudden flair of confidence in Gemma's tone. What an odd combination Gemma was, which led April to wonder if Gemma was even a combination at all. Maybe the real Gemma felt confident all the time. April wanted to find out.

"Lie back," April said in a demanding yet soft tone. She waited for Gemma to settle on the queen-size bed, the charcoal-gray comforter making her colorful skirt pop. She crawled atop Gemma, purposely moving at a languid pace. Everything April needed to know was on Gemma's face, the want in her eyes and each quiet pant that left her slightly open lips.

Gemma spread her legs instantly to accommodate April, who wasted no time pressing herself into Gemma's crotch. She propped herself up on her hands and stared down into Gemma's dark eyes. Something danced within them, and April wanted to learn the song. Instead of asking Gemma what she was thinking, April leaned in for a slow, deep kiss. She hoped to taste the answers and the cravings of the woman she was getting to know.

Gemma's soft moan was cut short by the sound of the door swinging open.

April froze.

Gemma cursed.

A soft voice apologized.

Chapter Twenty-nine

Eloise slammed the door shut. "Oh my God," she said to nobody in particular. She started flapping her hands about and repeating herself. "Oh my God, oh my God." She wasn't disgusted by any means, but she was most definitely shocked. She had never walked in on anyone at a party before and was convinced such a scene was reserved for movies or television shows. But here Eloise stood, a voyeur in her own right, with the image of fully clothed women writhing against each other. She decided in that moment she needed to share her experience, her missing coat long forgotten.

Sadly, her first instinct was to tell Jesse. A ping of pain chipped at her heart. "No," she said in a quiet command to herself. "Jesse will not rob you of the fun of this moment. She's done enough of that already."

"Are you talking to yourself?"

Eloise recognized the voice and froze. She didn't want to turn around and see Jesse's stupid fucking face. All she wanted was to escape, and now she was stuck between the one she was running from and a couple having a much better night. "Have you seen my coat?" Eloise said bluntly. She had no time or desire for another conversation. "I hung it in the front closet, and now I can't find it."

"You're leaving?"

Eloise rolled her eyes and turned around. The surprise was evident on Jesse's face. "Yes. I'm leaving. Have you seen my coat or not?"

"I moved it to my room."

Fury warmed Eloise from the inside out. "Why would you do that?"

Jesse's eyebrows twitched slightly upward. "I know you don't like your jacket to be crowded with other people's stuff because then—"

"My jacket smells like strangers." Eloise bit the inside of her cheek and looked down. She couldn't remember when or why she ever told Jesse that odd tidbit about herself, but damn her for remembering.

"It's almost midnight. You should stay at least for that."

"No. I don't think I want to do that."

Jesse slid her hands into the back pockets of her jeans. "You know where my room is." Yes, Eloise did. Eloise knew more intimate details than that, but she now treated those as distant memories. Jesse stepped aside and nodded toward the door not too far from where Eloise stood, giving Eloise a false sense of control over the situation.

Eloise knew better. She knew Jesse would follow her. Eloise walked quickly to the bedroom she'd never expected to see again. She couldn't decide if the moment was bittersweet or just bitter. Her jacket was laid with care on Jesse's navy blue comforter. She heard footsteps behind her, which spurred her to continue, and she put her jacket on.

"I've been trying to avoid you."

"Oh, really?" Eloise said, zipping up her coat, "I hadn't noticed."

"I'm sorry. I know it's juvenile—"

"And kind of mean. Don't forget that."

Jesse rubbed her forehead. "I really am sorry. I didn't mean for you to feel unwelcome or anything. I didn't even want to invite you."

"That's nice."

"But I did, and then I had this weird thought in my head that you and I would be able to, or at least maybe be…"

Eloise looked at Jesse and waited for another word or two to complete the sentence, but nothing ever came. "What? Maybe be what?"

"In each other's lives again, and I thought if you came here tonight, it could be the start of that."

"You'd have to talk to me for any of that to happen."

"I know."

Eloise didn't understand any of what was happening. She was at her wit's end. "I tried to talk to you on Christmas, but you shut me down. I forced the conversation, and then you invited me here. I show up and get the cold shoulder. Now I'm trying *desperately* to leave, and you're blocking my way. What do you want from me, Jesse? What do you actually want?" Eloise said loudly. She took a deep breath, could feel her nostrils flaring with anger. She wasn't entirely sure who she had become over the last six months, but Eloise knew she didn't care for this latest version of herself. "You know what? Save it, because I doubt you even know the answer."

❖

Jesse felt paralyzed. She couldn't speak. She didn't blink. She couldn't even try to swallow past her dry mouth. Eloise stood no more than six feet from her, and Jesse couldn't look away. Eloise's light brown hair was longer now than it had been the last time Jesse touched it. The curls came a little below her shoulders, and the ringlets were the perfect combination of tamed and chaos, with a soft laziness at the ends.

Her eyes looked browner in the dim lighting, but Jesse knew the prismatic effect sunlight could have on their natural enrapturing hazel. Just then, Jesse made her first mistake of the evening and looked at Eloise's lips. Those damn lips. Eloise's mouth was a treat, full and shapely with sharp angles and rounded curves. If Jesse concentrated, she was sure she could still taste them.

She had to talk. She had to say something because Eloise had been poised like a cat ready to leap, and she couldn't bear the thought of her leaving. Not yet.

"I didn't see this coming," Jesse said like a confession. She felt the tension build in her chest, and her mind sped up the way it always did right before she spilled her guts. "I didn't see you coming. You came in like a wrecking ball and changed everything for me, and the fact that we didn't work out—"

Eloise held up her hand. "Stop."

"What?"

"You keep saying things like that, and it's not true. Don't blame us or our relationship for your actions. You gave up. You quit. *We* didn't fail."

She felt Eloise's words like a slap and flinched. "My life is here, and your job is in another state. Explain how that's my fault."

"I didn't have to take the job. I told you a hundred times, and you still kept pushing me to go. I figured it was your nice way of telling me you were done with me."

"I just wanted what was best for you."

"I'm an adult. I don't need anyone making decisions for me or telling me what I need. You were supposed to be my girlfriend," Eloise said, crossing her arms over her chest. Eloise wasn't known for emotional displays, so Jesse panicked when her chin started to quiver. "But you weren't even willing to call yourself that."

Seeing Eloise again, sad yet hardened, made Jesse realize the damage she had done. "I'm sorry."

"You've apologized already, and honestly, I'm okay. I didn't even think of you when I made the decision to come back." Eloise pulled the cuffs of her sweater down from under her coat sleeves to cover her hands. "That's not true. I thought coming back would give me closure, or at least an idea of whether or not we could try again."

Jesse's heart lurched. "Oh."

"But I knew the moment I saw you that wasn't possible."

"What do you mean?"

"You looked terrified when I walked into Liv and Theo's."

"I didn't know you were going to be there."

Eloise shrugged. "You should never be scared, not if you really loved someone."

She wanted to argue and explain how fear could come from love. How loving someone and feeling that powerful emotion rushing back all at once could scare the shit out of someone. But Jesse couldn't get those words out. Instead, she nodded and changed the subject. "Are you really back permanently?"

"My mom needs me."

"Yeah, of course. If Lena needs anything, don't hesitate to ask."

Eloise didn't acknowledge her offer. She barely even looked at Jesse as she went to the bedroom door. Jesse pictured the last time she'd walked out. Those were happier days. Eloise paused with her hand on the doorknob.

"What did you mean by that?" Eloise said with her back to Jesse. She turned slowly, and Jesse noticed then just how sad her hazel eyes were. "When you said you didn't see me coming."

"I've known you for most of your life. You've always been right there. When you walked into Sylvia's that day, I felt like I was meeting you for the first time. You smiled at me, this bright and excited smile. I had never seen anything like it." Jesse swallowed hard and gave herself a moment to think. "I had never *felt* anything like it."

Eloise sniffled. "Don't say things like that."

"You asked."

"I have one more question, and then I'll leave."

"You don't have to go."

"Yes, I do." Eloise squared her shoulders and looked Jesse in the eye. "Why wouldn't you call me your girlfriend?"

She remembered how she'd danced around the title with every lie that sat ready on the tip of her tongue during the months of their relationship. "I felt like people would judge us."

"Us or you?"

She held her breath for a second. "Both." Eloise shook her head. "I was your teacher and you're—"

"Younger. Yeah, I know," Eloise said harshly. "You've mentioned it a time or two, and I always told you I didn't care. All that should matter is how we feel."

"It's not that simple."

"Yes, it is!" Eloise looked surprised by her own outburst. "Were you ashamed to be with me?"

"No," she said, feeling sick at the thought. "Anyone would be proud to be with you."

"I don't buy it. I don't buy any of it."

Jesse's chest tightened. "It's the truth."

"I'm calling bullshit. I know the people in your life, and I know my family and my friends. No one would care about us being together. But most importantly, I know *you*."

Jesse had to look away from Eloise's watery, fierce eyes. Her heart started to hammer in her chest, and her palms grew clammy.

Eloise stepped an inch closer. "You were the first teacher in the school district to step forward and suggest taking care of queer students. You fought with administrators and other parents. You teach your students to be themselves unabashedly."

"Because I want to help improve their world," Jesse said firmly.

"And you do because you are brave."

Jesse shook her head. "I'm not."

Eloise maintained eye contact and waited, as if giving her one more chance to speak.

Jesse remained quiet.

"You were never a coward, not until now. Not until me. Good-bye, Jesse. Happy New Year." Eloise opened the door.

She opened her mouth to stop Eloise, but no words came out. The closing of the door sounded loud despite the noise coming from the rest of the house.

Jesse dropped her head. The swirling design of the hardwood floors served as no distraction. All she saw was the hurt in Eloise's eyes, dark and tired, but unable to hide the lovely twinkle that was always present. Eloise always insisted Jesse put that twinkle there. For months they were happy. For months they loved one another, and for the first time Jesse had felt whole. Now she felt nothing more than broken. She looked back to the door.

What the fuck was she doing?

Jesse left the room in a hurry and scanned her crowded living room. Eloise couldn't have gotten far. Panic set in. Jesse ran to the front door and out to the street. She paced the sidewalk looking for Eloise's small blue sedan. She spotted it not too far away, and it was empty. Eloise was still inside.

She ran back and started looking everywhere. She didn't find Eloise in the kitchen or on the back deck where the few smokers she knew huddled together. Her breath came out as fluffy white clouds. Back in the house, partygoers stared at her as she kept looking. She checked her office, but it was empty. The only room left was the spare bedroom, and she prayed she'd open the door to Eloise standing there. She placed her hand on the doorknob and turned slowly.

CHAPTER THIRTY

April heard the banging on the door from where she was nestled between Gemma's breasts. "Shit." The banging continued.

"Eloise?" Jesse's voice boomed through the door. "Are you in there?"

"Eloise?" April said. She looked up at Gemma, whose rosy cheeks matched her hair.

"Come on. Unlock the door. Please." Jesse sounded more distraught than April had ever heard, and they worked with teenagers every day.

April stood and started gathering their clothes. She motioned for Gemma to get dressed. She pulled on her jeans and boots, and her shirt was nearly buttoned as she opened the door. She pushed the hair away from her face and said, "Everything okay? Who's Eloise?"

Jesse's frown was deep. "What the hell are you doing?"

"Uh…" April looked over her shoulder and then back to Jesse. "Nothing?"

"Unbelievable." Jesse turned to walk away, but April stopped her.

"Seriously. Are you okay? What's going on?"

"Nothing. I'm just looking for someone."

"I'll help you look."

Jesse looked her up and down. "You're obviously occupied."

"I'll help, too," Gemma said from over April's shoulder. April couldn't contain her smile, a smile that must've been big and contagious because even Jesse's mouth twitched at the corners.

"Gemma," Jesse said.

April was confused. Gemma had said she didn't really know Jesse and was dragged to this party by her sister-in-law. "Yeah, this is Gemma."

"Hi," Gemma said, raising her hand shyly. "Great party."

"I'm glad you're having a good time. Dana wasn't sure she'd be able to convince you to come."

"She can be very pushy—err I mean, persuasive." Gemma and Jesse laughed.

April raised her hand, feeling slightly left out. "Who's Dana? Wait. I still don't know who Eloise is."

"My sister-in-law."

"I'm glad she brought you because I've been wanting to introduce you to this butthead." Jesse flicked her thumb at April. "I'm glad you two hit it off, but now I have to go."

April's mind reeled for a split second but came to a sudden halt. "Who are we looking for?"

Jesse hesitated before her shoulders fell. "She's your height, maybe a little taller. Dark blond hair, loose curls, incredibly gorgeous, but definitely looks very pissed off right now."

April imagined Jesse's description and had way more questions now, but only one involving the search. "What's she wearing?"

"Long burgundy coat. Puffy with a fur-lined hood."

"Got it," April said, showing two thumbs up. She turned to Gemma. "Know who we're looking for?" Gemma nodded confidently. "Let's go." She raised her hand for a high five but at the last minute decided to go for a kiss instead. Gemma accepted happily.

Jesse clapped. "Guys."

"Sorry," April said. She lowered her voice before adding, "Mom."

Gemma giggled. "You're awful."

They followed Jesse out into the suddenly more crowded house. How long had she and Gemma been hidden away for? April checked the time on her phone and was shocked to see there were only ten minutes until midnight.

"Let's check by the food first."

"You're suggesting that because you're hungry," said Gemma.

April gawked before grinning. "And thirsty."

"Look at that. I'm already getting to know you." Gemma added a wink and walked ahead toward the kitchen. April watched her and shook her head. There was Gemma's confidence again.

Shortly thereafter April had a mouthful of food and a beer in her hand as she scanned familiar and unfamiliar faces. Across the great room, she saw the back of a burgundy coat. Its wearer was chatting with a couple April vaguely recognized. She reached out and squeezed Gemma's hand to get her attention, tipping her head in the direction she wanted Gemma to look.

Gemma looked back at her like she was crazy. "They have short black hair."

April did a double take. "My bad. I only saw the coat."

"I'd like to do this again sometime."

April raised her eyebrows. "Okay."

"Unless you don't—" Gemma stopped talking and tilted her head. "Okay?"

"Yeah."

"You are not helping," Jesse said quietly when she stopped behind April during her rush around the house. April grimaced before looking back at Gemma. She smiled and put out her hand.

Gemma took April's hand. "You look for the jacket, I'll look at the hair."

"And I'm sure neither of us will miss a pissed-off hot chick."

They continued through the house on a mission, this time with more focus. April hated being a pessimist, but anyone would assume Eloise was long gone by now. The crowd in the house started to shift as more people gravitated toward the television to watch the scene in Times Square. The ball would start to drop in two minutes. April stood on her toes to look around. Sadness tugged her earlier happiness down. She felt for Jesse. Whatever was going on between Jesse and Eloise was obviously big and heavy for Jesse to carry. The broadcast could be heard over the partygoers.

"Two minutes until the new year. Make sure your loved ones are close or whoever it is you're choosing to celebrate with. We're lucky to be ushering in another year together."

"We really are, Ryan. What are you most grateful for this year?"

"Easy. My health and my wife. As long as I have those I have everything. What about you, Katie?"

"I don't think we're going to find her," April said sullenly. "I really don't want to give up, but…"

April tightened her grip on Gemma's hand and silently shared her heavyheartedness. But with each second that passed, April's spirits started to rise. Because she was there in the moment, holding the hand of a beautiful, funny woman who somehow wanted to see more of her, and they were about to embark on a new year. A clean slate for whatever April wanted to build for herself. She and Gemma looked at one another and shared a small sweet smile with a twinge of mischief. The final countdown began.

Ten…

April turned to face Gemma and held both of her hands.

Nine…

Gemma's cheeks reddened.

Eight…

She stepped closer to Gemma.

Seven…

Everyone around them disappeared.

Six…

Gemma let out the most adorable giggle.

Five…

April stepped closer, closing any distance between them.

Four…

She felt Gemma grip her hips for dear life.

Three…

April held Gemma's face in her hands.

Two…

She leaned in slowly.

One…

"Will you marry me?"

Both April and Gemma turned, gaping, to see who just dropped that bomb. At the center of the room stood a shocked Leah, gazing down at Billie, who was on one knee. Billie was grinning broadly but nerves were apparent in her eyes as everyone looked on and waited for an answer.

Someone called out from the back of the room, "Answer her."

Leah started laughing and crying and flapping her hands back and forth. "Yes, of course, yes." Billie got to her feet and started kissing Leah over and over before sliding the sparkling ring on Leah's finger.

"I've never witnessed a proposal before," Gemma said with tears in her eyes.

April adored this moment for all its chaotic perfection. "Happy New Year, Gemma." She leaned in again and finally kissed Gemma soundly, soaking up the feeling of a new beginning.

NEW YEAR'S DAY: JESSE AND ELOISE

CHAPTER THIRTY-ONE

Happy New Year," Jesse whispered into the night. She took a deep breath, trying her best to fight back tears. A new year and no hopes to hold on to or wishes to make. The frigid cold biting at her cheeks offered a brief but much needed distraction from the pain in her chest. She had lost Eloise again, and this second time hurt even more. Why didn't Eloise tell her earlier that she was interested in seeing if they could work things out? *Because you never gave her the chance.* Jesse shivered.

She didn't want to go back to the party, the cheers, and the smiles. She couldn't leave either. Jesse felt stuck, cornered, and completely deflated. She went back inside and kept her head down. She didn't want to chat with anyone or fake happiness for another trip around the sun. She wanted to go to bed.

The small crowd was still going full force, and Jesse hated the noise. She resisted the urge to start screaming and yelling for everyone to get out. At least she would be safe in her bedroom. The guests could let themselves out when they were done. Along the way, Jesse stopped in the kitchen and grabbed the bottle of bourbon and a plastic cup from the counter. Life felt low, but she couldn't bring herself to drink straight from the bottle. Not yet.

She had one more stop to make between the kitchen and her one safe space. She found Liv in the living room next to the fire, Theo at her side as always. They were chatting with Timothy, the dramatic arts teacher they seemed to gravitate to at every party. Their consistency brought a fraction of peace to Jesse. She tapped Liv on the shoulder and motioned for her to step away.

"Excuse me," Liv said, kissing Theo's cheek. "What's up?" Liv's concern was evident.

"I need you to do me a favor. It's a big one."

"Yeah, sure."

"Will you wrap things up here? Not clean up. I'll take care of all that tomorrow, but just make sure everyone leaves and is safe about it." She knew her dwindling strength was apparent in her voice. She could barely speak loudly enough to be heard over the chatter. "I need to lie down."

"Yeah, we can do that." Liv placed her hand on Jesse's shoulder. "Do you want to talk about it?" The genuine worry in her eyes nearly cracked Jesse's resolve.

"Not tonight. Thank you. I owe you one," Jesse said, patting Liv's hand.

Jesse faked a few smiles as she took the seemingly long walk to her bedroom. She opened the door and didn't even bother to turn on the light. The moon was bright enough to see by, and its glow was gray enough to match her mood. She started to pour a drink before she even reached the bed and sat. The first sip burned going down, but the second mouthful felt more therapeutic. She nearly choked on her third gulp when the bed shifted behind her.

"I'm sorry," Eloise said.

Jesse stood and backed away. "What are you doing in here?" she said, more shocked than annoyed but unable to control her tone. "You scared the shit out of me." She flicked on the lights.

Eloise sat against the headboard with her knees drawn up to her chin and squinted at the light. Faint tracks of mascara tears stained her face. "I don't know. I tried to leave, but my car was stuck," Eloise said with a hollow laugh. "I didn't know where to go or what to do. I almost walked home, but it's really cold."

Jesse's heart pounded. Things between them had gotten so bad that Eloise considered fleeing three miles on foot on New Year's Eve just to get away. Jesse sat again and let out a heavy breath. She offered her drink to Eloise. "It's helping me."

"No. I've already had enough help."

"I'm sorry for all of this. You should never feel trapped. You should never feel pain. I should've never invited you tonight because I knew I wasn't going to be able to handle it."

Eloise started to get out of bed.

"No, please. Stay and sleep it off. I just..." Jesse listened to the endless noise in her house. "I just needed to get away from all that. I won't bother you. I promise."

She turned off the light and lay back. Jesse stared at the ceiling, and although she was painfully aware of Eloise beside her, she was still able to find peace. Jesse's every prepared speech left her mind and she simply breathed in Eloise's presence. Exhaustion took over. Jesse focused on the heaviness of her heart, mind, and body and slipped off into slumber.

When Jesse awoke with a start, the room was pitch black and silent. She looked around frantically, unsure of the time, but very sure Eloise had been there when she fell asleep. It was no surprise Eloise was gone. She pulled her phone from her pocket and frowned to find it dead.

"Great," she said. Her body ached from falling asleep rigidly, atop the covers and fully dressed all the way down to her shoes. She knew she had slept for at least an hour or two, judging by the awful taste left in her mouth from her nightcap. She walked to the attached bathroom and stripped away her sweater and button-up, leaving on just her crisp white T-shirt. Next were her shoes and socks. She brushed her teeth thoroughly and dragged herself to her bedroom closet. She wanted her most sinfully soft pajamas, needing any comfort she could find. A noise from another room caught her attention.

Jesse lowered her head. In this moment, she hated her dependence on technology. There wasn't one clock in her room, and she never wore a watch. Not knowing the time kept her from knowing whether to be scared or not. She wouldn't be surprised if a straggler or two were still celebrating, but if the hour was closer to morning, she wouldn't be very happy. She walked out of her bedroom quietly, tiptoeing her way toward the sound. She rounded the corner into the kitchen and stopped.

Eloise padded around, collecting empty bottles and plates left about. Jesse noticed the way Eloise moved slowly and with care, obviously trying to make as little sound as possible. She smiled. The late hour and mental and physical exhaustion softened Jesse.

"I know you're probably tired of hearing me apologize at this point," she said as she entered the kitchen, the room so quiet she could hear the light breeze outside. "But I'm sorry for all of this."

Eloise continued cleaning up, as if Jesse wasn't even there.

"I'll finish up. Please stop."

Eloise held the black garbage bag in her fists. "It's crazy how people are willing to leave such a mess in someone else's house."

"Unless it's a dinner party. Ever notice that?" Jesse stepped closer to Eloise, but not so close as to make her uncomfortable. She leaned her hip against the counter. "If you host a dinner party, everyone is eager and offering to help clean up. If you have a house party, it's like you're opening your door to a fraternity."

"Huh." The corners of Eloise's mouth dropped. "I never realized."

"I think it's the anonymity. It's hard to prove who did or didn't clean up after themselves. There's too much chaos. Except Liv and Theo never leave a trace."

"What about Billie?"

"Depends on the day," she said with a laugh. Jesse stepped forward and took the bag from Eloise. "I appreciate you helping."

"I couldn't just leave it."

Jesse wanted to tease Eloise for her tendency to find something to clean everywhere she went but decided to keep it to herself. "Thank you."

Eloise finally looked at her. "You're welcome." Only the light over the sink was on, highlighting Eloise's face with an amber glow. The shadows around her eyes hid too much from Jesse. Eloise wiped her hands on her jeans. "I should go."

Jesse stood motionless as Eloise started her exit, but when her faint perfume reached Jesse's nose, the scent cut away her final thread of restraint. She reached out and grabbed Eloise's hand to stop her. "Eloise," she said quietly, but even that was hard through the nervous tightness in her throat.

Although Eloise wouldn't turn back, she stopped walking and gripped Jesse's hand back. "Jesse, I..." Eloise dropped her head.

"What?" Jesse stood straight up. "You what?"

Eloise turned slowly. She reached out to play with the cuff of Jesse's T-shirt and touched the nickel-sized tattoo of an equality sign Jesse had on her bicep, done many years ago. As suddenly as the touch was there, it was gone, and Eloise stepped back. She pushed her long curls away from her face and took a deep breath.

"It's not fair," Eloise said.

"What's not fair?"

"How much I miss you still."

"I—"

"Even after you broke my heart. Even after you let me go. Even after you ignored me since I've been back."

Guilt hit Jesse like a punch to the chest. "I never meant to hurt you."

"But here I am, like a fool, craving you."

"You're not a fool," Jesse said, taking a risk and holding Eloise's hand again. "I'm the fool, for all of this and for all of my poor behavior." She grew earnest. "You didn't deserve any of this."

"I don't." Eloise stepped closer and started to examine Jesse's palm. The room was too dark to really see anything, but the touch felt deeper than a simple exploration. "You know I thought about the holidays with you?"

Jesse felt woozy. "What?"

"But it was nothing like this." Eloise choked out a laugh, sounding more disgusted than anything.

Jesse was ashamed to admit to herself that she only ever pictured a vague future for them, but that wasn't because she didn't want a real future with Eloise. She was just too damn scared to allow herself to believe she could have it. "What was it like?" she said.

"You wanted me here," Eloise said, dropping Jesse's hand. "We told everyone about us right before my birthday because you insisted. You said it'd be impossible to celebrate me in secret."

She would never forget the passing of Eloise's birthday. The leaves had been changing, and the early autumn breeze had seemed colder than usual.

"And everyone was happy. Not even Claire had a snarky remark at Thanksgiving."

Unable to resist, Jesse said, "That's unlikely, even in dreams."

"Christmas was the same as this year but also very different. We sat next to each other and held hands under the table. You'd touch my thigh way more than was appropriate, but I'd never stop you because I loved your hands on me."

Jesse closed her eyes at Eloise's use of the past tense. She needed to soften the blow of this conversation. "Like our trip to Atlantic City. I couldn't stop myself from touching you no matter where we had dinner." But Jesse knew immediately she wasn't making anything better.

"Our favorite secret hideaway," Eloise said softly. "But New Year's? I always pictured New Year's to be our holiday. We'd get ready for the party together, making a great team like we always did. We'd entertain everyone but also make sure to steal a moment here and there just for us."

"I never had that." Jesse couldn't stop herself from thinking about Stacy. They'd divide and conquer every time they threw a party, and always plan and play according to Stacy's rules. None of it was fun. Of course Eloise would paint a picture of the partnership Jesse always wanted.

"And then at midnight we'd kiss each other," Eloise said, looking up at Jesse and staring at her lips. Her eyes were sad and tired, filling with tears. "Everyone around us would be cheering and hugging, but we'd never want to stop kissing each other."

She knew she could be reading the situation completely wrong, but Jesse felt the pull to kiss Eloise then. The same pull she had felt hundreds of times. The same pull she was powerless against. She leaned in slowly, giving Eloise more than enough time to stop her if this wasn't what she wanted, if Eloise didn't need this as badly as Jesse did.

Their lips met, and Jesse nearly cried. Every part of her heart and soul melted into the familiar warmth of home. She held Eloise's face in her hands with a delicate touch worthy of fragile glass. She pulled back slightly just to move in and kiss Eloise again, more firmly and deeply, but still with enough caution. Jesse knew this was likely a fleeting moment. Maybe the last.

Jesse's lips tingled as she pulled away from Eloise slowly. No crowd surrounded them. The cheering had stopped hours ago. No fanfare or first second of the new year to soak up. None of this was like Eloise's image, but somehow reality felt more perfect. She took in the way Eloise's eyes opened slowly and the dazed expression on her face.

"Stay," Jesse said with much more calm than she felt. She was risking it all with just one word.

One word that could change everything.

CHAPTER THIRTY-TWO

Eloise had no idea what she was doing. The entire night was like a tug-of-war between her heart, mind, and body. She questioned what she wanted with each passing minute. And when she knew she had to leave, she couldn't. Actual cars blocked her in, but Eloise wondered if this was the universe's way of making her stay put and figure herself out.

She looked up into Jesse's darkened eyes. Eloise opened her mouth to tell Jesse every reason why she couldn't stay, but nothing came out. Her body betrayed her rational mind, and she nodded. In a second, Jesse was kissing her fiercely. The taste, feel, and adoration she missed came rushing back. She opened her mouth and invited Jesse in. And when their tongues touched, Eloise whimpered. Passion couldn't blind her to reality: this was a very bad idea.

Eloise balled the front of Jesse's sexy white shirt into her hands. She whimpered again, but this time she fought her inner voice. Eloise's mind went into a tailspin when Jesse put her hands on her hips. But then, suddenly, all apprehension fell away. Eloise's sole focus became control and getting what she wanted.

She pressed her pelvis into Jesse's, their height difference making it hard for her to meet every place on Jesse's body she wanted to, but Jesse knew how to put Eloise's petite build to good use. Eloise didn't miss a beat when Jesse gripped her behind and encouraged her to jump and wrap her legs around Jesse's waist. Jesse put her on the countertop, and she kept her legs tightly around Jesse.

Eloise felt herself being engulfed by flames. Jesse's mouth was everywhere at once—her neck and throat, her jaw and chin—and with a pull to the collar of her sweater, Jesse started kissing and nipping along Eloise's chest. She dropped her head back and moaned when Jesse's tongue teased her cleavage. She ran her fingers through Jesse's messy thick hair, down the back of her head, and scratched her neck. Feeling her nails dig into Jesse's flesh only turned Eloise on more.

"Take me to bed," she said in a low, demanding tone. She was no longer the woman who asked for what she wanted. Tonight with Jesse was about demanding. "Now."

Jesse picked her up with a low grunt and carried her to the bedroom. Eloise clung to Jesse's shoulders as they awkwardly fell onto the bed. The weight of Jesse atop her filled her every sense. Jesse leaned back on her knees and stared down at Eloise.

Her heart was beating with a force only Jesse ever brought out. "What?"

"I missed you."

Eloise didn't want to hear that. She didn't want to think about the emotions that brought her to this moment. She wanted to *feel*. Eloise took Jesse's hand from its perch on her knee and slowly drew it down her thigh. When she reached her apex, she could feel Jesse's hesitance. She showed Jesse exactly what she wanted by pressing her hand harder into herself. She canted her hips, spreading her arousal, and the friction against her clit started to drive Eloise crazy. Heat crept up her neck as she pushed her head back into the mattress.

Jesse finally moved, cupping Eloise firmly and leaning back down to kiss her. Eloise's first instinct was to bite Jesse's bottom lip hard enough to draw out a gasp. "Harder," Eloise said.

Jesse replaced her hand with her thigh and started moving her hips with hurried, firm motions. Eloise could tell Jesse was finding her own pleasure against Eloise by the change in her breathing. Eloise knew she could come easily and quickly, but that wasn't what her body needed. She needed to feel *everything* one more time.

"Stop," she said.

Jesse pulled back immediately and looked worried. "Are you okay? Did I hurt you?"

Eloise shook her head. "I want your skin."

Jesse kissed her firmly before stripping off her clothing. Every dip and valley was exactly where Eloise remembered it, which seemed a foolish thought. Only a few months had passed. Nothing about Jesse's body should be different, and yet Eloise expected to see a stranger before her. The curls between Jesse's legs caught Eloise's attention. Jesse wasn't perfectly groomed, and that brought great satisfaction to Eloise because she knew Jesse wasn't getting laid regularly.

Jesse reached for the button of Eloise's jeans. "May I?"

Eloise unbuttoned her own jeans and slid them from her full hips. She wanted to remind Jesse she could be in control, too. She pulled off her sweater and camisole next, leaving her in mismatched bra and panties. Her red thong was all about a New Year's superstition, while her floral demi bra made her feel sexy. The way Jesse looked at her caused her pussy to clench. No lover had ever made Eloise feel this wanted. Jesse had a way of devouring her with her eyes, hands, and lips.

Jesse wasted no time exploring Eloise's newly revealed skin with her mouth. Eloise moaned, loving the feel of Jesse's tongue just inside the cup of her bra, barely grazing her sensitive nipple. To her surprise and pleasure, Jesse bit the swell of her breast.

Eloise's eyes flew open, and she looked at the very satisfied smirk on Jesse's face. She looked down at Jesse's hands against her skin as she removed her thong. Jesse had the best hands, not feminine or masculine, but the right combination of rough strength and gentle reverence. Jesse leaned back onto her knees again, this time hooking her hands under Eloise's knees. Eloise moaned when Jesse pulled her closer in order to press into her. The feel of Jesse's rough hair against her most delicate, wet skin was intoxicating.

"What do you want?" Jesse's voice was a low growl.

"Fuck me," Eloise said without hesitation. "I want you to fuck me."

Jesse pushed her hips forward. "Like this?" Jesse gripped the pillow beside Eloise's head and caressed Eloise's sternum. She pushed forward again and again, establishing a rhythm, only to stop and leave the bed abruptly. Jesse went to the closet and returned with a harness, already adorned with a six-inch dildo. "Or like this?"

Eloise shivered, looking at Jesse standing completely naked, holding the toy that had given her many hours of pleasure. Jesse's body was exquisite. She had tone and muscle throughout her upper body, a few veins popped on her forearms, and her breasts were small with delightfully dark nipples. Jesse's hips and thighs were soft, the kind Eloise loved to be between.

Eloise's throat was so dry and tight with desire that she wasn't sure she'd be able to speak. "Please," she said, only managing the one word before she fell back onto the bed and spread her legs. She kept her eyes closed and listened to Jesse moving around. Her pulse started to race as she heard Jesse putting the harness on. It looked like a simple pair of briefs, but it was capable of so much more. The mattress dipped, and Eloise took a deep breath in anticipation. She squeezed her eyes shut, feeding off her other senses to heighten her pleasure.

"You're so wet," Jesse said against the inside of her knee. Jesse kissed her inner thigh and licked a long line down, stopping just before she reached the target.

Eloise whimpered, "Oh my God." She could feel Jesse panting against the bare skin between her thighs. She finally opened her eyes, locking with Jesse's just as she swiped her tongue along Eloise's pulsing labia. "Oh fuck."

Jesse circled her clit with the tip of her tongue for what felt like forever, keeping the pressure maddeningly light. Just as she was about to yell at Jesse for more, Jesse pressed a fingertip into Eloise's entrance. Eloise moved her hips the best she could in an attempt to draw Jesse deeper.

"Patience," Jesse said. She sucked her clit between her lips and released it with a pop.

Eloise couldn't comprehend patience, and she surely didn't want to give Jesse the upper hand. She grabbed as much of Jesse's short hair as she could and pulled Jesse up. "I told you I want you to fuck me. No teasing." Eloise slid her hand down and wrapped it around Jesse's throat. She applied slight pressure and watched the way Jesse's eyes changed. Jesse, all buttoned-up and cautious during the day, loved being handled roughly in the bedroom. Giving as good as she got, Jesse pulled back and spread Eloise's legs farther apart with force, drawing a low keen from Eloise when she dug her strong fingers into her flesh.

Jesse licked her fingers and rubbed them over the head of the dildo. Smoothly, she leaned herself forward and lined up with Eloise. Jesse never looked away from Eloise's eyes as she entered her, deeper and deeper until their bodies were flush.

"Don't move," she said, digging her nails into Jesse's hips. The burning stretch to adjust would've been painful if it didn't feel so damn good. She released Jesse just enough to allow shallow thrusts. Eloise lost herself to everything, Jesse's lips on the side of her neck and feeling so full. "More."

Jesse sped up her movements, alternating between deep thrusts and teasing Eloise with just the tip before sinking all the way in again. Jesse's ability to multitask made her an extraordinary lover, the best Eloise ever had. Jesse bit her collarbone and palmed her breast, flexing her left arm as it held her weight.

Eloise kissed Jesse's ear before pushing her shoulders until Jesse understood her direction and flipped over onto her back. Eloise licked a line down Jesse's sternum and straddled her lap. She rocked back and forth, letting the friction of the dildo bring her closer to orgasm. But this wasn't how she wanted to come. Eloise opened Jesse's nightstand drawer and found the small bullet vibrator, smiling as she pushed the button, and the toy came to life. She pulled back the waistband of the harness and put the vibrator in place against Jesse's clit. Jesse bucked but remained silent. Eloise positioned herself above the dildo, still slick with her arousal, and lowered herself slowly. Feeling so deeply touched almost brought tears to her eyes.

"Shit," Jesse said, hissing out the word.

She started moving back and forth, grinding on Jesse to create the perfect pleasure for both of them. Her movements were precise and controlled, until her legs began to shake and Jesse tightened her grip on Eloise's thighs. Eloise fell forward and started panting, her hands on Jesse's chest.

Jesse's legs went rigid beneath her, and she started pushing and pulling at Eloise's hips. They both started to lose control. Eloise curled her fingers and scratched across Jesse's chest. She held both of Jesse's small breasts as she came loudly, screaming obscenities into the night. Jesse let out soft noises as she came next, burying her head back into a pillow.

Eloise withdrew the dildo and fell atop Jesse, a pile of useless limbs. Her breathing didn't return to normal before her eyes closed and she drifted off.

Chapter Thirty-three

Jesse missed the feeling of sleeping with someone. Well, not just anyone—Eloise. She missed Eloise's scent and the feel of their skin touching at all points. She missed the way Eloise would teeter between too hot and too cold but hog the blankets either way. She adored the unintelligible words Eloise would mutter, and she felt whole now that they were spoken into her ear once again. She lay in the moonlight and watched Eloise sleep. After a drowsy and clumsy dismount, Jesse removed the harness and dildo and slipped between the covers, ecstatic when Eloise sought her out in her sleepy state. Now they were in one another's arms, Jesse caressing Eloise's addictively soft skin.

She noticed Eloise's long lashes twitch. What was Eloise dreaming? Was she happy? Could she be dreaming of Jesse the same way Jesse had dreamed of her for so many nights? Jesse's mind wouldn't stop. She looked out the window and noticed the sky starting to come to life, the black turning to blue. She had dozens of questions, but the most important was what she could make Eloise for breakfast. Jesse kissed Eloise's forehead and smiled when Eloise tightened her arm around her. She planned on making the perfect breakfast in bed with all of Eloise's favorites, and if Eloise ended up too full to go anywhere and they had to spend the whole day together, oh well.

She had a fresh loaf of multigrain bread that'd toast perfectly and all the ingredients for a variety of omelets and pancakes. Today was the fresh start she had been hoping for, the one she didn't dare allow herself to believe in before.

Eloise started to stir, mumbling nonsensical words as she turned to stretch. She smacked her lips together after a big yawn and opened one eye. Eloise looked at Jesse in confusion. "What time is it?"

"A little after six if I had to guess," she said. Jesse felt like completely soft mush just from watching Eloise wake up, no matter how disgruntled she seemed.

"Ugh. I hate being programmed to wake up early."

"I get it. I'll forever be on teacher time."

Eloise looked around. "I guess I should get going."

"What?" Jesse pulled back as if slapped. "What do you mean?"

"I should go," Eloise said again without even looking at Jesse as she got out of bed and started picking her clothes up off the floor. She was almost fully dressed before Jesse could think of what to say next.

"I figured you'd stay," she said dumbly. "We could spend the day together, like you pictured, and maybe talk a bit."

"There's nothing to really talk about, Jesse. I think we both said our piece, and now it's time for me to go home."

"But last night—"

"Was fun. Last night was fun, and I think we both needed it."

"But you…" Jesse couldn't collect her thoughts quickly enough. "What about everything you said? Everything you wanted?"

"I thought I wanted this. I thought I wanted us." Eloise collected the last of her things, including her jacket. She finally looked at Jesse, who had yet to move from bed. "But I realized that *this*"—she pointed between them—"isn't what I ever thought it was."

"Last night you said—"

"I was upset, had a few drinks, and felt really lonely. It got to me."

Jesse's nostrils flared. "You said you came back to try again," she said, her voice cracking slightly. "You said you never stopped thinking about me and that we were worth it."

Eloise bit her lower lip. "I can't. I'm sorry."

Jesse got up and wrapped the covers around her body. She walked over to Eloise slowly, trying to find a hint of anything in Eloise's eyes. They were dark and cold. "Why?" She stood within inches of Eloise. "Why can't you?"

"Because you're not being honest with me. I don't even think you're being honest with yourself." Jesse wanted to argue, but Eloise kept talking. "You haven't changed, which means nothing else has either. I can't knowingly put myself in a position where you'll hurt me again."

"I won't."

Eloise started to cry, but she forced a smile through the tears. She placed her palm against Jesse's cheek and said, "I can't believe you." Eloise turned and left.

Jesse was left alone and speechless. What could she even say to keep Eloise from leaving? The sound of the front door closing nearly echoed in her quiet home. Jesse sat on the foot of her bed and stared at the wall in disbelief. The past twenty-four hours had dragged her through every emotion, and what did she have to show for it? An aching, bitter heart. She lay back and closed her eyes.

"I didn't really know where else to go." Eloise stood in the cold.

Billie looked at her sleepily, her dark brows knitting tightly together as if she was solving a riddle. "You came here?" Billie tightened the sash of her robe and opened the door farther. "Come in."

"I'm really so sorry." Eloise barely moved once the door was shut behind her. "I didn't wake you guys, did I?"

"Leah sleeps like the dead," Billie said, waving her concern away. "Do you want coffee or anything?" Billie started to sound more awake. "I'll probably make pancakes and stuff."

"If you're having coffee, I'll have some." Eloise stood awkwardly just inside Billie's living room. She didn't want to take up space or time or Billie's food. "But only if you're having some."

"I'm almost always drinking coffee." Billie looked at her up and down, oddly. "What's going on? What's wrong?"

Eloise's first instinct was to play it cool and come up with some believable excuse as to why she'd show up on Billie's doorstep at seven in the morning in the same clothes as the night before. "I had a terrible night, and I just didn't want to go home. Not yet."

"Come on," Billie said, leading Eloise to the kitchen. She started putzing around and prepping the percolator. Eloise smiled at the coffee maker, remembering all the holidays she'd spent with Billie's family and the long dessert chats complemented by percolated coffee.

"I guess one tradition never died," she said, pointing.

Billie laughed. "Percolator coffee just tastes better. I've tried it all, and the only other one that compares is French press, but I don't have time for that."

"Who does?"

Billie smirked. "French people."

Eloise let out a laugh and then covered her mouth immediately. She moved her hand away and mouthed an apology. "I'll feel awful if I wake Leah up."

"You don't have to whisper," Billie said with a chuckle. "Our bedroom is upstairs on the other side of the house. You're good."

Eloise relaxed.

"Can I make you breakfast? I've basically mastered the omelet."

"Oh? The person who burned every scrambled egg she ever tried to make?" She leaned forward, placing her elbows on the cold granite countertop. "You really have grown up."

"That was high school. So shut up and tell me if you want a damn omelet." Billie gathered the necessary bowls and pans. "I can do veggies and cheese, just cheese, or something with bacon if you'd prefer."

Eloise covered her growling stomach. "Veggies and cheese would be great." She was always hungry, rarely full, and emotional turmoil never turned her away from food. "How big of an omelet are we talking?"

"Big enough, I promise." Billie turned her back to Eloise and started working on their breakfast. "Do you want to talk about it?"

Eloise didn't know if Billie turned away on purpose or not, but she was grateful for the privacy to consider her next words. "I know Jesse's your best friend, and your family—"

"You were my first best friend, Ellie, and time didn't make that go away. You can talk to me about anything."

Eloise didn't even fully realize how much she'd missed Billie until that very moment. She started to fidget with her fingers. "You're one of the only people who knows about us, so I didn't know where else to go," she said and then stopped suddenly. "And you've always been the softest when you put me in my place." She watched Billie's shoulders shake with laughter. The lovely smell of sizzling greens started to fill the kitchen. "I don't think Jesse's being honest with me, and it's really fucked me up." Billie kept cooking and didn't say a word. "We didn't tell anyone we were together. At first, that was a mutual decision because we weren't sure about how you would feel, but then it became exclusively about her."

Billie grabbed a loaf of bread from the cabinet and turned to look at Eloise. "You know I wouldn't have cared, right? I was shocked initially, but I didn't freak out or anything."

"I know. At first it was kind of fun, the sneaking around and it being a dirty little secret."

"What happened?"

"It started to just feel dirty." Eloise kept her head down until she felt Billie go back to cooking. "She says it's because of our age and how she was my teacher. She thinks everyone will give us grief."

Billie cracked an egg. "She told me the same thing."

"I think it's bullshit."

"I was wondering whose voice that was," Leah said as she entered the kitchen. Her hair was sleep tousled and she wore a silk robe that covered just to her knee. "Good morning, Eloise." Leah padded over to Billie and kissed her cheek. "Good morning, love."

Eloise noticed the ring on Leah's finger immediately. "Oh my God." She stared at them with an open mouth. "Oh my God," she said again and pointed.

Billie smiled. "What is it, Ellie? Use your words."

Eloise had no time for the teasing. "You're engaged! When did this happen?" She slid off her stool and rushed over to hug them both at the same time. "I'm so happy for you."

"Last night," Billie said, looking at Leah with soft, love-filled eyes. "At midnight. Very clichéd, but what can you do?"

"It was perfect." Leah kissed Billie's cheek again, and again and again.

"Babe, Eloise came here from Jesse's."

Leah froze midkiss and turned to Eloise slowly. "Oh, shit."

She started to blush from the awkward attention. "Yeah."

"Can you grab me a whisk?" Billie said to Leah. Eloise took the opportunity to go back to her safe place on a stool. Billie caught Leah up as best she could before bringing the attention back to Eloise. "Why do you think it's bullshit?"

"Because she's Jesse," Eloise said without thought. "She stands up, she never backs down, and she rarely allows fear to dictate her life."

"She is right," Leah said, grabbing a piece of asparagus from the pan.

Billie swatted Leah's hand away. "But she's also Jesse," Billie said with no explanation. Leah and Eloise just looked at her expectantly.

Eloise was too tired and too hungry to have the patience required to break Billie's code. "That's what I said. You can't say what I said as an argument to what I said." Eloise was pretty sure that made sense.

"Jesse is easily the bravest person I know, but she's also the biggest scaredy-cat." Billie poured the eggs into the hot pan. The sizzling sounded loud as everyone waited for more. "Jesse also wants to avoid personal confrontation at all costs and will always try to do what's right, even if it means sacrificing herself."

Eloise scoffed. "You're making her sound like a saint when all she's doing is hurting me."

"And herself," Billie said with her eyes trained on the eggs. "I guess I'm actually agreeing with you. I don't think those are her real reasons, but I don't think she's lying either, and you're not going to find out for sure unless you talk to her."

"I've tried talking."

"Maybe give her some more time," Leah said.

"I gave her months this summer." A rush went through Eloise's body. "And I gave her last night." She lost herself in the brief memory of being touched with the kind of care only Jesse was capable of. When she snapped out of it, Billie was standing in front of her with a plate.

"I hope you're hungry."

Eloise sighed. "Starving."

CHAPTER THIRTY-FOUR

Jesse liked to keep to herself, for the most part. If she was struggling or in the midst of a tough decision, she let it marinate. None of her friends, close or not, would know about it. Jesse didn't want input, and she didn't want to feel herself being swayed by someone else's opinion. The only time she felt ready for feedback was when she knew her gut was already sure. Or if she was completely lost.

"I'm completely lost," she said to Liv over the phone, "and I don't know why." She tried to juggle the device between her head and shoulder as she washed the dishes.

"Because you love her."

"Well, yeah, but I've been in love before. None of this is new."

"Isn't it?"

Jesse stared out the window at a bright cardinal feeding. "I don't know about that." She didn't know where this new compulsion to lie came from. "Being in love is being in love."

Liv snorted. "Wow. Do you really believe that? Being in love with Eloise is the same as what you had with Stacy?"

Jesse dropped a handful of silverware, and the loud crash echoed. Eloise was nothing like Stacy. "I didn't expect her to just leave this morning."

"Why not?" Jesse could hear Theo's mumbling in the background. "Do you need to go?"

"No, just give me a minute." Liv's phone went oddly quiet. She must've muted herself.

Jesse continued with the dishes and started wiping down the

countertop. Liv finally came back a few minutes later, sounding like she was midlaughter. "You good?" Jesse said.

Liv took a deep breath. "Yeah. You should come over."

Jesse looked around at the mess surrounding her. "No way."

"Come on. Are you doing something better?"

"Yes?" Jesse cursed herself for the inflection.

"What're you doing right now?"

"Cleaning."

"Cleaning?"

"Yes, cleaning. This place is a mess after last night." Jesse started breaking down the chafing dishes. "I don't know if I'll do this again next year."

"Yeah, right. You love your parties just as much as the guests do." Liv's voice went muffled for a second before she came back. "Anyway, come over. Theo isn't taking no for an answer, and neither will I. The mess will be there when you get back."

"The whole point is to not have a mess at all."

"Come on. You know you want to."

Jesse started to feel persuaded but didn't want to give in that easily. "I won't be very good company."

"You always are. Please, let us make you feel better. After all, I feel like I still owe you for Christmas Eve."

Jesse chuckled. "All I need in return is a promise you won't do any rhyming if I come over."

"Easy promise. So, is that a yes?"

Jesse considered the mess surrounding her and realized it wasn't all that bad. "Fine. But I need a shower, so I won't be there for about an hour."

"Deal. See you then." Liv hung up.

"Pushy," Jesse said to her phone.

She walked into her bedroom and felt a pang of sadness at the sight of the unmade bed. She hadn't been back there since Eloise left. She only called Liv because her constant train of pitiful thoughts was getting annoying. She couldn't come up with a solution or any idea for her next move. Hell, she couldn't even figure out if she should have a next move at all when it came to Eloise. Normally Jesse was the sure and certain one, but in this situation she was a scrambled mess.

She hoped spending time with Liv and Theo would help put her back together, or at the very least gather her into one pile.

Jesse started to make the bed, thinking it would help put a lid on her feelings about last night, but the shift of the covers wafted Eloise's scent into her nose. Jesse dropped the comforter and backed away, treating it like a ticking bomb counting down from three. She shook her head and turned her attention to the dresser. She'd pour all her brainpower into picking out an outfit for the day, something comfortable but appropriate for a day out. She decided on a hoodie and cargo joggers. When she closed the top drawer of her dresser, she noticed a hair band sitting atop it. Jesse picked it up and twirled it around her finger. Jesse knew she should resist, but she never claimed to be strong.

She held the elastic up to her nose and felt weak at the faint scent of Eloise still clinging to it. She put it back down and refocused her energy.

"Stop being weird and take a damn shower." She looked around. "Like talking to yourself isn't making this whole thing weirder." Jesse walked directly into the bathroom, no longer trusting herself to stay on task.

She showered quickly and ignored the urge to only cleanse the parts of her Eloise hadn't marked. Every minute she felt more frustrated with herself. Why now, all of a sudden, was she acting like an infatuated teenager? None of this behavior was normal or acceptable for a forty-one-year-old person. She scrubbed her face harder and then rinsed off. Dressing quickly, she grabbed her phone on the way out but then paused. She felt like she was forgetting something. She rushed back, pulled the hair band onto her wrist, and finally left the house.

The drive to Liv and Theo's was a short, very silent twenty minutes. Jesse was afraid of music because she'd undoubtedly associate every song with Eloise. She jogged up the walkway, rang the bell, and shook off the cold. Why she'd opted to leave her coat behind was beyond her. "Butch problems," she grumbled to herself.

Liv swung the door open. "I tell you every time to just walk in."

"And I tell *you* every time that it's not my style." Jesse stepped in and removed her shoes immediately. "Hey, Oliver." The cat stared back, tilting his head minutely. "Good to see you, too."

"Coffee?" Liv continued into the house, and Jesse followed.

"Please," she said, rubbing her hands together. "I think I'm going to get a cat."

"Best decision you've ever made."

Theo popped her head out of the kitchen. "When did you decide this?"

Jesse pulled back slightly. "Just now, why?"

"Think about it longer. Cats can be assholes."

Liv cracked up. "Oliver wouldn't stop pawing at our bedroom doorknob last night. Theo barely got any sleep. Can you tell?"

Jesse bit her tongue and smiled. "Couch?"

Liv nodded. "I'll be right in with coffee."

Jesse relaxed in her favorite spot in the corner of the sofa. She examined the Christmas tree, shaking her head while thinking of how her Christmas unfolded. Every holiday this season, actually. She noticed all the rolled-up wishes were gone.

"Disgusting black coffee for you," Liv said as she handed Jesse a big steaming mug. "And deliciously light and sweet for me." She sat across from Jesse in the chair and took a slow sip of her coffee. "Now, do you want to tell me what happened last night?"

Jesse opened her mouth and almost spilled it all to Liv, but she caught herself. "Not really, no."

"You can't keep doing this."

"Doing what?"

Theo joined them, sitting on the opposite side of the couch. "You're constantly holding everything in, Jesse. You were seeing Eloise in secret, you two struggled in secret, and then you kept your heartbreak all to yourself. It's not healthy." Theo drank her tea.

She grew defensive. "I don't have to talk about everything."

Theo nodded. "You're right, you don't. But you should try to talk about *something*. At the very least, what happened last night."

Jesse let out a long breath. Imagining the action somehow made her feel ready. "On Christmas, I invited Eloise to my New Year's Eve party. We were stuck standing together, and it was so awkward. One thing led to another, and I invited her. As soon as I did, I knew it was a mistake, but…"

Liv leaned forward. "But what?"

Jesse couldn't fight a small smile. "She seemed so happy to be invited."

"And that made you happy?"

She remembered the feeling vividly. "It did."

"I have to ask you, bud," Liv said, pausing for another sip of coffee. "Did you want to see her again? At all?"

Jesse took her time considering her answer. She took the first drink of her coffee and let it sink all the way in. She hoped the caffeine would help with the buzzing headache she'd had all morning. She dropped her shoulders and finally admitted defeat. It was time to confide fully in her friends. "I always wanted to see her again. I've missed her every day since we split."

Theo reached across the sofa to squeeze Jesse's shoulder. "And why did you two split?"

Even though Jesse was positive Liv had already filled Theo in, she played along. "There was too much stacked against us. It would've never lasted." She could hear Eloise's voice in her head calling her a liar.

"Do you think it would've if you'd actually tried?" Liv said, cut, dried, and to the point as usual.

"I tried."

"Jesse?" Theo said.

"Yeah?"

"What was stacked against you?"

She grew so tired of stating her case over and over. "Age, society, our little town alone, our differences. Everything."

Theo bobbed her head side to side. "How old is Eloise again?"

Jesse swallowed another mouthful of hot coffee, enjoying the slight burn as it traveled down her throat. "Twenty-nine." Theo hummed as she drank. "See? Those are the reactions I want to avoid."

Liv sat back and crossed her legs. "Does the age difference really bother you that much?"

"I wasn't reacting to the difference," Theo said, returning to her own corner of the couch. "I was trying to see your perspective, but I'm having a hard time. You don't look twelve years older. Hell, you barely look older at all. Who will know?"

"My friends—"

"Spoiler alert," Liv said, pointing at Jesse with a cocky smile. "We already know."

"My family." Jesse grimaced, thinking about her disastrous Thanksgiving. "Never mind. They know now, too."

"Can I ask you another question?" Theo's voice was so gentle it actually made Jesse nervous.

"Sure."

Theo swiveled on the sofa to give Jesse her undivided attention. "What made you fall in love with Eloise?"

Jesse was shaken by the unexpected question. "I, uh..." She cleared her throat. Her mind threw at least a hundred reasons to the forefront to choose from, but the loudest of them all was a memory of that first night at the bar. "Her warmth," she said. She looked between Liv and Theo, and for the first time she was eager to talk about Eloise. "I went to Sylvia's alone one night over the summer. It was right after my breakup when I wasn't feeling very good about myself. I just wanted to be social and feel like maybe..." She laughed at herself. "I wanted to know if I still had it."

Liv raised one eyebrow. "Do you?"

"I thought all hope was lost until Eloise walked through the door. I was sitting at the bar with my back to everyone, drowning my sorrows in bourbon too expensive for its own good, when someone tapped me on my shoulder." Jesse felt the same breathlessness she had that day. "She was grinning when I turned around, like seeing me absolutely made her day. She sat next to me and started talking about everything and anything and nothing all at once. She was waiting for a date that never showed up. Call it fate or whatever, but I laughed more that day than I had in a while." Jesse looked into her coffee cup at her faint reflection in the dark surface. "Eloise made me feel okay."

"And it's safe to assume you were attracted to her?"

Jesse looked at Liv like she just asked what color the sky was. "Have you seen Eloise?"

"Don't answer that," Theo said firmly as Jesse laughed.

Liv's phone chimed, and she checked it. She typed away for a minute before turning her attention back to Jesse. "You'd want to fix it, right? Have a second chance with Eloise?"

"That ship sailed," Jesse said, feeling sadder each time she admitted it. "I had last night with her, and I'm lucky I even got that."

"But *if* you could have a second chance, would you take it?"

Jesse didn't have to think long or hard before answering. "Absolutely."

"Great," Liv said, slapping her knee. She got up and walked straight to the front door and opened it. "Come on in."

Jesse felt time morph into slow motion as Billie and Eloise, dressed in the same clothes from the morning, walked through the door. Judging by the look on Eloise's face, she was just as surprised as Jesse.

CHAPTER THIRTY-FIVE

"What's going on?" Jesse shared her most threatening look between Liv and Billie. "What are you doing?"

Eloise crossed her arms over her chest and looked at everyone but Jesse. "I'd like to know the same thing."

"We read all the wishes from the tree," Liv said with her hands pressed together. She looked like she was praying and not dancing around Jesse's question. "I know that's probably a little messed up."

"And a little bit of an invasion of privacy," Eloise said.

"Is it, though?" Liv's voice went high-pitched. "Really? We're all basically family, which means very few wishes were a surprise. Tammy wished for Jason Momoa, Terri wished for more quality time with Todd, Todd wished for golf clubs, and I burned Rich's wish before we could read it. What did you really expect us to do?"

Jesse couldn't believe it. "I expected you not to read my wish!"

"You hung it on *my* tree!"

Jesse blew out a loud breath through her nose, trying to control her temper. "I hung it on your tree as a tradition, not as a confessional."

"At the very least, you should tell people you're going to read them before you convince them to share," Eloise said, sounding much calmer than Jesse.

"At the very least," Jesse said, feeling the need to emphasize Eloise's point.

Liv looked at Theo, and when no support came, she started to look mildly scared. "Look, that's not the point here. The point is I want you to read each other's wishes."

"Not only do you read them over coffee with your wife, but now you want us to share with the class?" Finally finding the strength in her legs, Jesse stood and held her hands up in surrender. "You know what? I'm done with this. I'm out of here." She started for the door, but Liv stopped her in her tracks.

"Happiness," Liv said loudly and quickly.

Jesse felt her cheeks warm. "That's not cool—"

"What's wrong with my wish?" Eloise said.

Liv's smile was much too satisfied for Jesse's liking. "Nothing's wrong with either of your wishes. Actually, some would argue that there's a whole lot right when a couple wishes for the exact same thing."

Eloise looked confused, but stood tense. "We're not a couple."

"We wished for the same thing?" Jesse kept her eyes on Liv now, waiting to see if her friend was trying any tricks.

Liv held up two small pieces of creased paper. "Same exact wish, written the same exact way. Except Eloise's handwriting is much neater."

Jesse's head swam with a million thoughts and questions, and the only person who could make sense of it stood by the door, poised to run at any moment. Eloise had always been the key. "Eloise?"

"Everyone wishes for happiness," Eloise said, still sounding cold and distant.

Jesse knew the kind of sadness that drove her to write that wish, and she couldn't bear the thought of Eloise carrying the same weight. She stepped close to Eloise, slowly and cautiously, and waited until they were only a foot apart. "I'm so sorry."

"I'm going to go," Billie said awkwardly.

"Us, too," Theo said from behind Jesse. "Come on, Liv. I'd like to go out for an early lunch."

"Wait," Jesse said, looking back. "This is your house. We'll go." She looked back at Eloise, hopeful that she seemed open to the idea.

"No, no. We insist. You still have coffee, and there's more in the kitchen if you'd like a cup, Eloise." Theo was already bundled up from head to toe, pushing Liv toward the door. "Talk it out, and we'll see you guys later." Liv walked by Jesse and placed the wishes in her hand.

In seconds the door shut, and Jesse was alone again with Eloise. She wouldn't make the same mistake with this chance. "I love you," she said abruptly. She watched Eloise's defenses drop for a second. Risking it all, Jesse continued. "I love you, and I don't think I realized how much until this past week."

"It's too late."

"What were you thinking about when you wrote this?" She held up Eloise's wish.

Eloise wouldn't look at the paper. "Just life," she said unconvincingly.

"I thought about you," Jesse said, undeterred by Eloise's stiffness. "I thought about the emptiness I haven't been able to shake since you left. I thought about how every day lacked and lagged." She swallowed hard and tried to make sense of the many thoughts clamoring in her head for attention. "We were so happy together, weren't we?"

Eloise's eyes were softer now. "We were."

"Then let's find a way back to that."

"Please stop, Jesse. We can't. It's too late, and I've been hurt too much by all of this."

"Believe me when I say I am so sorry for everything," Jesse said, reaching for Eloise's hand.

Eloise pulled back. "I do believe you're sorry. It's everything else I don't believe."

"And you were right about all of it, except I never lied to you. It's very important to me you believe that." Jesse tried for Eloise's hand again, happy when Eloise allowed the touch. "I found a hundred outside reasons to blame for my fear when all of it was just me. I was too afraid."

"Of what, though? If not all those things, what were you so afraid of?"

"You."

Eloise dropped Jesse's hand and started to walk away. "I can't do this—"

"Do you know what fear can do to a person?" She paused but didn't give Eloise enough time to answer. "It paralyzes you. It speaks so loudly in the middle of the night when you can't sleep. It screams about every terrifying possibility and makes them seem so real."

"There's no reason for you to be scared of me."

She let out a brief laugh, no more than a release of air. "Isn't there? Eloise, you have no idea what you've done to me."

"What about what you've done to me, huh? First, you string me along for months—"

"That's not what I'm talking about." She knew her eyes were wet, and her heart was hammering in her chest. "I fell for you so hard and so fast—it scared the shit out of me. When I was with you, I believed in love. Everything I never had. So easily." She swallowed hard to tamp down her rising emotion. "In a minute, in a simple hello between acquaintances, everything changed. But the weak moments started to win. I thought about how I wasn't good enough for you, or I was too old and not good-looking enough."

"Why didn't you talk to me? I would've told you how wrong you were."

"And risk scaring you away?"

"You *pushed* me away instead."

"I was completely lost in you. The love I have is overwhelming and blinding, and I have never felt that before, so when all these fears and these thoughts came creeping in..." Jesse couldn't finish her sentence, too distracted by the itching in her palm, begging for her to reach out and touch Eloise more.

"What? What happened?"

"I believed every last one of them. I was made to believe I didn't deserve to be happy. How was I ever going to keep you? How was I ever going to be good enough?"

"You let that negativity in when you should've been grateful for the moment. You should've felt all the positives we had."

"I know that now, and I am so sorry," she said earnestly. "I need you to believe me when I say I get it now. It's like I'm finally awake." Jesse looked at Eloise, noticing every closed-off nuance in her behavior and stance. The sick, spiraling feeling she had grown so used to over the months grew stronger. Eloise turned away. "Eloise, please."

"You have no idea," Eloise said, no longer moving away but not turning back. "You hold so much power, and you have no idea."

"Power?" Jesse scoffed. "The only reason we're here right now is because I'm weak."

"You only believe that because it's what Stacy told you. It's not true." Eloise twisted her fingers together and looked everywhere but back at Jesse. "I never told you this, but after that night at the bar, I went home and deleted my dating profile."

Jesse shook her head, momentarily confused. "You did? Because of me?"

"No. Well, yes. Kind of. We hit it off, that much was obvious to anyone around us. But it was the natural chemistry that convinced me. Even if you never called me, I knew I wanted the old-fashioned feeling of meeting someone when I least expected it."

"I know I wasn't expecting to meet anyone that night."

"I wasn't expecting to meet you." Eloise looked at the door. Silence stretched on, deafening and awkward.

"My ex called me that night." Jesse started to pick at a callus on her palm, the one that would never go away. "She always had impeccable timing."

"What did she say?"

Jesse shrugged. "I don't know because for the first time, I didn't pick up. She left a voice mail, but I deleted it right away."

"Why?"

"Because I didn't care anymore. I wasn't afraid of making her angry or that she'd show up and demand answers from me." A revelation hit her. "You reminded me of who I am, not the beaten-down version she created." Eloise's eyebrows rose, just a little, the way they always did when she was feeling so much more than she was saying. "I've been handled with kid gloves by everyone since my split. But not you."

"Why would they?"

"Because they didn't know the truth. I only ever told you about the control and the anger. Everyone else thought we were happy. Everyone else thought she broke my heart." So much, maybe even too much, started to make sense. "Only you knew she actually broke *me*."

"Jesse…"

She cleared her throat and regained some of her composure. "But this isn't about her. This is about us. Now you know everything, and I would like to know if you thought of me when you made your wish."

Eloise's nod was so subtle Jesse nearly missed it. "I hated Baltimore," Eloise said abruptly. "I hated it because I knew you would love it. I stopped feeling like myself. I felt anxious and unwound, and it was all because of you. I couldn't sleep without you, and I couldn't stop thinking about you. Do you remember when we traveled south and found that incredible café in Little Egg Harbor?"

Jesse head was spinning at the odd direction Eloise's confession took. "Of course. It was the first café I found that offered decaf cappuccino and oat milk."

Eloise smiled at her. "You didn't pick on me for ordering one of every baked good they offered, and you let me dissect them later in our hotel room."

"That was one of our first weekends away. We stayed at that gorgeous hotel in Galloway with the golf course."

"Mm-hmm."

Jesse tried to put it all together but didn't understand. "What about it?"

"I started to realize then that nursing might not be for me. You helped me without even realizing it, but then I had to run away from you in order to survive heartbreak. I have never felt so lost in my life."

Jesse wanted to apologize for the millionth time, but Eloise wasn't done yet.

"I was completely dismantled because of you, and I don't know how to get past that."

"What do you want?" Jesse said, hoping to keep Eloise partially in the past, their happy past. "Imagine the perfect life starting tomorrow. What does it look like?"

Eloise shifted, clearly hesitant to play along, but Jesse could tell she was thinking. "I take over the bakery full-time and let my mom rest, which will give me full creative control."

"I think you should do it," she said, stepping even closer to Eloise. "What else?"

"I rebuild my relationship with Billie. I really missed her."

"She would love that."

"Would you be okay with that?"

Jesse read between the lines and dared to feel hopeful. "She can come over for Sunday dinner every week."

"What about our age difference?"

"You're the one stuck with an old lady."

"Shut up," Eloise said, slapping Jesse's arm. Eloise gasped slightly when Jesse caught and held her hand. "I was your student."

Jesse held Eloise's hand to her chest. "And I was your teacher. It's another part of our story, and I happen to love our story."

Eloise took a deep breath and started to fidget with the string of Jesse's hoodie. "I can't let you hurt me again."

"I won't."

"You can't promise that."

"Yes, I can. I've watched almost everyone around me struggle over the past few weeks, whether with themselves or their relationships, and it all helped me realize something." She brought Eloise's hand to her cheek. "Hurting you is my biggest regret, and having you in my life again is my greatest wish."

Eloise's eyes filled with heavy tears. "Happiness."

"You were always my happiness. I'm sorry it took me this long to realize it."

Eloise shook away the tears and sniffled. She cringed and said, "I really need to shower and change."

"How about this? I drive you home for a change of clothes, and then we go back to my place. I know how much you love my shower."

"You do have great water pressure."

"Is that a yes?" Jesse said.

"Yes. Now let's go before they come back and trick us into something else."

"I am going to punish Liv for this," she said, watching Eloise walk to the front door. "Wait." Jesse grinned when Eloise turned back curiously. "Look up." She followed Eloise's gaze all the way up to the top of the doorway. A small bundle of mistletoe still hung in all its glittery glory. She walked up to Eloise and placed her hands on her hips. "For tradition's sake?"

Eloise wrapped her arms around Jesse's neck. "For tradition."

Jesse leaned in and kissed Eloise sweetly, soaking up the sense of warmth and home, all while pouring her love into the moment. She silently promised to never let a moment pass without Eloise knowing how loved she was, how cherished and respected, and how grateful Jesse felt to have her in her life.

Eloise opened her eyes slowly. "I love you, too, by the way. I never stopped." They kissed again and again, wrapped in one another's love.

Jesse pulled back only when her need to be home with Eloise outweighed her desire to make up for all the kisses she'd missed. "Thank you."

"For what?" Eloise said with a giggle.

"For being my wish come true."

EPILOGUE: NEW YEAR'S EVE

One year later

"Cheers," Jesse said, holding up her champagne flute. Theo responded first with her glass of water, followed by the rest of the guests.

New Year's Eve looked a little different this time around. No big, messy party, only Jesse and Eloise's closest friends gathered to celebrate the start of another year.

The dining table was pulled into the living room to ensure Theo could stay in a comfortable chair. Being eight months pregnant called for some modifications. Liv waited on her hand and foot, kissing Theo every single time she brought her something or added more food to her plate.

"Are you finally all ready for baby McGowan?" Jesse said.

Liv nodded. "Preparation is done, but I do not feel ready."

"Even I'm getting nervous." Theo moved around in the chair, a big round belly taking up most of the space. "And I'm getting cranky. I'm uncomfortable all the time, and I feel like I can't catch my breath. All I want to do is eat and sleep."

"I'm honestly surprised you're still up. It's almost midnight." Liv sat on the arm of Theo's chair. "I guess that small cup of coffee did the trick."

"After being deprived of caffeine for months, I'm probably more sensitive than ever."

"But you're okay?" Liv's hyperconcern was evident and endearing. "You feel fine? No shakes or palpitations?"

Theo took Liv's hand and kissed her knuckles. "I'm fine. Just awake for once."

"What a difference a year makes," April said.

Jesse chuckled. "Yeah, you finally stopped wearing those dumb hats."

"False. I just stopped wearing them to parties and functions." April ran her fingers through her long brown hair.

"Thanks to me." Gemma held her champagne toward Jesse. "Which I do believe deserves its own cheers." Jesse nodded and clinked her glass to Gemma's.

April's face fell. "I thought you said I looked cute in the hats."

"Aww." Gemma kissed April's cheek. "You always look cute, baby. You just shouldn't wear them all the time."

"Okay, that's enough of that lovey-dovey ooey-gooey business. Have some sympathy for those of us who are alone."

Jesse grimaced and tugged at the collar of her simple black button-up. Somehow she had forgotten. "I'm sorry, Billie."

"It's okay. I knew tonight would be hard. I just didn't expect it to suck this bad." Billie's attention was on her crystal flute. She had been somber throughout dinner, and the minutes leading up to midnight only bolstered her melancholy. "The holidays all sucked this year."

"Oh, come on. Don't be a Negative Nancy. You knew last year wasn't the usual."

"Yeah, but I didn't expect Leah to work every single holiday this year. I've barely seen her since Thanksgiving. Our family thinks they scared her away."

"It's not a crazy assumption," Jesse said, hoping to make Billie laugh. No success.

Eloise entered the makeshift dining room looking flustered. "Sorry that took so long. You all know how chatty my mother can be."

Billie perked up minimally and said, "For someone who opens a bakery at six in the morning, I'm surprised Lena is up so late."

"She's always been a night owl." Eloise took her seat beside Jesse and reached out to hold her hand. "What did I miss?"

"Nothing much," Jesse said, leaning in slowly for a kiss. "But I did miss you."

Billie gagged. "Gross."

"Is everything okay?" Jesse spoke barely above a whisper for only Eloise to hear.

Eloise's hazel eyes held a hint of pleasure and mischief. "Everything is perfect."

She pecked Eloise's lips lightly and pulled back to continue the conversation. "How are wedding plans coming along?"

"Great, except Leah's mom wants to be in charge of the seating chart because their family has so much drama." Billie rolled her eyes. "But don't tell her I told you that. She keeps saying it's to let old friends catch up."

Gemma's face scrunched in a thoughtful moment. "But it's not her friends who are invited."

Billie shot her with a finger gun. "She's fooling nobody."

Jesse gave Billie a lot of credit for remaining patient throughout the process. Weddings were stressful enough, but adding family drama only made everything harder than it needed to be. She looked at Eloise, who was deep in conversation with Gemma about their own mothers' antics, and thought about marriage. They had alluded to it many times with mentions of when and where, and they even talked at length about their future before Eloise moved in. But did Jesse really want the traditional hoopla? Or would she rather run away to a private destination to seal her forever with Eloise? Either way, she knew for sure she would be marrying Eloise Grant.

"Jesse?" Eloise said with amusement in her voice. "Are you okay in space land?"

Jesse snapped back to the moment. "Yeah. I'm great."

"What were you thinking about?"

Jesse's heart swelled. "I was thinking about marrying you."

Eloise's eyes softened. "I love you."

"And I love you." Jesse overheard another mention of midnight and checked the time. "Oh shit. Four minutes. We better put the TV on and turn Theo." Jesse looked at Theo and had to hold back a laugh.

Liv shrugged. "She almost made it."

"Should we wake her up to watch?"

"No. You guys go ahead. I'll sit right here with her."

"Are you sure?"

Liv looked at Theo adoringly. "There's no place else I'd rather be."

The small group migrated closer to the television and watched as a crowded New York City started to celebrate. The tradition of it all and the memory of just one year ago made Jesse's chest warm. Life was an odd journey, one that had taken her through many ups and downs just to drop her right where she belonged. She took in the moment and each person she shared it with, and all she felt was love.

Jesse looped her arm around Eloise's waist once the countdown started. She waited patiently, ready to have the New Year's midnight she'd missed last year. She turned to look at Eloise and smiled when she looked back. "Three, two, one…"

"Happy New Year," Leah said from behind them all, dressed in her layered medic uniform.

Billie spun round so quickly she nearly fell over. "What are you doing here?"

Leah laughed. "Kiss me—my rig is outside waiting for me." Billie kissed her without another second of hesitation.

"Did you have something to do with this?" Jesse said knowingly as Eloise grinned.

"I may have left the front door unlocked just in case."

Jesse weaved her fingers into Eloise's hair and drew her in for a kiss. She pulled back until their lips were barely touching and said, "Happy New Year, Eloise." She continued to kiss Eloise in every way she could as the new year started, then she pulled back and smiled down at her. In Jesse's heart she knew with this group of incredible people and Eloise by her side, she couldn't have wished for more.

About the Author

M. Ullrich is a four-time Goldie Award finalist and a two-time Lambda Literary Award finalist, and she has been featured in the *Advocate* magazine. She currently resides by the New Jersey Shore, but dreams of living someplace a little less touristy and with a whole lot less road rage. When she's not writing or working her full-time job, M. Ullrich appreciates the simple pleasures in life like breakfast foods and sweet treats, working on her artistic skills, and enjoying the company of someone who laughs at her ridiculous humor. You can reach M. Ullrich through social media including Instagram, Facebook, and Twitter.

Books Available From Bold Strokes Books

A Convenient Arrangement by Aurora Rey and Jaime Clevenger. Cuffing season has come for lesbians, and for Jess Archer and Cody Dawson, their convenient arrangement becomes anything but. (978-1-63555-818-0)

An Alaskan Wedding by Nance Sparks. The last thing either Andrea or Riley expects is to bump into the one who broke her heart fifteen years ago, but when they meet at the welcome party, their feelings come rushing back. (978-1-63679-053-4)

Beulah Lodge by Cathy Dunnell. It's 1874, and newly betrothed Ruth Mallowes is set on marriage and life as a missionary...until she falls in love with the housemaid at Beulah Lodge. (978-1-63679-007-7)

Gia's Gems by Toni Logan. When Lindsey Speyer discovers that popular travel columnist Gia Williams is a complete fake and threatens to expose her, blackmail has never been so sexy. (978-1-63555-917-0)

Holiday Wishes & Mistletoe Kisses by M. Ullrich. Four holidays, four couples, four chances to make their wishes come true. (978-1-63555-760-2)

Love By Proxy by Dena Blake. Tess has a secret crush on her best friend, Sophie, so the last thing she wants is to help Sophie fall in love with someone else, but how can she stand in the way of her happiness? (978-1-63555-973-6)

Marry Me by Melissa Brayden. Allison Hale attempts to plan the wedding of the century to a man who could save her family's business, if only she wasn't falling for her wedding planner, Megan Kinkaid. (978-1-63555-932-3)

Pathway to Love by Radclyffe. Courtney Valentine is looking for a woman exactly like Ben—smart, sexy, and not in the market for anything serious. All she has to do is convince Ben that sex-without-strings is the perfect pathway to pleasure. (978-1-63679-110-4)

Sweet Surprise by Jenny Frame. Flora and Mac never thought they'd ever see each other again, but when Mac opens up her barber shop right next to Flora's sweet shop, their connection comes roaring back. (978-1-63679-001-5)

The Edge of Yesterday by CJ Birch. Easton Gray is sent from the future to save humanity from technological disaster. When she's forced to target the woman she's falling in love with, can Easton do what's needed to save humanity? (978-1-63679-025-1)

The Scout and the Scoundrel by Barbara Ann Wright. With unexpected danger surrounding them, Zara and Roni are stuck between duty and survival, with little room for exploring their feelings, especially love. (978-1-63555-978-1)

Can't Leave Love by Kimberly Cooper Griffin. Sophia and Pru have no intention of falling in love, but sometimes love happens when and where you least expect it. (978-1-636790041-1)

Free Fall at Angel Creek by Julie Tizard. Detective Dee Rawlings and aircraft accident investigator Dr. River Dawson use conflicting methods to find answers when a plane goes missing, while overcoming surprising threats and discovering an unlikely chance at love. (978-1-63555-884-5)

Love's Compromise by Cass Sellars. For Piper Holthaus and Brook Myers, will professional dreams and past baggage stop two hearts from realizing they are meant for each other? (978-1-63555-942-2)

Not All a Dream by Sophia Kell Hagin. Hester has lost the woman she loved, and the world has descended into relentless dark and cold. But giving up will have to wait when she stumbles upon people who help her survive. (978-1-63679-067-1)

The Secrets of Willowra by Kadyan. A family saga of three women, their homestead called Willowra in the Australian outback, and the secrets that link them all. (978-1-63679-064-0)

Turbulent Waves by Ali Vali. Kai Merlin and Vivien Palmer plan their future together as hostile forces make their own plans to destroy what they have, as well as all those they love. (978-1-63679-011-4)